OMEGA'S POSSESSION

JESSICA HALL

OMEGA'S POSSESSION

(Possession Series, Book 2)
Copyright © 2024 by **Jessica Hall**

ISBN 978-1-923138-34-6

First Edit by Gabrielle Gerbus from Incubix Branding. Second Edit & Proofread by Jaime Powell
Format & Inside Layout by Patrisha Badalo (Art Muse Graphic Designs)
Inside Illustration by Gnin
Cover Design by Zhandre Dex G. (MC Damon)

DEDICATION

To those who know that an Alpha's power is just an illusion until he's beneath them. For the fierce souls who dare to turn the tables, making the Alpha who once tried to own them bow down and beg.

And to the wild ones who savor the moment he realizes he's only as strong as the teeth that mark him, and the pussy gripping him.

Yes, this is for you, my unapologetic queen.

Happy breaking him in, darling.

X

Omega's Possession

CHAPTER ONE

HARLOW

race upstairs to shower and change. I use the back stairwell, not wanting another run-in with Elaine. As I shower, I can hear shouting downstairs. Thane is losing his mind at someone. I have a sneaking suspicion it is Raidon. Or maybe Elaine. Regardless, I take my time, dreading the moment I have to go downstairs and face her. I hope Thane meant what he said—that he will get rid of her if she becomes too much. I do not feel like arguing with that woman or my mates

Grabbing the hair dryer, I quickly dry my hair before pulling it into a bun. I hope they aren't expecting a prim, proper Omega because I look quite the opposite in my purple pajamas with tiny wolves and my rainbow socks, choosing comfort over looks. If I have to endure this woman, I am doing it comfortably.

The arguing has stopped by the time I make my way downstairs. I head toward the kitchen, for once preferring Thane's presence over everyone else's. He is muttering angrily under his breath about Raidon. I step next to him, and he nudges me.

"Are you okay with this? Because if you aren't, I have no problem throwing them out," he tells me.

"It's fine. As long as she doesn't overstep. If you guys can ensure she keeps her distance, I can stomach this for an hour or two." I take a big breath and get my game face on, as best I can.

Thane uses his Calling to help me relax, kissing the top of my head, "Just say the word, and I'll make them leave."

Thane and I set the table. I can hear Elaine's voice as Raidon tries to pull her back from coming into the dining room to help.

"Mom! Let Thane and Harlow handle it. Let her get used to the idea of you being here."

Elaine begins to protest to the point of insistence. "Sweetheart, it's no trouble at all. I still know how to be an Omega, you know, just —"

Raidon cuts her off, "Mom, I said no. Leave them be. She has been through enough, don't you think?"

I can tell he finally makes her back down after he says that. I don't know what she thinks coming in to help will accomplish. She has helped enough, as far as I'm concerned. Especially her help in trying to get me killed or put in rotation. Just thinking about it makes my blood boil. Thane puts his hand on my hip, sensing the shift in my mood. When I look up to meet his eyes, he motions to my hand, which is holding a fork. Well, it was a fork. Now it is just a bent piece of metal that used to be a fork. I blink, not realizing I am taking my frustration out on the cutlery.

Thane grips my hand, prying the fork from between my fingertips and holding it up. "Hmm, maybe I should give you a spoon?" he softly chuckles, pocketing the mangled fork. I purse my lips and continue to focus on what I am doing.

When we finish setting the table, I glance around, debating where to sit. Thane nods to the head of the table, where he usually sits, and I tell him so. "But that is where you always sit."

He shrugs. At least it will be the furthest from everyone, and I will feel better knowing I won't be next to Raidon's parents.

"Oh, the napkins," I tell Thane, quickly ducking back into the kitchen as everyone starts coming in from the living room. I ignore them and move to grab the napkins from the third drawer, where he also keeps the tea towels. Grabbing the silky, off-white fabric, I shut the drawer and turn, only to run right into Elaine's open arms.

I freeze as she hugs me, my heart nearly leaping out of my chest, not just from the unwelcome hug, but also because I did not hear her come up behind me.

I stand there awkwardly, frozen to the spot as she moves to hold me at arm's length. Her face is beaming as she smiles, rubbing my arms, and her eyes move to my huge, round belly.

"I am so excited and glad we are finally past everything," she says, running her hands over my belly.

My hands grip the napkins, strangling the fabric to prevent me from strangling her. Her hands touch and fuss over my belly as she gushes excitedly. It only makes me more mad. She's acting like she didn't order Thane to kill me just a few weeks ago.

Arms wrap around me from the side, and Rhen's familiar scent cloaks me as he tugs me to him, just as Raidon scolds his mother.

"Mom! What did I say?" he snaps, and Elaine jumps.

"I am just saying hello. I'm not—" She stops as Rhen tucks me closer to him. His scent slows the racing of my heart, and he presses his lips to my temple.

"Elaine, remember your place. You, of all people, should know better," Rhen adds, letting me escape from under his arm as I move to the dining room. Leon stands in my way, talking to Raidon's father. I stop, almost running into the man's back, while he explains something with some very enthusiastic hand gestures.

The man is tall, roughly the same height as Raidon, though his features are surprisingly softer. I half-expected him to have the same brooding features Raidon has, yet his smile is gentle, and his eyes crinkle around the edges as he peers down at me.

"You must be Harlow. Raidon told me about you. My name is Charles," he says, holding out his hand to me. I stare at it before hesitantly placing my hand in his. His hand engulfs mine. The man has huge hands, yet his grip is gentle. Arguing breaks out behind us in the kitchen. Charles glances behind me and sighs.

"She is a stubborn woman, who won't take no for an answer. Excuse me. I best go sort this out before she goes on a rampage and takes a shoe off," he says, moving past me.

"A shoe?" I mutter, watching him go.

"Yeah. You know you need to run when she takes a slipper off. Tough old cookie, but she isn't so bad once you get to know her," Leon tells me. I stare at him, and he chuckles lightly.

"You'll see. She's eccentric and a little kooky, but her heart is in the right place."

"Unless you get on her bad side," I mumble.

"I'm not defending her. I'm just saying; Omegas are ruled by emotion and instinct. She was extremely close with Hana. It's no excuse, but I know she is deeply sorry. She just isn't very good at communicating that," Leon tells me, reaching his arm around my waist. His finger strokes the side of my belly as he pushes me toward the dining room table.

I hear some firm words from Charles and Elaine's apologetic reply. Turning my attention back to the dining table, I notice Thane is watching me. I hand him the napkins, and he grips my fingers, staring at me and not letting go.

"One word," he says, and I nod just as Elaine comes in with Charles. She stops when she sees me, looking at her husband.

"I'm sorry if I made you feel uncomfortable, Harlow, and I'm also sorry about everything else that has happened. Please know I am not usually such a sour old grape," she tells me.

"Unless she removes a slipper," Leon whispers next to my ear.

"Oh, you little—" Elaine growls at him as Leon waggles his eyebrows at me. Elaine stops when her husband clears his throat and pulls a chair out for her. Elaine may appear to be the bossy one, but it is clear who rules the roost in their house. Charles nods for her to take the seat.

She does, and Leon nudges me toward mine, right next to her. Everyone starts heading to their usual places at the table when Thane speaks.

"Low," he growls, making my head snap up as Rhen moves behind me to pull out my chair. Thane nods to his chair. I can see my mates' shock as I move toward it. Thane nudges Rhen to move down one from his usual spot, making him sit next to Leon.

I swallow, feeling everyone's eyes on me. I'm shocked at Thane giving me his spot when he sits there religiously. I also feel smug satisfaction when Elaine goes to move before her husband grips her hand. Elaine sighs.

"Raidon, be a dear and go fetch the gift bag from the living room," she says through gritted teeth, while giving her husband a tight smile.

He lets her hand go, and Raidon quickly rushes off. He comes back with a huge pink bag and sets it on the table's edge, next to his father, who then places it on the floor next to him.

"Let her eat first. You can show her afterward," Charles tells his wife, who seems to almost pout at the suggestion.

CHAPTER TWO

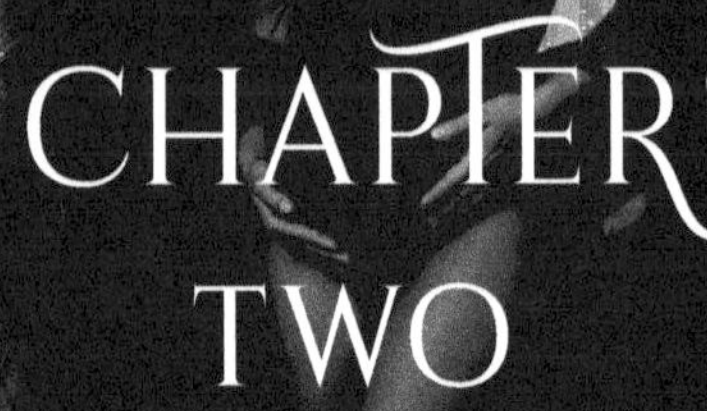

Thankfully, I let Thane cook. It is worth giving up my non-existent chef's hat for Thane's food. Besides, if I gave them burnt noodles, it would have left a great impression on my in-laws and probably a bad taste in their mouths.

Dinner is quite pleasant, surprisingly. Afterward, Leon and Rhen clear the table. Now, with nothing to distract me from speaking with the woman, I kind of want to flee, but Rhen and Leon return with a cinnamon and custard tart I didn't realize Thane had also made—no way am I missing dessert.

Thane snorts when I go to get up but immediately sit back down again after seeing dessert. I grab my spoon as Elaine gets up and grabs the bag Raidon retrieved for her. I freeze. Instead of approaching me, however, she passes it to Raidon, who in turn passes it to me. I let out a sigh of relief, knowing she won't suffocate me by coming over.

"I got a few things for the baby and also a few sentimental things from when Raidon was a pup," she tells me, nodding toward the bag.

"Huh?" Raidon says, leaning forward and looking in the bag. His mother slaps his shoulder.

"Let her open it," she snaps at him, and I undo the ribbon pinching the top of the bag together. Reaching in, I pull out some pink crochet booties and a blanket. The wool is soft in my hands as I hold it up.

"I crocheted that for your little one," she tells me, and I nod, thanking her. Raidon pushes his chair back, as I refold it. I set the blanket on his lap, so I don't ruin it by placing it on the table. Reaching into the bag, I pull out a metal rattle with a teddy bear on it. Leon snorts beside Raidon, and Raidon groans, making me look at him.

"Don't you dare," he hisses at his mother. I glance at her while Thane tries and fails to contain his laughter. Charles shakes his head, sitting back in his chair and draping his arm over the back of Elaine's chair. I look at Elaine. It is quite heavy for a baby rattle.

"Raidon called that his Bam-Bam; he had an obsession with The Flintstones when he was a child," Elaine lightly chuckles, while Raidon growls.

"This was Raidon's?" I ask her, and she nods. Rhen snorts, making me look at him questionably.

"Always trying to embarrass me," Raidon mumbles.

"I think it's sweet," I tell him.

"Yeah, sweet, when he was a baby. He even took that thing to school," Thane laughs beside me. I look at Raidon, whose cheeks are turning a little red.

"Yep, he took it everywhere with him, had to all but pry it from his hands when he was ten after he smacked his teacher over the head with it," Charles tells me.

"That prick deserved it, calling my mom a whore," Raidon grumbles.

"Hush, you," she scolds her son before rubbing the side of his face with the back of her hand. "He used to be protective of his momma," she chuckles.

I can't tell, I think dryly. He still is! Thane snickers, watching Raidon grow redder at his mother's affections.

"I wouldn't laugh too much, Thane. Don't think I have forgotten how you used to carry around that pink unicorn blanket. It was barely a piece of scrap by the time your mother had enough. She had to sneak into your room while you slept to get rid of that thing."

"I was a boy," he bites back.

"Sixteen is a boy?" she taunts. He huffs and folds his arms across his chest, sitting back. "Your mother had to sneak it into the trash like she was smuggling drugs over the border. It had holes in it everywhere," Elaine softly laughs.

"It was sentimental," he huffs.

"A unicorn blanket?" I chuckle, looking at Thane. Thane swallows but says nothing.

"Wait, she doesn't know?" Elaine asks, staring at Thane. He presses his lips in a line, and I glance at him, before he sighs.

"I had a twin sister. Her name was Scarlett. She died when we were four. The blanket was hers," he tells me.

I suck in a breath, not expecting such a heavy answer. I am curious to know how she died, but I know better than to pry. He will tell me when he wants to.

"Have you got siblings?" I ask Rhen, already knowing that Leon has a sister.

"Two brothers. We aren't close, and they are half-brothers," he tells me. I look at Raidon.

"Only child," he answers, and I nod.

"You have a twin, too?" Elaine asks me, before looking at her son. "Raidon told me about her. You two recently reconnected?"

"Yeah, I thought she was dead," I tell her. I wonder if it is genetics that causes so many twins to be born from Alpha lines. I am very glad to be having only one baby, because I am already the size of a house.

Turning back to the bag, I find a pink dress and a teddy bear. I thank Elaine for the gesture, and we talk more about baby stuff and appointments. Charles even goes over my medical charts with me, which Thane keeps on hand. Elaine also goes over my pathology results, telling Thane I am lacking some vitamins, and he tells her he will get supplements for them tomorrow.

When Raidon gets up to help with the dishes, Elaine slides into his seat beside me. She starts fiddling with the gold bracelets on her wrist.

"There is something else I want to give you," she says, glancing up at Thane. He nods to her, and she unclips one of the bracelets from her wrist. They are matching, but the one on her wrist has a few different charms on it from the one she hands to me.

It is quite heavy for a bracelet. Charms cover one side of it, and I admire the shiny gold.

"I can't accept this," I tell her, but she shakes her head.

"Hana was going to give it to you. She had the charms rearranged a few weeks before she passed. She told me the other side is for you to fill with your own charms," she says.

"This was Hana's?" I ask, thinking I definitely can't keep it. It should go to Thane, not me.

"Yes, she had the bracelet rearranged for Thane's Omega. She told me she was going to bid in the auctions. She was going to find a mate for him, since he was too stubborn," she chuckles.

I look at the charms on it as Elaine shows me her bracelet. It is an almost identical match, besides a few different charms.

"All four of us had matching bracelets," she explains.

I remember Jake telling me how Elaine, Hana, and his mother were all friends from an Omega facility. Yet he never mentioned a fourth woman.

"You, Jake's mother, Hana, and…?" I ask.

"Yes, originally, there were four of us. Me, Hana, Sofia, and Harper. Now there's only two of us left. We never found out what happened to Harper. Hana got her out before she was auctioned off or put into rotation," Elaine tells me.

"These bracelets were given to us when we were all in the Omega facility together."

"My father bought them for my mother while he was dating her," Thane tells me, and I peer at him over my shoulder.

"I thought your mother was auctioned?" I tell him. He nods his head.

"My father was one of the main sponsors of the facility. While attending a tour there, he met my mom. They dated for a bit," Thane answers.

"Headmaster Waylen was so mad! He scolded her for drawing attention," Elaine chortles.

"Anyway, when she went to auction, he and his mate, who at

the time was only his business partner, made sure to be the winning bid," Elaine quietly chuckles. Raidon comes back in and clears his throat, but I hold up my hand.

"No, I want to listen," I tell him. It helps me understand Elaine better. We aren't so different, and I realize I had forgotten that. She ducks her head, staring at her bracelet, and I know she's thinking the same about me.

"Hana came back for us. She gave us these bracelets, and she tried to bid on us, to set us free from the facility, but then politics came into play."

"And my fathers had just filed for bankruptcy. Their business collapsed," Thane tells me, as Raidon takes a seat beside his mother. I glance at her husband, Charles, who has a somber expression on his face.

Elaine shakes her head and makes a strange noise. "After we all left, we decided to get charms to represent each milestone," she tells me, showing me hers. She pinches a charm between her fingers. It's a flower, and Hana's bracelet in my hand has the same charm.

"The flower represents our time in the facility and us blooming. We were in the same facility she got you from, Harlow," she tells me, and I am taken aback. Some strange emotion chokes me hearing that, knowing we are connected in a way I never imagined possible.

"The carousel represents my three years in rotation before Hana set me free," she says before showing me the next charm; it is a little birdcage with the door open. "This one represents my mate setting me free of the cage Omegas are put in when in the system." The next is a medical symbol. "Caduceus and a tassel; these two represent my time in medical school and graduating." The next is a ring, "Me finally marrying Charles, and this one," she holds up an R, "is for having Raidon. And this is the last one," she shows me the charm of a baby. "Hana and I got them together. It represents our future grandchild," she tells me, and I nod, peering down at the same charm on Hana's bracelet.

Hana's also has the ring and the letters T and S, which I now know must represent her children. Elaine leans forward, showing me the other charms on Hana's bracelet. One looks like a tiny little mirror.

"Hana got this one to remind herself that what she sees in the mirror does not define her. She was more than an Omega, and she refused to conform," Elaine tells me before moving to the next one. It is a little book. "This represents the history of Omegas," she tells me, and I furrow my brows.

"History?" I ask, and Elaine nods.

"Yes, we weren't always slaves to the system. Omegas were celebrated, revered. Not how it is today," she tells me. Hana's bracelet also has a tiny birdcage, and then I see a little unicorn.

"She got this one after Scarlett passed," Elaine says, moving to the next, which is a little gavel. "This one is for her fight against the system. She tried everything to get the laws changed," Elaine tells me, and I peek over at Thane, who is staring at the table.

"And this one?" I ask, holding up the little crown.

Elaine smiles sadly. "I remember she was so happy when she got this. She was in shock at first," she whispers.

"What's it represent?" I ask her.

"Becoming equal to her mates."

"When she took their serum?" I ask her.

Elaine shakes her head. "No, that didn't make her equal. The serum doesn't make you of equal power. This is from an older tradition, one long forgotten. It made her more than them."

I tilt my head to look at Thane.

"I told you my mother was their equal," he says.

"I thought you meant the serum," I whisper, and he shakes his head.

"This one represents something more than the serums, more than marriage ever could," Elaine tells me.

"It takes a very strong Alpha to do it. It's not in our nature. It goes against everything that makes us Alpha," Charles chimes in, smiling sadly at his wife.

"I have never expected it of you," she tells him, and he nods while I turn my attention back to her.

"This crown represents her becoming their Luna," she tells me.

"Luna?" I ask. It isn't a word I am familiar with. Elaine nods, but it is Thane who answers.

"My fathers submitted to her. She became their Alpha," Thane tells me.

I would never even think such a thing was possible. It goes against nature and instinct, so I understand what Charles meant by his words.

"It also caused an uproar when everyone in the city realized they would now be answering to a woman in charge," Elaine tells me.

CHAPTER THREE

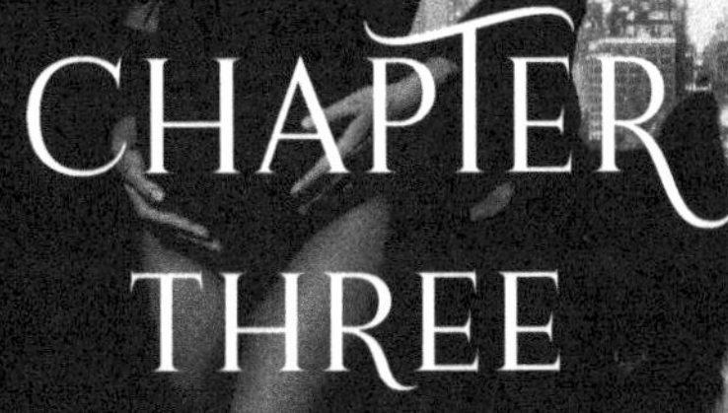

We all sit quietly for a second as my mind mulls over what I just learned. No wonder Elaine hated me. She believed I killed the one woman who saved her.

"I spent a few years in rotation. Hana used to send me birth control until she introduced me to Charles," she explains.

"And Sophia?" I ask.

"She was in rotation, too, until she met her mates," she sighs heavily. "And Harper, we tried to find her. Waylen and Curtis hunted her down for years. We eventually gave up searching for her, knowing it wasn't safe. Curtis was always watching us, following us with every lead we found."

"Curtis? Is he a member of the council?" I ask, not having heard that name before.

Elaine shakes her head. "You never met him? He's the current headmaster of the Omega facility, Curtis Black?" she asks. I blink at her. Mr. Black is this Curtis person?

"Waylen Black was his father. Curtis took over after he died," Elaine tells me.

"So, Mr. Black was looking for her?"

She sits back in her chair, staring at the bracelet in her hand.

"After Hana, Harper was the next to be put up for auction, but she was pulled suddenly. We didn't understand at first, until we overheard Curtis talking to his father; he wanted her. Her levels were off the charts, and being the headmaster's son and an Alpha, he was technically allowed to bid. Yet Curtis knew he would easily be outbid by other parties. He didn't have that kind of money, then. Instead, they swept it under the rug and pulled her, falsifying her records at the facility. When Hana came back for us, she learned of his intentions. So, with help from one of the guards, they snuck Harper out. She ran off with the guard."

"The guard took her?"

"Yes. They were in love, and they had been secretly seeing each other every chance they could get because he wasn't allowed to bid on her."

"Because he was a guard, and Curtis wanted her?" I ask, trying to understand.

She shakes her head. "No, because he was an Omega himself," she tells me.

Male Omegas are rare. They are also the only ones who can produce more Omegas or Alphas with an Alpha female. Betas mostly produce more Betas, though on the rare occasion they can also have Omega children. Two Omegas will almost always produce a pure Omega, which is classified as an Omega with pheromone levels at 80% or higher.

Pure Omegas are rarer, not just because of a lack of Omega males, but because it is seen as wasteful when an Omega female can belong to an entire pack. So, two Omegas being together is mostly forbidden, which never made sense to me. It is also why Zara and my pheromone levels are so high. Both of our parents were Omega. My mother was born from an Alpha and Omega; my father was born from two Omegas.

"We never located either of them. It's better off that way. Curtis would have used her and sold her off when he was done with her. He was always a bastard. He knew his older brother would inherit everything, except that one facility, when his father died. We always believed his intention was to find an Omega to produce an heir in the hopes his father would change his mind."

"Or use her genes to blackmail his brother into allowing him to join his pack," Charles adds, and Elaine nods.

"Or that," she says.

"So, Curtis isn't the only heir to his father's disgusting legacy?" I ask.

"No, his older brother, Alpha Corbin, was set to inherit everything. The Black family adopted Curtis. Waylen planned on leaving everything to his biological son, and he did. Corbin owns most of the facilities in the country. Curtis was given that one facility, and Corbin inherited the rest."

"Alpha Corbin, why does that name sound so familiar?" I ask. I can't place it, yet I'm certain I've heard it somewhere before.

"The Mountain Pack. Alpha Corbin is the head of the other Alpha pack in this state, besides mine and Jake's," Thane answers. I chew the inside of my lip, knowing I nearly ran right into their arms at Talon's. Glancing over my shoulder, I can tell Thane is also thinking about that night. His jaw clenches, but he says nothing of it.

We chat some more about random topics before saying our goodbyes. Elaine wants to take me baby shopping, to which I agree. Raidon and Rhen say they will come with us, which I'm grateful for. Despite getting along with Elaine tonight, I barely know the woman. Though I feel I have a better understanding of her now.

After cleaning up from dessert, we settle in on the couch to watch a movie. It starts to get late, and I am struggling to keep my eyes open by the time I eventually crawl into bed. Yet, when my head hits the pillow, I find myself wide awake.

Leon is snoring beside me, which isn't helping, and the more I lie here, the harder it is to switch my mind off. It annoys me that lately, no matter how exhausted my body is, it seems the moment I lie down for sleep, my mind will suddenly switch on. It will begin conjuring up every conversation I had that day, every little detail playing over in my head. Or, it will conjure memories of the past, or intentions for the next day.

Stupid brain.

Cursing, I climb over Leon and head downstairs. Having lain

awake for so long, I am now thirsty. Walking down the hall, I notice Rhen and Raidon's doors are shut and wonder if they are in Thane's room. I've caught them sleeping in there a couple of times, as if they miss him. Glancing back at Leon's room, I sigh. Even I am finding it harder to sleep in there—my bond tugging for my mates—yet we can't all fit in Leon's bed.

Walking downstairs, I move toward the kitchen and grab the apple juice from the fridge. I pour myself a glass and put the bottle back. I shut the door and grab my glass, only to nearly jump out of my skin when I see Raidon standing there.

"I thought I felt that you were awake," he smoothly chuckles.

"You nearly gave me a heart attack," I hiss at him, before noticing the door to the Den is open behind him. My eyes flick to it. Raidon glances over his shoulder at it. He scratches the back of his neck awkwardly as Thane comes out of the Den with only his boxers on. He stops when he notices me, his eyes moving to Raidon briefly, as if they've been caught doing something they shouldn't.

Seconds later, Rhen emerges from the Den, walking directly into Thane's back. We all kind of stand there awkwardly, no one speaking. I reach for my juice. This explains why both of their doors are shut. They usually leave them open, and sometimes I will wander between rooms, trying to find somewhere comfortable to sleep.

"Well, this is awkward," Rhen mutters, stating the obvious.

"We're mates, Low. You're not the only one who struggles to sleep without us. I hear you walking around most nights," Thane tells me.

"I didn't say anything," I tell him.

His brows furrow, and Rhen steps beside him. He opens his mouth to say something, but Raidon sighs before speaking.

"You're wondering why our doors were closed," he exhales.

"I thought you were in Thane's room," I admit. "I'm not angry. We just can't all fit in Leon's bed. " I curse myself for sounding so needy, but it is the main reason I struggle to sleep most nights, the bond forever pulling and pushing for my mates. And now that Thane and I are finally talking, it seems to tug even harder, like it is searching for them.

"I'll wake up, Leon. We can sleep in Thane's room," Rhen says, walking off. Thane watches him go. I finish my drink and set my glass in the sink before following Raidon down the hall when I stop.

"Are you coming?" I ask Thane. He seems taken aback, yet I can tell he wants to follow us.

"I'm allowed?" he asks, glancing at the door to the Den.

"Well, I'm not sleeping down there, so—" My eyes dart to the Den door. Just the thought of stepping down there makes my heart race faster before I shove the feelings aside.

"Come to bed, Thane," I tell him before walking off and up the stairs. I am halfway up the stairs when I hear him follow.

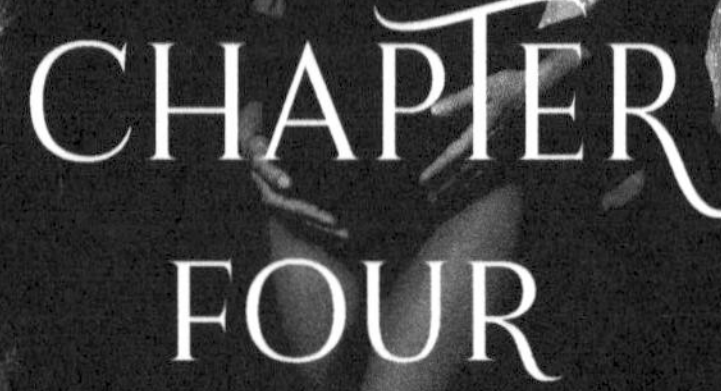

CHAPTER FOUR

As I follow Harlow up the stairs, I can't decide if this is real or just a figment of my imagination. Granted, she let me touch her earlier, and well, I did more than just touch her.

Pulling myself out of my jumbled thoughts, I follow Harlow, hot on her heels, to my room. Raidon manages to get the grumpy Leon up, so we can all sleep together. When I step into the room, our mingled scents calm me in a way I haven't felt in ages, as if I can finally breathe again. As I climb into my usual spot and Raidon gets on the outside of me, I watch Harlow slip between Rhen and Leon.

Of course, I would prefer if Harlow slept next to me, but I'm not pushing my luck tonight. I'm not going to risk getting banished back to the Den by demanding she sleep next to me. I'm not going to sleep alone again.

I can't help but feel jealous, however, of how she clings to Leon the most. It's like I'm a damn light fixture in this house — useless and unnecessary.

But it's alright. Baby steps. One step at a time and all that. So, I'll take whatever I can get.

Sleeping with all of them in one bed finally allows me to drift off without much effort. However, what Elaine said tonight keeps replaying in my mind. Before I can sift through the conversation, though, sleep takes me.

I am dreaming deeply, sucked so far into the past that I am recalling days from my childhood. In my dream, my mother is talking to my fathers, sounding very upset about something.

"Do you not understand? Harper is pregnant! Their children are even more at risk than they are! She won't tell me where she is, no matter how much I beg. All I got is that she is safe for now!" My mother didn't say child, but children, which has to mean Harper was having more than one baby.

I remember during my early childhood, my parents fought endlessly over how my mother would drag me halfway across the country, searching for this mystery woman. Raidon and I would both be stuffed in the back of the car while my mother and Elaine tried to locate Harper.

My parents fought endlessly, until one day my fathers put their foot down and refused to let her look for Harper anymore. For some reason, my mind latched onto that memory, hyper-focusing on it when Elaine mentioned her name. Even now, the woman makes her way into my dreams. That vague memory plays on repeat in my head, as if it holds some significance in my subconscious, until finally, I drift into the darkness of oblivion.

Waking up, I find Rhen already awake and getting ready for work. He raises his finger to stop me from speaking and uses the mind-link.

'I'm going in early to finish our last contract projects. Stay home with them. I should be back a little after lunch.' I'm about to object to Rhen going in by himself when he leans over and kisses me. 'Be back soon. Spend some more time with Harlow.'

I touch my lips. The past two days have been the most interaction I have had with my mates since Harlow came home. I just hope it lasts. I don't think I can go back to the Den after sleeping in my own bed with them last night.

Yet, Rhen has a point. The only way Harlow is going to accept me back is if I spend more time with her while she wants me near. I don't really want to leave her, but now, I am wide awake, and there is no way I can fall asleep again. Letting them sleep in, I decide to head downstairs and cook us all some breakfast.

When I finish cooking, I go back upstairs to tell them it's ready. I stroll into the room to find Leon stiff as a log beneath Harlow, who has climbed on top of him. Harlow growls when I push the door open, and her eyes instantly snap in my direction. Her pupils are blown wide, and I can tell she is overtaken by instinct.

Leon looks petrified beneath her. His fangs poke out from beneath his upper lip, and his hands fist the sheets. Harlow sniffs the air and finally recognizes my scent. Once she's content I am not a threat or some stranger, she turns her full attention back to Leon. That's when Raidon shifts awake and pulls her off Leon, making her whimper.

Stepping further into the room, I watch Leon attempt to climb off the bed. I grab his shoulders and focus on Raidon, who is trying to stop Harlow from mauling Leon. I know she won't stop until she takes what she wants, what she needs. Some part of me knows that despite what happened last night, it isn't me who she wants, so they will have to suck it up and surrender to Harlow.

"Harlow!" Raidon growls as her lips travel down his chest and abs before finding her prize. She shreds his boxers with her claws, and she has her lips wrapped around the tip of his cock in no time. Taking his cock further into her mouth, she purrs, only to pull back and run her tongue along the side of his shaft before swirling it around his tip.

"Harlow!" Raidon groans, his head dropping back onto his pillow as he grabs her hair in one hand and guides her mouth back down on his cock.

Leon tenses in my arms, watching them. His need and hunger grows tenfold as he watches Harlow devour Raidon. Her arousal perfumes the room, making my cock twitch uncomfortably, straining against my pants as I continue to watch her suck my mate's cock.

"I need to go. I need to get out of here!" Leon growls, pushing back against me. My grip tightens on him.

"I'm right here," I growl in response. Fuck, why did Rhen have to leave? At least I know I can convince him to give Harlow what she is craving. While Leon fears his bloodlust, he is also terrified of hurting her and the baby.

I know she wants both of them. They are the only ones she hasn't claimed in any way, which is why she is constantly drawn to them. All that, and her need to mark us. Though, I wonder how she will take the news once she realizes she must mark me first. We will cross that bridge when we come to it. Which by the looks of it, will be quite soon.

Raidon tenses when her lips leave his cock with an audible pop. She crawls up him, her lips nipping and sucking his flesh. But, before Harlow can get anywhere near his neck, Raidon pushes her off. The look of rejection on her face is so gut-wrenching that all I want to do is punch him.

Raidon pushes me off him. I reach for Leon, but he jerks away from me as if I will burn him the moment our skin brushes. Rejection smashes me, and I growl at him in frustration.

"No, Harlow. You know I can't. Don't make me do this!" Leon whimpers. I can feel that his need for me is just as intense as the need I have for him. He wants me just as much. So why do they keep denying me?

"I won't let you hurt her, Leon," Thane growls as Leon tries to pull away. Only at the sound of his voice do I notice Thane standing behind him, his hands on Leon's shoulders. It upsets me to know the only reason Leon hasn't run from me is because Thane is holding him in place.

My blood is boiling. If one of them won't give me what I want, I am just going to have take it from them, whether they like it or not. The bond is refusing to give up this time, not until I claim them. I'm not glass. They can't break me by touching me.

I'm horny and hormonal, and I need one of their damn cocks inside me, like yesterday. At this point, I don't care whose. The bond is tearing me apart more each day, making me more uncomfortable.

I need to mate with them. The bond between us needs it. I need it!

Leon stares down at me before he glances at Thane over his shoulder.

"I won't let you hurt her," Thane repeats the promise. Leon sighs, glancing at Raidon. My nails dig into his arm when he sits up behind me.

"You'll stay here?" Raidon asks Thane, and my eyes instantly focus on him. Will it be wrong to not include Thane?

"I'm right here, Raidon. You aren't betraying me by fucking our mate," Thane assures him. I glance at Raidon, who nods, leaning his head down and kissing my shoulder.

Is that why they aren't touching me? Because they worry it might upset Thane? Thoughts run through my mind, but everything fades as Raidon pulls me back against him by my hips, his Calling vibrating against my back.

Leon crawls closer, and I can feel his hunger radiate off him. Feel his desire burning brighter than ever, yet I know there's a reason he won't touch me, a reason that is different from Raidon's.

Leon is scared of feeding on me. Before he can change his mind, I reach for him and pull him down onto the bed with me. I arch my back, already anticipating the pleasure their burning bodies promise to bring.

I feel greedy, selfish, and needy, but I feel no guilt about it. I pull their hands onto my body, placing them on my breasts and thighs. Their fingertips run over my sensitive skin, just a mere touch, a barely-there sensation that makes me moan louder than ever before.

Reaching up, I put my hand on Leon's cheek and guide him down toward me. I kiss his mouth, molding our lips together, letting my tongue explore every bit I can reach. The way they are touching me makes my head spin. Four hands are touching me, and two mouths suck and lick; it doesn't take long before I lose the ability to tell what belongs to who. I don't care anymore.

At this moment, lust and the bond make reality warp around us in a pleasing way. All three of us are moving on the same wave of pleasure, serving that pleasure, and letting the force of it fill the room. When Raidon grips my knee and forces my legs open, I gasp right as he crawls between them.

His tongue slips over my pussy, sending a new-found pleasure through my body like electric shockwaves. My body shudders, and my eyes roll back at the sensation. I can feel the way my chest rises and falls as I moan through each flick of his tongue. The sensations make me feel floaty as I writhe and lose myself in the pleasure only Raidon can provide.

I reach my hand out, grabbing Leon's cock and guiding it to my mouth. I wrap my lips around it, still moaning from the pleasure of having Raidon's mouth devour me. I look into a pair of eyes, finally locking gazes with Leon.

His groans of pleasure excite me to unknown lengths. I choke on his cock as he thrusts into the back of my throat; the mere action makes him rip himself away from me. The possessive snarl that leaves me makes him freeze as if he is too scared to move.

Raidon isn't paying attention to Leon and spreads my legs wider to lift my hips and slip his tongue inside me. I gasp, gripping his hair.

"Don't stop," I moan out. He softly chuckles before he sucks on my clit again, making me cry out his name. My hand reaches for Leon, but he remains frozen to the spot and shakes his head, trying to move away from me.

Leon is still hesitating when I hear Thane growl, and the bed next to me dips. "Thane!" Leon growls through gritted teeth. "I will hurt her!"

My eyes move to Thane as he kneels by my head. He leans against the headboard and says, "I told you I won't let you hurt her."

Leon chews his lip, staring down at me, and Thane grips my chin.

"Why don't you go ahead and open that pretty mouth of yours?" he whispers, and my eyes dart to Leon. His eyes flicker and turn a dark shade of crimson. As I try to sit up, Raidon's grip on me tightens, holding me in place while he happily devours my pussy.

Finally, Leon moves and grabs my throat. His lips become punishing as they crash against mine. His fangs graze my lips, slicing them. But I don't care — the bond craves anything it can get, and so do I.

Leon kisses me hard and growls against my lips. His hand remains on my throat and starts shaking as he fights to control his hunger. Leon's other hand grips my hair, which makes me moan at the subtle pain, but then, he lets go of my throat and pulls his lips from mine.

As I part my lips, I feel his hands wrap around my hair at the base of my neck. Leon pulls me forward. The raw, warm, stiff cock pushes its way past my lips and down my throat.

I wrap my lips around it again, and my tongue instantly darts to the tip of his cock. I do what I can to suck and lick, hoping he will come soon and I can taste him. Yet, Leon is more interested in using my mouth as a man uses any other hole, fucking my mouth with deep, powerful thrusts.

The bed dips as Raidon stops and sits up. My knees fall closed when Raidon grips my hips and moves me around until I am on my hands and knees between them. His fingers push between my legs, barely touching my throbbing pussy, as if he intends to tease me, and then finally, gently pushing inside.

I am already soaked, dripping in need. I can't wait for him to bury his cock inside me, but I know he won't stop teasing me, even if I beg. I try to moan, and the muffled sound that comes out of me seems to amuse them.

Leon holds my head in his enormous palms. He starts pulling himself out, until just the tip of his cock remains between my lips. He then places a hand under my jaw, grabs my throat, and grabs the top of my head with his other hand.

He moves my head with complete control, as if it is a toy that belongs to him, making me lick and suck the tip of his cock however he wants. It sends me into overdrive, and I desperately move my hips up and down, forcing Raidon to finger my wet pussy the way I want. But this won't be enough for me to cum; it certainly won't be enough to satisfy the bond.

Leon pulls his cock out of my mouth again, giving me enough time to catch a breath and cry out a single word.

"Please!"

I sound desperate. I am afraid he is going to leave me like this.

I can feel his fear mingling with his desire, while every inch of my body feels as if it is catching fire from the intensity of it all.

"Shh, he's not going anywhere," Thane murmurs.

"You heard her. She said please, didn't she?" Thane states, holding my face in his palm and stroking my cheek with his thumb.

"She did," Raidon agrees, gripping my hips and lifting them. He leans over me and kisses my shoulder before I feel the tip of his cock push between the folds of my pussy. He shoves inside me, inch by inch, and I sigh, relieved and in pure bliss.

Once he is fully sheathed, balls-deep, he pulls out and starts moving his hips at a constant, slow rhythm.

I purr at the feeling of Raidon's thick cock filling me. Leon glances at Thane, who nods to him before he takes my open mouth as an opportunity and pushes his cock down my throat again, slowly matching Raidon's speed and movement.

It's my first time ever doing something like this, but I never want the moment to end. I want to stay here, like the center of gravity pulling these two men inside me.

Raidon fucks me with ferocity, grabbing my hips and thrusting with force. Leon matches his intensity, and he forces me to choke on his cock. He pulls it out and lets me spit — I am making a mess on the bed, but as soon as I suck in a breath, he is pulling my head back into position and ramming his massive cock down my throat again.

I can feel the pleasure rising as Raidon's thrusts become more violent. His other hand slides between my legs, his fingers rubbing circles on my clit while he fucks me from behind.

I feel my clit pulsate and twitch as he pounds me. My walls clench around his girth, begging for more. I keep moaning, and I think I would be screaming if it wasn't for the large cock gagging me.

Gagging on Leon's cock turns up the pleasure to a place I have never been before, one I am shocked I even enjoy. I feel his cock twitching in my mouth as it leaks precum onto my tongue and down my throat. My mouth fills with the taste—the taste of sex, passion, and lust—until it becomes intoxicating and addictive. All I keep thinking is "more". I crave him, crave them. The bond loves every second.

I keep going like this until my whole body trembles, the sensations too powerful for me to carry on. The pleasure is intense and seems to stay at this level for an unnaturally long time. My knees are weak, and I can hardly keep myself up on my arms. When I feel hands grab me, Leon pulls his cock out of my mouth, and Raidon rolls me onto my back. I feel like I am a piece of melted putty.

"She's fine, Leon. You didn't hurt her. She's pregnant, not broken. Let her catch her breath," Thane speaks over the tension as Raidon pushes my knees apart, settling between my legs.

He grips my ass, dragging me closer as Thane leans over and rubs his hand over my belly. Thane's lips cover mine. His tongue invades my mouth, and I moan, kissing him back while Raidon teases his cock between my wet folds and over my clit. My hips rock, wanting him inside me, but I am too exhausted to move.

Suddenly, being pregnant kills my stamina. So, all I can do is whine. "More," I mumble against Thane's lips.

Thane quietly laughs and pulls back just as Raidon's cock slams inside me, pumping back and forth ruthlessly. I look up at him as he fucks me, knowing he is desperate to cum and that holding himself back is a challenge. Each thrust of his hips makes me shudder and moan, bringing—no, forcing—me closer to the edge.

He doesn't wait. Raidon grips my thighs and thrusts his cock deeper into me. All I can do is take what he offers. Suddenly, he leans down, slips his arm under my lower back and rolls, so I am straddling his hips, and he leans against the headboard next to Thane.

Raidon's hands glide over the sides of my belly, and Thane grips my throat, bringing his face closer and stealing another kiss. My walls clench around Raidon's cock as Thane's tongue slips into my mouth. My hips rock against him, and Raidon grips them, moving me faster when Thane pulls away.

Thane moves off the bed before he returns with a small, black plastic bottle. He chucks it to Leon.

Leon puts a few drops of lube on his fingers and begins to gently play with my ass. Leon properly covers his hard cock with lube and then applies lots of it to my ass, carefully stretching me. He then hands the bottle to Thane, who sets it on the bedside table.

Raidon thrusts up into me hard, making me gasp. His cock fits perfectly inside me, but it is clear I won't be doing any riding. He may be below me, but he is very much in control.

"Eyes on me. Don't worry about what Leon is doing," Raidon growls. His firm grip on my hips prevents me from moving, and he slowly thrusts from below.

I have three of Leon's fingers inside me now, stretching, but even with that, I know his thick cock will be difficult to take. With all the gentle care in the world and with an unwavering precision, Leon pulls me back by my hair, forcing my back to arch. The moment he does, all three of them flood me with their Calling, turning me languid between them, and Leon forces his hard cock up my ass.

They are both completely inside me. Leon stills, and Raidon's thumb presses against my clit. Thane kneels on the bed just as Leon lets go of my throat.

Thane captures my lips. "Good girl," he growls against them before delving his tongue into my mouth.

I groan and rock my hips. Leon slowly pulls out before thrusting back inside me. I wait for the pain, but I am sedated by their Calling, loving every second of them filling me so completely.

It hurts a little as Leon and Raidon start to move in sync, but it is a good kind of pain, the one you enjoy as long as you're not pushed too far. The combination of pure pleasure from Raidon's unceasing attacks from beneath me and Leon's slow, methodical pounding, while Thane dominates my mouth, is impossible to describe. Leon is careful enough not to hurt me but raw enough to let me know that he already needs to cum. Thane lets me go, allowing me to suck in much-needed air.

I stare down at Raidon, who has spread his arms to the sides around the pillows and cushions, letting me bounce as much as possible, matching my movements with Leon's. But, when he realizes this will not be enough, he grabs my hips, anchors his heels on the bed, and starts fucking me relentlessly. Leon increases his speed, too, as he feels my ass stretching to accommodate his dick.

I scream, my entire body tensing as my walls squeeze Raidon's cock. I feel as if I am speaking in tongues, some strange dialect only understandable to me. My orgasm washes over me, making my entire body heat and buzz as I slump against Raidon's chest, my teeth tingling. As his scent hits my nose, I lick him, intoxicated, and before I can stop myself, I sink my teeth into his neck.

He groans, and his grip tightens on my hips as his knot swells, yet he doesn't force it inside me. Instead, he holds me up, making me whine as I feel the warmth of his seed spill inside me before he lets go.

The moment he does, Leon pulls me back into his arms and kisses my neck. I smile dreamily as I hear him tremble, then growl. Thane moves quickly, gripping my shoulders and shoving me down on top of Raidon, and I hear him grunt.

Leon falls back, exiting me, and I fall on Raidon, who wraps his arms around me before tugging the blanket over us. For the first time in months, I feel the bond go silent, finally getting what it wants. The torment that had created a void inside me suddenly feels less painful.

Raidon kisses my temple, and I feel Thane's aura rush out in a blast as Leon whimpers, making me glance over my shoulder. His teeth tear into Thane's neck, and I finally understand why Thane shoved him off me.

His hand strokes up and down Leon's spine. His blood spills down his chest as Leon savagely feeds off him. A whimper escapes me, and Raidon's hands rub my belly. "He's fine, love. Thane will take care of him."

This is the last place I want to be, especially when I feel my bond pulling me back to my mates. The happiness building in Thane makes me giddy. I miss them already, and if this meeting doesn't hurry along soon, I will cancel it.

Talon is already ten minutes late, and my patience is waning. However, as I'm checking the mountain-load of paperwork Leila left on my desk, I find I can no longer concentrate. Thane's arousal smashes into me through the bond, and my pants suddenly feel very restricting.

Deciding I can no longer wait for Talon to sort out his contract with his vendor, I get up from my seat and head toward the elevator. Talon was supposed to meet me here after my earlier meeting with a security company looking into advanced technical services.

That meeting went off without a hitch, and Talon knows better than to leave me waiting. Leon can deal with him, I am done trying to sort out his messes. I press the button on the elevator, only to notice it is already on its way up. Great, so much for going home early. Sighing, I move to the small kitchenette to make some coffee. I hear the elevator chime and call out to Talon.

"I'm in the kitchen," I yell out over my shoulder.

I hear more than one pair of shoes coming toward me. Setting my cup down on the counter, I move to see who he brought with him. I'm expecting it to be Bree, but when I step out of the small room, I find Talon, beaten and bloody, being escorted into the office by Alpha Corbin.

"Hello, Rhen. I was hoping to find Thane," Corbin says, shoving Talon to his knees in front of me. Reaching down, I grab Talon by the arm and pull him to his feet.

"What the fuck have you done?" I growl at him.

"Indeed, what has he done? I am a patient man, Rhen, reasonable, but this worm has screwed me over for the last time," Alpha Corbin says as Leila comes down the hallway behind him.

"Rhen!" she whimpers.

I growl, noticing half of Alpha Corbin's mates behind her. One has her arm wretched behind her back; her lip is also bleeding, as if one of them slapped her.

"Let her go. Whatever this is, we can sort it out," I say, shoving past him and reaching for my sister-in-law. Leila whimpers and hides behind me. I push her into Thane's office. "Lock the door," I tell her. She nods, her eyes glassy from crying.

I motion toward the conference room down the hall. Alpha Corbin heads toward it when I open the mind-link. 'Raidon, I need you in the office, now,' I tell him, before abruptly cutting the link. I know my mates, and I know they'll come. I am severely outnumbered here, and all of them are Alphas. Talon flinches as I step next to him.

"If you put my mates at risk, you don't have to be scared of Thane killing you. I will do it myself," I sneer at him.

Entering the conference room, I find Alpha Corbin with his feet up on the table, sitting back in the chair with a smug smile on his face. He flicks his dirty blond hair back and rests his arms behind his head.

"I guess now we wait for your Alpha."

"Raidon is on his way."

"I would prefer to deal with Thane and Leon," he growls at me.

"Thane is otherwise occupied. Now, do you mind telling me what this is all about?" I ask, my eyes cutting to the side as Jaxson, Leo, and Finley enter the room behind me. They lock the door, and I grit my teeth.

"You sure you want to go down this road, Corbin?"

"I am owed quite a lot of money. Talon here has not settled his debt as agreed. Your mate, Leon, paid half, and I am here to collect what's outstanding."

My eyes move to Talon, and he whimpers. I can feel my mates getting closer, feel Thane coming for me.

Talon meets my gaze, his eyes pleading for me to understand. I snarl and bare my teeth when Leo punches him.

"How much?" I ask, turning my gaze to Corbin. Thane will kill me if I bail him out again.

"It's not just money I am owed, but don't worry, I've learned you have exactly what I require. She'll do to replace the girl he lost," Corbin says, and I furrow my brows.

"Excuse me?" I ask.

"Not to worry. It will all be settled when Thane gets here."

I don't like the sound of that. And where are his other mates?

"You see, Leon went down for collateral." He clicks his tongue and shakes his head. My heart beats faster at his words.

"You're not taking Leon," I say, and he laughs, the sound mocking. I grit my teeth.

"I don't want Leon. Leon was stupid enough to back Talon against the vamps. Leon was stupid enough to tell them he will cover any debt Talon can't. He even signed my contracts, and he was stupid enough to pay the debt for him."

My brows furrow at Corbin's words.

"If the debt is paid, why are you here?"

"My purchase was supposed to be delivered to me last week, but she wasn't. I have recently learned that Talon here set my purchase free."

Talon shuffles forward on his knees.

"I'm sorry, Rhen. She's barely eighteen, and I panicked," Talon pleads.

I glare down at him, and I open the mind-link, feeling for Thane. *'Where is Harlow?'*

'At home with Leon. What's going on?'

'Alpha Corbin is here.'

'We're almost there. Just hold him off.'

'No, get back to Harlow. Now!' I scream through the link, just as I feel a fist connect with my face. I spit blood and wipe my mouth before glaring at Finley, who punches me again. While I'm recovering from the second blow, I feel something slide between my ribs and steal my breath.

I twist, glancing under my arm to find a knife embedded in my flesh. Pain ripples up my side, and my shirt slowly turns red. The hand holding the knife twists, and I suck in a breath before locking eyes with Jaxson.

"Leon should know better than to take his cousin's word," Corbin says.

"Whatever the cost, we'll pay it," I grit out. Jaxson sneers behind me and twists the knife further. My claws slip out as I fight the urge to shift, knowing if I do, Corbin will tear me apart.

"You're right. Leon will pay for his mistake."

"Leon owns nothing. Everything is in Thane's name, and if you think Thane will let you take Leon—" I hiss when the knife is ripped out. My hand grips my side to stem the bleeding, and my knees buckle.

"Now that's where you're wrong. Leon does have one thing in his name. He owns your Omega," Corbin snarls. My back arches as the knife plunges into it, between my shoulder blades. I choke, sputtering out blood, and I gasp when I feel my lung collapse.

He rips the knife out, and I fall forward onto my knees. Talon screams, and my vision starts to fade as I fight to remain conscious. Why am I not healing? My veins feel like they are on fire as I search for her through the bond, search for Harlow. Instead, I get Raidon.

'Rhen?'

'Tell Harlow I love her,' I choke, spewing blood onto the floor. I see them drag Talon out of the room. My entire body feels cold, and I shiver.

'No. I am almost there,' Raidon replies.

My eyes flutter, and the room blurs. The ground beneath me is soaked in my blood, and I collapse.

'Rhen!' Raidon screams through the bond when I feel my tether break.

CHAPTER SEVEN

ONE HOUR EARLIER

I must have dozed off at some point because I am awoken by Raidon shaking my shoulder as Thane places a tray on my lap. Lifting my head off Raidon's chest, I find the tray covered with a plate of French toast and a cup of coffee. My hand instantly goes for the coffee.

"You seem calmer," Thane says, and I nod, taking a sip of the coffee.

"Eat," grumbles Raidon, tapping the tray and stabbing a piece of toast with a fork. I roll my eyes at his bossiness, but tear a chunk off the pile of syrupy goodness.

"Where's Rhen?" I ask after swallowing.

"At work," Leon says, stepping out of the bathroom with a towel wrapped around his waist. My eyes roam over his muscled body and I lick my lips. My hunger for other things rears its damn ugly head again. Raidon softly chuckles.

"Our Omega is turning into a nympho," he purrs, making me look at him.

I glare as he pinches my chin between his fingers, forcing my face to his. His lips brush mine softly and I growl, biting his lip. He laughs, snapping his teeth next to mine.

"I don't mind if you bite," he chortles. A smug smile plays on his lips, which makes me remember I've already marked him.

My eyes zero in on his neck. My face scrunches up, and I sit up higher on the bed. Raidon slips his arm behind me, and Thane quickly removes the tray, grabbing my coffee before I spill it everywhere.

Raidon hauls me on top of him, so I am straddling his waist. My eyes are on his neck, my bond demanding to know where my mark went. I check the other side of his neck. Raidon's fingers trail up my spine as I turn his head, looking for it. I could have sworn I marked him.

Pulling back, I look at him before glancing over my shoulder at Leon, wondering if he is the one I marked. I remember the taste of blood. I remember marking one of them. Leon is pulling his jeans on, watching me. His eyes flick to Thane, and I feel the bed dip as Thane climbs on behind me. He sits between Raidon's legs, and his hands slip around my waist as he pulls me back against him, his hands gently rubbing over my belly.

"You're confused why your mark didn't stick," he states, and I nod, staring at Raidon's neck. Some part of me wonders if he rejected me while I slept. I glare at him, my chest hurting at the thought. I touch his mark on my neck. It feels perfectly fine, and I let out a breath.

"You did not just think that!" Raidon growls at me. "I would never reject you," he says. He must have read my thoughts on my face. Thane sighs behind me, his hands slipping under my belly as he holds it.

"We should have told you, but we were afraid of how you would react," Thane purrs, nipping at my shoulder. His lips trail up my neck, and I turn my face to look at him. He pecks my lips, and sighs.

"Tell me what?" I ask him, my voice shaking, wondering why they sound so worried. Their worry bleeds into me, making me anxious.

"You can't mark them," Thane says slowly. My lips part,

wanting to protest, but his lips cover mine, cutting off anything I might say. "Wait, I'll explain," he mumbles against my lips before pulling away.

His eyes flick to Raidon, and I can feel Thane's fear, loud and clear. He is afraid to tell me whatever it is. He exhales, pressing his face into my neck before sitting back up.

"Do you remember how I had to mark you first?" he asks, and I nod.

"Yes, because you're the Alpha. They can't accept me unless you do."

He nods.

"It's the same with you marking us. I have to accept your mark first. Until I do, any mark you make on them will just heal."

"Wait, so you don't want me to mark them? Therefore I can't?" I ask, jerking away from him. He growls, pulling me back to his chest.

"That is not what I said, Low."

"But you just said —"

Thane cuts me off, growling at my accusatory tone.

"You have to mark me first. I never said I don't want you to mark them. Just that until you mark me, you marking them won't stick," he finally says.

"It's also why we wouldn't touch you," Raidon says. "We didn't want to upset you knowing you want to mark us."

I raise an eyebrow at him before looking at Leon, who shrugs.

"Are you all thick?" I ask. Leon bristles and shakes his head.

"Wow," Thane says, and I turn to look at him.

"What? Not one of them would touch me. My bond has been going haywire thinking they are rejecting me because they wouldn't come near me. Only to find out they wouldn't touch me because I might mark them?" I stare at them. They glance at each other.

"You didn't think to just say that? Jeez, I am not unreasonable!" I snap at them.

"That's debatable," Raidon chuckles gently, and I growl at him. He holds up a finger and gives me a pointed look. "If we told you that you had to mark Thane before you could mark us when you got back here, you would have pitched a fit."

I blink at him. I swear I can see his brain cells dying right before my eyes.

"And probably run from us, again," Leon adds.

"No. I wouldn't have liked it, but I wouldn't have run. I didn't have to come back here, and I knew that by doing so I would have to accept Thane, too, since you all damn well come as a quadruple package. I would have been pissed, but at least I wouldn't have spent the last couple of weeks thinking you were all repulsed by me," I tell them.

"Why would you think that?" Raidon snarls angrily, and I point to my stomach. Is he blind!

"Maybe the fact I am the size of a fucking house, while you all walk around here like Greek gods, posing to have your goddamn statues erected."

"The only thing 'erected' around here is my damn cock. Don't let me hear you speak such nonsense again," Raidon snaps at me. "Besides, I like your tiger stripes. There's nothing sexier than knowing you are growing our child," he purrs, leaning forward and clamping his hands on either side of my face.

He jerks me forward, kissing me. He forces his tongue into my mouth, kissing me as if I am the very air he needs to breathe, while I actually do need that air. He lightly chuckles, pulling away, and I narrow my eyes at him.

"Asshole!"

"Your asshole," he corrects while climbing off the bed. "Shower with me," he says, holding his hand out. I slap it, and he laughs, wandering into the bathroom. Huffing, I unwrap Thane's arms from around me.

"Where are you going?" Thane purrs as I crawl to the edge of the bed. I flinch as his hand smacks my backside. I jump and twist, my ass stinging, and he smirks at me.

"To shower. I reek of sex, and—" I shake my head. "And you should shower, too. I am not biting you while you're covered in blood. And I need to brush my teeth," I tell him.

"She's marking me, she says," Thane laughs, looking at Leon.

"Pretty sure that's what she just said."

I pin Leon with my glare.

"I feel assaulted. Don't I get a say in this?" Thane laughs.

"Nope," I tell him, popping the 'P' at the end and climbing off the bed.

"Hm, maybe I won't let you," he jokes, and I tilt my head to look at him. I know he is kidding, but I don't like the smug look on his face.

I shrug at his words, and he reaches over as I walk past him. His fingers wrap around my wrist, and he pulls me to him.

"Maybe I should make you beg?" he tells me, and I tap my chin, thinking.

"Hop to it, then, on your knees," I tell him. He raises an eyebrow at me.

"I meant you beg me," he says.

"Ah, I thought you said that but figured you must have gotten your words jumbled because I won't beg. But now that you've suggested it, I really think I need to see you on your knees."

"Excuse me?" he says.

I am having way too much fun with this as the wheels start turning in my head.

"Yep, that should do it. I can put up with your tyrannical ways. I just need to see you beg first, and I will be content tying you to me."

"Tying me to you? I think you got your wires crossed somewhere. You don't own me," Thane laughs, looking at Leon. Leon snickers at him, and Thane turns his gaze back to me as I step out of his reach.

"Now would be great; I really need to shower," I tell him, pointing at the floor. Thane leans back on the bed, bracing his hands on either side of him.

"No! I am not bowing down and begging you to mark me," he deadpans. I huff, then shrug, turning to move toward the bathroom.

"Wait, that's it?" Thane asks.

"Yep, no skin off my nose. I have survived this long without marking them, haven't I?" I tell him, stepping into the bathroom.

"Low? You need to mark us!"

I stop, turning in the doorway to face him.

"Do I, though?" I ask. Thane huffs, and I walk over to him as

Raidon calls out from the bathroom.

"Wait, if Thane is begging, I want to witness this! Leon get your phone," he says.

"I am not begging!"

"I think you are," I tell him, and he scoffs. Leon clamps a hand on his shoulder.

"Don't worry. I will get proof to show Rhen. He won't believe us otherwise," Leon tells him. Thane's face falls, and he growls at Leon.

"Are you forgetting who your Alpha is, Leon? Don't make me remind you," Thane warns, and Leon shrugs.

"You may be Alpha, but she is Harlow and carrying our baby. What Momma wants, Momma gets. Now on your knees, or you might as well take a vow of celibacy."

"Excuse me?" Thane asks as Raidon bursts out from the door behind me.

"Good, I haven't missed it," he says, tucking the corner of the towel he's wearing into his waistline.

Thane looks at me. I smile while he glares, clearly not finding it funny having the tables turned around on him.

"You never know. You may enjoy it," I snicker.

"Doubtful. I don't get on my knees for anyone."

"Except for me!" I say, rubbing my foot on the carpet as I point to it. "Right about there should do it. Any closer and I won't be able to see your eyes over my baby bump," I tell him, rubbing my huge belly.

Thane begrudgingly gets up, growling and muttering under his breath.

"Ah, what was that? I didn't quite hear you, Thane."

"This is ridiculous," he mutters.

"But it's not ridiculous for me or Leon to beg?" I retort.

"That's different, I'm Alpha!" he huffs.

"On your knees, Omega," I tell him.

"You did not—"

I smile and cut him off.

"Looks like the only one who won't be getting their dick sucked around here is you," I tell him. He growls, glancing at Raidon.

"Don't look at me. I like getting my dick sucked. I am just here to witness," Raidon purrs at him. Thane mutters something under his breath before dropping to his knees. I stare down at him while he glares at my mound.

"My eyes are up here." The look he gives me at those words makes me giggle.

"You're lucky I love you," he sighs. He huffs before kissing my belly and cupping it in his hands. "Harlow, will you mark me? Please."

I ponder for a second, pretending to think really hard while tapping my finger on my chin.

"Woman, I swear if you got me on my knees to reject me, I will spank you."

"Hm, maybe I wouldn't mind being spanked," I say, and he growls. His eyes flicker black, and he smirks.

"You would like that, wouldn't you," he purrs, his hands moving from my belly and down my thighs.

"Yes, Thane, I will mark you," I say. I giggle when I hear Leon's phone camera go off. Thane growls, shooting him a glare over his shoulder. He goes to stand, but I push down on the top of his head. "While you're down there—" I start, only for Thane to growl, grabbing me and making me squeal. I don't expect the rush as my legs are pulled out from under me. I grab his shoulders as he tosses me to the bed. My heart races as his lips crash against mine.

"My naughty Omega," he growls against my lips while pressing me gently into the bed. His lips travel south, nipping and licking, when I feel a twinge of worry from Rhen. Thane also tenses, feeling it, too. He lifts his head, looking at the others, and Raidon suddenly rushes from the room.

"Leon, watch Harlow," Thane growls, taking off after Raidon while I sit up on my elbows.

"What's going on?" I worry, feeling their anxiety.

Leon shakes himself and smiles. "Whatever is going on, Thane will handle it." Yet I can see the worry on Leon's face, feel it through the bond.

"Come, I'll help you shower," Leon says, offering me his hand, just as I hear Thane's car tear out of the driveway, the engine screaming.

"Leon?"

"I'm sure it will be fine."

CHAPTER EIGHT

RAIDON

Racing down the stairs, I can feel Rhen's fear. That man, much like Thane, fears nothing, so I know he must be in dire circumstances if he thinks he can't handle it on his own. My feet miss some stairs as I fly down them to reach the main floor. I snatch the keys off the hook by the door. Thane barrels into me, plucking the keys from my hand as he opens the door.

I see his eyes glaze over as he hits the key fob. No doubt Rhen is telling him what's going on. He jumps in the car, and I throw myself in the passenger side, before peering down, to realize I still only have a towel on.

The roof of his car hits the garage door before it has a chance to fully open. He pulls out and spins the car around.

He hits the button above his head for the gate and presses his foot down on the gas.

"There's a suit hanging in the backseat," Thane says, not taking his eyes off the long driveway. I twist, unclipping my seatbelt and snatching it when I hear the gate scrape across his side of the car.

He curses but doesn't stop to assess the damage. I start ripping the pants up my legs, and I mean ripping because I have thicker thighs and more ass than Thane, and all his suits are tailored. As we hit the city limits, we pass a bunch of black state council SUV's. I watch them drive past.

"Why are state authorities in the city?" Thane mumbles watching them in the rearview mirror. I slide my arms into the shirt as the mind-link opens again. I can tell Rhen is looking for Thane, but Thane pushes the link wider, so I can hear what's going.

'Where is Harlow?' Rhen panics.

'At home with Leon. What's going on?' Thane answers.

'Alpha Corbin is here.'

'We are almost there. Just hold him off.'

'No, get back to Harlow. Now!' Rhen screams when the link is abruptly cut off.

"Pull over!" I yell at Thane, and he slams his foot on the brakes. "Get home. I will find Rhen." He nods. I throw myself out of the car and shift while Thane rips the car around, heading back home.

People scream and jump out of my way as my huge wolf form plows through the bustling sidewalk. I see our building up ahead. My paws slam against the concrete as I weave between people before giving up and moving toward the road. Fifty feet away relief floods me, but only briefly, as I feel the link open up.

'Rhen?' I panic.

'Tell Harlow I love her,' he chokes out.

A cold shiver runs up my spine before pain sears through me, making me collapse. The pain is so terrible, it forces me to shift back, and cars screech as they narrowly miss me.

'No. I am almost there,' I tell him as my body skids across the asphalt, my skin getting torn to pieces. I stand, only to be hit by a car and tossed into the median separating the traffic.

Getting up, I am covered in cuts and bruises, and people are lining the streets, phones in hand. Some race toward me, but I take off running with a slight limp. I feel the bond flickering, weakening.

'Rhen!' I scream through the link. My heart is thumping so hard I can hear it as I run through the glass doors at the back of the building.

Pain steals my breath and nearly brings me to my knees. I feel it cut in and out, and I nearly rip the handle off the door to the fire escape, not willing to wait for the elevator. With each step, the pain grows more agonizing. *'Rhen!'* I wail through the bond, begging him to stay, begging him to hold on. I feel Thane's, Leon's, and then Harlow's anguish at his loss as his bond severs.

My vision blurs from tears as I continue to force myself up the stairs. Six more flights.

I am giving up. I want to drop down and die on the stairs myself when I feel the smallest glimmer of hope. So faint, so weak, yet it is there, and it shoots adrenaline through me. In no time, I am ripping the door open and hear Leila screaming frantically.

"Help, somebody get help!" she wails. My bare feet slip on the floor as I follow my nose to find him. The conference room door is wide open. I see his feet, and so much blood.

"Help! In here! Help!" Leila screams, her voice sounding broken. I gasp as I step into the room. Leila looks up with tears rolling down her face, her wrists and lips all bloody.

"Raidon," she chokes, pumping his chest. I drop to my knees. His face is drained of all color. Her hands work frantically to try to revive him.

"You did good. He's still with us. I can feel him," I tell her, as my hands replace hers. She bites her wrist as I continue pumping his chest.

"I panicked. I didn't know what else to do. Harlow is going to hate me," she sobs, feeding him more of her blood. She lifts his shirt to see his wounds slowly closing.

"He's not dead. She won't hate you. We just gotta keep him alive long enough for him to heal," I say. She sobs and nods, re-biting herself before looking at me.

"You'll heal him faster, being his mate," she says. I offer her my neck, and she slashes her nails under my chin before grabbing his head and forcing his mouth open. My blood streams out, dripping all over his face, and I know she hit an artery. Leila moves his head, letting my blood pour down his throat before she shuts his mouth. Her fingers grab my neck to stem the flow of blood, but I am already healing. Still, I pump his chest, knowing if he dies with her blood in his system, two things will happen.

First, he will turn into a hybrid; then he will become sired to her.

"I'm sorry, I'm sorry," she sobs, making me look at her. "I hope she doesn't hate me. I didn't want this."

"Leila, you saved his life. You did good. You got to him in time, and the bond didn't fully break. He will be fine. I felt it come back. You didn't sire him." And no sooner do I say it than Rhen gasps, lurching upright. His eyes are wide and bulging as he grips my arm.

"Get to Harlow!" he chokes before coughing. Leila wails as she clutches him. I exhale, but only feel relief for a brief moment before I feel Thane's rage and Leon's fear. Then, as if a switch is flicked within Thane, gone is our mate. In his place is our Alpha.

And whoever brought that beast forward better fucking run.

CHAPTER NINE

Leon is tense as we shower, and it has me on edge. I climb out as Leon finishes washing the shampoo from his hair.

"Wait, don't leave without me," Leon says, frantically scrubbing at his scalp as I wrap a towel around myself.

My face scrunches up, wondering what has gotten into him. He's barely said anything to me since Thane and Raidon left. Hearing the doorbell, I glance at the bathroom door.

"Harlow!" Leon snaps at me, but I ignore him, retrieving one of Raidon's shirts and slipping it on.

"I'm just answering the door," I huff before moving into the bedroom. The moment I step into the hall, I hear the front door get kicked down, making me jump.

A scream of fright leaves my lips, only to be muffled by Leon's hand. My breathing is harsh as he sniffs the air. I hear the housekeeper downstairs, demanding to know who they are.

"We are here for the Omega," comes a gruff voice.

My eyes widen at the demand. Leon holds a finger to his lips and lets me go before ushering me to the back stairwell.

'Thane, get back here!' Leon snarls through the link. I'm cursing myself for not marking them earlier. I can hear them, but with an

incomplete bond, I can't reply. Leon grabs my arm, quickly leading me down the back stairs and into the library. He glances at the door that leads to the kitchen, where we can hear the housekeeper arguing with them to leave. We hear a sickening slap, followed by her whimper.

Leon growls. His eyes burn bright red as he leads me to the huge glass window. Footsteps above us tell me a few of them went upstairs. From the different scents, I can smell at least seven people, three of which I can tell are Alphas.

I hear another car pull up out front as Leon quietly slides the window open before grabbing my hips and lifting me through the window.

"What are you doing?" I hiss at him.

"Head for the sheds at the back of the property. I will come find you. Stay out of sight."

"Wait."

"Can't, love. Now run," Leon says, not giving me a chance to protest before he drops me to my feet and quickly closes the window.

I duck down, scanning my surroundings and spotting the huge sheds by the edge of the tree line, where the gardener keeps his tools. With one last glance at the huge mansion, I start across the lawn, using the hedges for cover and keeping as low as possible.

I hear a commotion inside before a man is tossed from the second-floor window. The glass shatters, and I freeze, watching him hit the roof of the first story, only to roll off and hit the concrete below. I duck down, watching as he tries to get up. He clutches his neck, which is spurting blood everywhere. My gaze moves to the window above to see Leon fighting another man.

Ducking back down, I run. As I reach one of the sheds, I push the door open enough to slip inside. Peering through the gap, I see the housekeeper being dragged outside, and a tall man with dirty blond hair, clearly an Alpha, lifts his gun and shoots her in the head.

I gasp as she collapses to the ground. My hands cover my mouth at what I see. What the hell is going on? Only a few tense seconds later, I watch as Leon is dragged from the house and tossed beside the dead housekeeper, whose name I feel bad for not remembering.

Leon is drenched in blood, covered as if he bathed in it. The two men who tossed him to the ground are also bloody. One man's arm is bent at an odd angle, and I watch him shove it back into place. Staring out, I see seven Alphas and two other men in uniform, who look to be officials.

I recognize the man with the gun as one of the Alphas from the glory hole event at Tal's. I swear I have seen the other man before, yet I don't place him until he speaks.

"Where is she?" he yells, kicking Leon in the face. My blood runs cold, and I am suddenly frozen to the spot, trapped in a memory I don't want. A memory I worked so hard to forget. The memory slams into me by the mere sound of his voice and throws me back in time. Everything I suppressed starts assaulting my mind.

THE DAY OF THE ATTACK

We're in Mrs. Keller's car, which is upside down and in a ravine after they ran us off the road. Mrs. Keller is slumped and dangling from her seat. I hear men shouting in the distance.

"Down here! Quick, grab the bitch and let's go!"

I blink, and blood from the gash on my head taints my vision. I shake Mrs. Keller awake. She groans, peering around. The voices get closer. She turns, and I will never forget the look she gives me. One of pure terror, and she screams at me.

"Run! Run, Harlow. They are coming for you," she screams, and I run. I am at the edge of the tree line when I stop, expecting her to be right behind me. However, as I peer between the bushes, I see men running down the ravine as she tries to crawl out her door. She has a huge piece of metal stabbing through her stomach.

The men grab her, hauling her out of the car. My entire body is frozen as I watch the horror unfold before me. I'm paralyzed by fear, and I tremble, staring out between the bushes.

She is thrown to the ground on her hands and knees. The man grabs her hair, jerking her head back. She spits in his face, and he wipes it off. "Where is she?" he asks.

"Go fuck yourself, you pin-dick prick," she responds, only for him to slap her across the face. Blood sprays over the grass, and tears brim in my eyes. Mrs. Keller laughs, however, and wipes her mouth before glaring at him.

"You always were a pathetic excuse for an Alpha," she sneers at him.

"You were supposed to be mine!" he growls at her.

"I was never yours, and neither was Harper!" she screams at him.

"You had Sophia take the first twin from me. You aren't getting this one. Black fucked up, and he'll pay for that mistake, but in the meantime, you'll pay for ever daring to cross me."

He grabs her face, kissing her, but she growls, biting down on his tongue. He grabs the steel protruding from her stomach and twists, making her scream and let go.

"When I find her, and I will, I'll make sure there is nothing left of her for Thane. You took Harper from us. Now we take Thane's Omega from you," he growls at her.

"You're a dead man," she spits at him, blood dribbling down her lips and chin.

"He'll never know," the man laughs, and two men haul her to her feet. He pulls a knife from his back pocket and drags the tip down her face. She doesn't flinch, just glares at him.

"My son will come for you. He'll come for her, and you better pray to the Moon Goddess he has mercy on you!"

The man laughs, tapping the knife on her cheek.

"Find her. She can't have got far!" he snaps at the other four men with him. They start taking their clothes off and begin shifting.

"All this time and you're still trying to catch a ghost," she laughs.

He growls before slitting her throat.

That's what finally gets me moving. I do what she told me, and I run.

I hid in that forest for days, covering my body in mud to hide my scent as I waited them out. Now, staring out the shed doors, I see the man who killed Hana. The man who hunted me. His voice triggered a memory my mind had blocked out.

The blond man with the gun must be Alpha Corbin. I can tell who he is by the sheer size of him, and his aura is menacing, like Thane's. He lifts his gun, pressing it to Leon's temple before he looks up at the house.

CHAPTER TEN

"Harlow, you have two minutes before I put a bullet in his head!" he screams out. My hands shake, but I remain where I am as Leon's voice flits through my head.

'Stay where you are. Don't fucking move, Harlow,' he snaps at me.

One of them kicks Leon, and he doubles over, coughing with one hand on the ground as he wheezes. Another man drags the gardener from behind the side of the house. He begs and pleads as he is dumped next to Leon.

"Now Harlow, or I'll kill—" he looks down at the gardener. "Whoever this is," he says waving the gun at him. He is still staring at the mansion, not realizing I'm not inside.

'I'm five minutes out. The road is blocked!' come's Thane's furious voice.

Pain suddenly tears through me from Rhen, and I drop to my knees. Leon screams, clutching his chest, and I gasp for air as I feel Rhen's tether break. I feel the agony from all of my mates, only to peer up and see men racing toward me.

I must have screamed out in pain without realizing, and I choke back fear. Leon gets to his feet, only to be hit in the head with the butt of the gun. I scramble to my feet, fighting the agony of Rhen's tether breaking. It burns, tearing my heart out.

I look for another exit, cursing that I didn't run for the trees when I had the chance. I clutch my stomach and glance around. I see another door at the back of the shed and race toward it. I hear them reach the main door as I squeeze through a gap in all the equipment. My fingers wrap around the door handle, only for someone to grip my hair and rip me back.

"There you are, love," a deep, rumbling voice says next to my ear. I thrash, kicking and fighting to get loose. The other man grabs my legs, hauling me out of the huge shed. The moment I am brought out, Leon gets to his feet and charges at the men holding me, only to be shot twice in the back, giving the gardener a chance to attack Corbin.

Leon staggers, dropping to his knees. A second later, another gunshot rings out and the gardener drops to the ground. Leon wheezes. One hand clutches his hip where the bullet went straight through. His shoulder is also bleeding, but he is alive, for now.

Corbin lifts his gun and shoots again. Leon twists, but the bullet still hits him. He slumps to the ground, and I scream, feeling pain tear through my ribs from the same spot he was hit. I thrash harder when I see Alpha Corbin strode to us. All I can think is 'why aren't the officials doing anything?' They just stand and watch.

I am placed on the ground at Corbin's feet. The man who killed Hana walks up behind him and smirks, looking down at me.

"Exactly like her mother," Corbin says, tilting my face from side to side with his gun.

Tears stream down my face as I try to figure out why he is doing this. It makes no sense to me. I see Leon trying to get up, but a man puts his foot on his back and shoves him back down.

"Stay down. Enough people have died today," the man says.

Leon looks at me and I plead with my eyes for him to listen to the man. He clenches his jaw.

"We'll have to take care of that," Corbin growls, nudging my stomach with his foot. I use my arms to cover my bump and growl at him, only for him to laugh.

"Feisty like her mother, too," he snarls, making my brows pinch together as I stare at him. He returns my look with a sadistic smile. "Leo, chuck her in the car!" he says to the man who murdered Hana. He reaches for me, but I scramble back on my hands and feet. He stalks after me.

"Are the roads still blocked off?" Corbin asks one of the officials. They both nod.

"Yes, but we can't keep it blocked for long," one man says as this Leo person grabs my arm. I lash out, kicking him. I extend my claws and slash them down his face.

He growls, and Leon screams when he stomps on me. I move quickly enough, and instead of him stomping on my stomach, he stomps on my shoulder.

"Try that again, and I will cut your pup from you right now," he snarls, wiping his face with the back of his arm. I whimper as he presses his foot down harder on my shoulder. I turn my face to see Leon get knocked out. He falls limp on the ground.

Leo grabs me and starts dragging me to the car by my hair. The gravel rips at my back, ass, and legs. I kick my feet, trying to get enough traction to stand.

"Now we just gotta find the other one," I hear Corbin say as I am tossed into the back of the car.

"Bree said she is with Alpha Jake," one of them says.

Bree? I blink, wondering what she has to do with this. The car door slams as Leo climbs in next to me. I hear the sound of an engine screaming up the road, and Leo leans forward, peering out the windshield. Alpha Corbin jumps into the passenger side and looks at the official in the driver's seat. The other men run for their cars.

"I thought you said the roads were blocked!" Corbin snarls at the man.

"They are," the man stammers.

Corbin spins in his seat and kicks the man, shoving him out his open door before climbing into the driver's seat.

"Corbin?" Leo growls beside me.

"We can outrun him," Corbin says, starting the car. The engine roars to life, and I see Thane's car skidding onto the long driveway. Corbin guns it, throwing me back in my seat, only to be cut off by one of the other cars, forcing him to slam on the brakes.

I giggle. Leo glares at me as he grips the back of the driver's seat. "You're so fucked," I tell them, reaching for the door handle.

Leo growls, grabbing at me, but I jump from the vehicle. Leo snarls as I land on my hands and knees. Corbin hits the gas, and Leo is tossed from the car when he tries to grab the back of my shirt. Corbin doesn't wait. He guns the engine, choosing to leave his mate behind, or not realizing Leo is gone, as he plows toward Thane's car.

Leo grabs me. I throw my head back as he tries to wrangle me. My head hits his face and he grunts, dropping me just as I hear the two cars collide. My gaze moves to the scene to find Corbin's car spinning out of control, before he floors it and skids sideways out the gate. The other two cars slam on their brakes to avoid smashing into Thane's car. One zips off around him, escaping with Corbin. Thane tosses his car door open and glares at the third car.

A furious growl echoes around us. Leo freezes, staring in Thane's direction. The trapped car starts reversing. Thane stalks toward it, and if looks could kill, they would be dying the most agonizing death right now.

Within seconds, he shifts, and his huge mammoth of a wolf dives straight through the front windshield of the car. The men's screams are loud as the car rocks from side to side and starts rolling forward. Leo gasps before grabbing my arm and hauling me to my feet.

I kick my legs, screaming for Leon and Thane as he starts dragging me toward the tree line. I drop my weight, slipping out of his grip as I hear their car crash into Thane's. Leo stops, glancing over his shoulder, before he snarls and grips my hair. Twisting, he rips my hair out painfully, and I kick him between the legs.

I hear Leon groan as he staggers to his feet. I dart my eyes to him briefly, costing me precious time. Leo snags my ankle, dragging me back to him.

"Leon!" I scream as Leo pins me. His knee presses down on my groin area as he tries to grab my shoulders. Feet suddenly appear beside my head, making Leo freeze. His eyes widen, and stare past his shoulder to see Thane standing next to us, naked and drenched in blood.

Leo lurches off me and scrambles backward. Thane steps over me. "You touched my Omega."

Leo shakes his head, "Corbin, he—"

"You touched my mate," Thane deadpans, his voice ice-cold and his steps calculating. Leo backs up, and Thane stalks him. Leo is now his prey. Leo's face twists into a snarl. He shifts at the same time Thane does, and they start tearing into each other.

CHAPTER ELEVEN

LEON

Thane tears into Leo. I can see Harlow caught, frozen like a deer in headlights. Her entire back and legs are bleeding from being dragged. Thane pushes Leo, trying to keep him back and away from her. Every time Leo moves or slams too close to her, Thane's wolf is there taking the brunt of it while he screams through the link for me to get up and move her.

If she doesn't move soon, it will cost Thane. She's distracting him, and his positioning is making it hard for him to kill Leo and not trample her. Leo recognizes that, and he uses it to his advantage. He knows it is the only chance he has in a fight against Thane.

Staggering, I force myself to move. My breath wheezes as I feel my lung try to heal and re-inflate. Harlow screams when Thane is tossed. He just barely catches himself before landing on her and crushing her. She is now caught between his legs, but she crawls out, finally coming out of her shock as Thane chomps down on Leo's neck.

Leo howls, the sound pained, before he twists, reflexively trying to bite anywhere he can reach. Thane pounces on him, breaking his hind leg in a single bite.

"Harlow!" I scream, trying to get her attention. She looks lost, as if the gravity of the situation has finally hit her. Now that Thane is here, she knows it is safe to fall apart.

Harlow lifts her head to look at me. "Leon," she gasps, finally finding her feet and rushing toward me. Her voice distracts Thane, and he turns to search for her. I grab her, hauling her away from the fight as Thane is suddenly hit from the side, that second of worry costing him.

Thane gets back to his feet just as Leo pounces. However, before Leo hits his mark, he is tackled by Rhen's big mottled wolf, who comes out of nowhere to divert Leo's attack. Raidon is right behind Rhen, also in wolf form. Raidon's wolf is huge, as big as Thane's, and it reminds me of a grizzly bear.

He grabs Leo's neck, shaking viciously, while Rhen and Thane get to their feet. He tosses him, and Leo skids across the grass, about ten yards away from us. The second Leo comes to a stop, Thane pounces on him, while Raidon moves to protect us.

Leo's whimpered shriek is loud, making Harlow jump. She turns her head in their direction and so do I. Leo is forced to shift back, and Thane's huge black wolf towers over him.

Raidon licks Harlow's fingers, nudging her with his nose. Rhen watches on, making sure Thane doesn't need him, though we all know Thane has it handled. He's about to deliver the final blow when Harlow screams.

"You can't kill him!" she rasps out, as loud as she can. Thane tenses, freezing, and so do I. Her conscience surely can't be getting the better of her now. Thane ignores her as she tries to get out of my grip. "Thane, he has information we need!" she says before looking up at me.

Thane growls, shifting back. He glances over his shoulder at us before staring down at the ripped up man, who is slowly healing.

"We need him!" she repeats. Thane growls, his fist clenching.

"Fuck!" he curses and shakes his head. Harlow weasels out of my grip, having spotted Rhen. She rushes to him, and his wolf drops his head to catch her on his shoulder as she locks her arms around his neck.

My gaze goes back to Thane, just in time to see his foot come down on Leo's head, knocking him out. Within seconds, Raidon is there to grab him and hauls him over his shoulder.

Rhen knocks Harlow over, forcing her on her back as he frantically licks her face before pushing his nose into her stomach.

"Baby is fine. I can hear her heartbeat," I tell him, walking over to them. Rhen huffs, and I grab handfuls of his fur, tugging him off her. When I go to grab her, he shifts and pushes me away before scooping her up.

"This is your fault," he snaps at me, and I nod once. Rhen isn't one to point blame, especially when it comes to me. So, if he is, I know this is related to me helping Talon. Thane growls, glaring at me, but it's Rhen he grabs.

We all felt his tether nearly break, all know whatever happened nearly cost his life. Thane presses forward against Rhen.

"You're not allowed to die on me," he growls. "You, however," he says, turning to me. "I'm still deciding how badly I want to kill you." He lets go of Rhen. I look at the ground, wondering what Talon did, and they walk off.

Glancing up, I see Raidon ahead. He is stopped by the doors to the house, looking in the hedges. He nods to them, and Thane runs ahead to see what Raidon is motioning toward. I reach his side just as he pulls a man in uniform out from his hiding place.

He is a state official. He cowers, hands covering his face as Thane drags him out by his collar. Thane shoves him toward the door.

"You and I need to talk," he says. The man falls to his hands and knees inside the doorway. He starts crawling away from Thane.

Stepping inside, I see Raidon tying Leo to a chair. The official freezes when Raidon turns his icy glare toward him. He motions with his finger for the man to come to him. The man whimpers but doesn't dare disobey Raidon. He sits next to Leo.

Rhen places Harlow on the couch and starts checking her over, much to her dismay. She grabs Rhen's head and whispers something to him. He looks at her, and his rage and shock smash into all of us, making us glance at him.

"Thane, I need you to walk out of this room and let Raidon and I handle this," Rhen tells him.

"I'm not going anywhere while that bastard is still breathing," Thane growls at him. Rhen's eyes go to Raidon. I watch as they mind-link.

"Are you sure?" Raidon asks, looking at Harlow. She nods her head, her eyes darting to Thane nervously.

"You need to leave, Thane," Raidon tells him.

"I said no. Not while he is still alive. I won't risk him escaping," Thane replies. He turns to Harlow questioningly. Her lips quiver, and her hands shake as she reaches for Thane. He doesn't hesitate and moves toward her, gripping her fingers.

"Please leave. You can have him after," she whispers. His brows furrow as he glances at all of us. He shakes his head.

"Someone tell me what's going on. We have come too fucking far for you to start hiding shit from me now. What did I do?" he snaps at us.

"You did nothing. It's what Leo did," Harlow whispers. Thane looks at her. "I didn't recognize him until he spoke."

"Huh?" he asks, his tone accusing. "Recognize him from where?"

Raidon finishes tying Leo and steps in front of him when Rhen speaks.

"Leo is the one who killed your mother," Rhen says.

The roar of fury that leaves Thane hurts my ears as he lunges for Leo.

Raidon blocks him, keeping himself between Thane and Leo, just as Rhen and I grab Thane. Thane stands toe to toe with Raidon, his chest heaving, his nostrils flaring at Raidon for preventing him from getting to Leo. My hands shake, and I can see Rhen is also struggling to hold him back. Thane's strength in this state is immeasurable.

"You need to let Rhen and me handle this," Raidon says, keeping his cool, and speaking calmly.

"HE KILLED HER."

"We know, but we need him alive to figure out what is happening. So stand down, Alpha," Raidon says. His aura slips out, showing Thane he won't back down. Thane will have to hurt him if he wants him to step aside. Thane clenches his jaw and snarls before shoving me and Rhen off. He turns, grabbing Harlow, who shrieks at the sudden movement.

"If I am leaving, then so are you. I am not leaving you anywhere near him," he tells her.

"But—" she starts before Rhen shakes his head at her. She sighs and allows Thane to stalk off with her. Leo is slumped over, still unconscious.

"So, what did Harlow tell you?" I ask as the official groans.

"We'll start with him," Rhen says, ignoring me and reaching for the man. He tosses him back on the couch.

"You will speak," Raidon warns him, and the man nods, his entire body trembling.

"Just don't kill me," he pleads pathetically.

"That depends entirely on your answers and how truthful they are," Rhen tells him.

Thane is like a raging bull as he takes me to our room. He goes straight to the bathroom, muttering under his breath about being forced to leave. I let him. Besides, I have bigger concerns. My stomach is cramping, my skin hurts, and I need to shower desperately.

Thane turns the shower on and sits me on the edge of the tub. He tugs off the shirt I am wearing, and his eyes trail over my naked body. Leaning down, he presses his hands to my belly. Our daughter writhes inside me as if she is doing yoga.

He lets out a breath. He crouches between my legs and kisses my belly. My skin tightens and my belly tenses as it cramps.

He jerks back, looking at it as I grit my teeth. "You look uncomfortable."

"Duh! I feel like I've been skinned," I exhale. My back stings so badly with all the little cuts and scrapes. Thane nods and turns toward the shower, placing his hand under the water.

"It's gonna sting, but we need to get the gravel out," he tells me, pulling me to my feet as Leon walks in. Thane growls, and Leon stops by the door.

"Get out, Leon. Right now. I don't want you near me," Thane

says. Leon goes to protest, but Thane snarls and steps toward him. I get between them. Thane glares at him, and I place my hands on his chest.

"It's not his fault," I tell him, confused at why everyone is mad at Leon. Thane's eyes flick down to me.

"He put you at risk. He put all of us at risk!" Thane snaps. I look at Leon, his eyes are glassy, as if he is about to start crying.

"I didn't think—" he starts.

"You're right, you didn't think. You should have come to us!" Thane yells at him, and Leon flinches. "I warned you time and time again about Talon, not to back him, and you did worse. You put everything on the line when you said you would be the collateral!"

"I just paid the debt; I didn't know he would gamble it!"

Thane shakes his head. "He didn't gamble it. He set her free!"

"What? No! I just gave him money. What are you talking about?" Leon argues.

"Money he used to get a fucking underage Omega! Rhen told me what happened on the way here. Your actions nearly cost us his life! You going down as collateral for Talon nearly cost us our fucking child!" Thane screams at him.

"Wait, what are you talking about?" I ask, confused. Thane pulls me closer, steering me toward the shower.

"Leon put his assets, meaning himself, down as collateral for Talon. If Talon doesn't come up with the money, they can go after Leon."

"Yeah, I put my life on the line, Thane. No one else's."

"And even that is too much!" Thane snaps at him. "You just don't fucking listen. I told you, next time, come to me. I'm changing her title back. This is exactly why we can't keep anything in your name. Every damn time he calls, you go running to help."

"He's family," Leon sighs.

"No, we are your family! I am done with this shit. Done with you bailing him out!" Thane roars. "What if I didn't get back here in time? What would your excuse be then, Leon? He came for her because she's an Omega under your fucking name! We could have lost her!"

"That makes no sense. They have no way of knowing her title is in my name," Leon says, but Thane shakes his head.

"Omega records are public information. They could have looked it up through the council, or Tal could have given him the information," Thane says, pinching his brow.

"No, Tal wouldn't— he wouldn't betray me like that."

Thane scoffs, and I remember the conversation Corbin and Leo had.

"And he didn't. Bree did," I tell them. They both look at me.

"Rhen never mentioned Bree. They had Talon, but Bree wasn't with them," Thane says.

"Bree would give up that information for him. You know she loves Talon," Leon says before sitting on the edge of the tub and putting his head in his hands. "I'm sorry. I didn't think," he murmurs.

Thane growls before nudging me under the water. I hiss, my back arching as it comes in contact with the water. "I know, love," he whispers, stepping under the water with me and holding me under its spray.

I try to pull away. It feels like my back, ass, and legs are on fire.

"Shh," he hushes before flooding me with his Calling. My body turns languid and he has to hold me upright. I am drowning in the sensation his Calling awakens. Thane starts washing me, while continuing to speak with Leon. My brain is mush, making it impossible to understand anything they say. His Calling is potent, nearly knocking me out when I feel another set of hands on me.

Leon's scent wafts to my nose, so I know it is him. The shower turns off and Thane weakens his Calling, letting me slowly awaken from it, bringing me back to them. I find myself in the bedroom suddenly, with no memory of how we got there. His Calling changes to something more like a muscle relaxant than an actual sedative. I roll to my side on the bed, tensing as my belly aches and my hips hurt. Thane pulls me to him, tugging a shirt over my head.

"What else did he say?" Thane asks someone, and I hear Rhen respond.

"Corbin took the families of both the officials who were here. Half of the state officials are already in Corbin's pocket, too. Raidon is about to wake Leo up. When he does, we'll question him."

"If he has half the state officials in his pocket, who the fuck do we call?" Leon asks.

"He gave us a few numbers of some higher ups who might be able to help. As for the city, anything that happens within its limits is ultimately up to Thane. We are well within our rights to defend our home. They can't come after us for that, and whatever happens within the city is Thane's decision," Rhen tells Leon.

Thane sighs. "Maggie and Samson?" He must be referring to the housekeeper and gardener.

"I called the coroner. He will be here soon to pick up both their bodies. The city authorities are out front if you want to deal with them. They are going over the car. You killed four men in there. One was Corbin's mate, and, well, we have Leo, too. Tal wasn't in the car, so he must have been in one of the ones that got away."

"And Corbin?"

"Alerts have been put out. We will find him. Raidon and I are also going to make some calls to get the ball rolling on the investigations into the state council," Rhen tells him. "But in the meantime, I need you to stop sedating Harlow. I need to know what she saw the day Leo killed your mother. I need to speak to her, Thane."

"I'm staying," Thane snaps.

"Very well. Leon, go handle the authorities downstairs. Leila is also down there, asking for you. She's convinced Thane is torturing you," Rhen says. Thane's Calling finally lifts, and he tilts my head back.

CHAPTER THIRTEEN

I make Thane call Jake to warn him about Corbin. It is a good distraction for him while Rhen takes me downstairs to speak with Leo. So far, he has been uncooperative and unwilling to give up his mate. He knows he isn't leaving here alive. I shift uncomfortably on the couch, my enormous belly tightening. It makes sitting quite painful with the pressure on my groin.

"Who told you about Harlow?" Raidon asks for the hundredth time. He's a broken record at this point. Leo just laughs, and Raidon punches him, making me flinch. Leo growls, spitting blood on the floor. He smirks at me, his eyes sparkling with mischief.

"You look just like your mother." He sits back in his chair. My brows furrow. Leo tilts his head to the side. "And to think, her two daughters were right under our noses all this time," he says, baring his teeth.

"You knew my mother?" I ask him. The cogs turn in my head with everything I know so far, and for some reason, it all links back to Harper.

"Yes, I knew her. She was the youngest of the girls promised. Like Hana," he sneers as Thane walks in. Leo clicks his tongue at him.

"Your mother was a fucking hoot. Good in the sack, too. I wonder what your Omega feels like," he taunts, trying to bait Thane. Yet, Thane doesn't pay him any mind, instead, focusing on me.

"You called them?" I ask, and he nods.

"That won't help her. Corbin has plans. He won't let this go, not after all this time," Leo states.

My heart skips a beat at his words. Thane tugs me to him and waves his hand at Raidon, who knees Leo in the head. Thane's calm demeanor is just a façade. I can feel his rage boiling. He wants to kill Leo but is calm enough to see reason now.

Leo grunts at the blow, and Leon walks in with a blood bag, slurping on it like a juice box. "Fucking vermin, like your cousin. All hybrids should have been put down years ago. Fucking bloodsucker," Leo growls, his eyes flickering.

"You would know. Weren't you a feeder for years? Wait, no, that was your sister and mother. I'm pretty sure I tasted both of them, and they both tasted like shit. Must be the bad genes," Leon responds. Leo snarls, jerking in his restraints.

"Enough, Leo. Either speak, or I'll let Thane kill you now. I am done playing these little games with you," Rhen tells him. Leon takes a seat beside me, and I move over, only to get up. My stomach is cramping from sitting, and the pressure in my groin is intense.

"You don't look too good," Leo comments.

Thane is watching me, and the concern on his face is evident. They have been hovering over me all damn night. I shake off his hand when he reaches for me.

"I'm fine. It's just Braxton Hicks," I tell him.

"Harlow?" Rhen starts, but I wave him off, too.

"Rhen is right, love. Your due date is only two days away. The baby could come any time now. At least let me get Mom and Dad to check you over," Raidon argues.

I shake my head, clutching my belly. Shouldn't I be in more pain if I'm in labor? All the stories I heard make it seem like the pain should be unbearable.

"No, I'm calling them. Rhen watch him," Raidon says, walking off.

I lean on the arm of the couch before turning my head back to Leo. "My mother, you believe she's this Harper woman?" I ask him.

"I don't believe she is, I know. It's why Hana bid on you and why Sophia had her son bid on your sister. Jake thought he was just obtaining an Omega, but he was really buying his mother's goddaughter back."

I raise my brows at his words.

"My mother's name wasn't Harper, though. It's Zahra," I tell him.

Leo laughs. "The sneaky bitch used her middle name," he says, shaking his head.

"What's any of this got to do with my mother, though?" Thane asks. I can see how tense he is. His fingertips have turned into claws, and I didn't like the conversation turning to Hana with him present. He is barely holding it together. I'm not sure if I'm making a mistake when I move toward him. I sit in his lap, and he sighs. His claws retract as he places his hands on my belly.

"You might as well talk, Leo. Corbin left you for dead," Rhen states.

"Thane will kill me no matter what happens. I don't see any point in answering shit," Leo spits, and Rhen shakes his head.

"You had a daughter before you joined Corbin's pack," Thane states.

"You won't fucking touch her," Leo snarls.

"She is Omega," Rhen tells him. Leo's canines slip out. "Tell me what we need to know, and I will ensure she doesn't end up in rotation."

"You can't ensure that!"

"I can in my city. I have the sanctuary here," Thane says, and Leo shakes his head.

"No, Corbin will keep her safe. He won't let her go into rotation."

Rhen laughs, making Leo look at him. "You're an idiot if you believe that. You're one of his newest pack members. How old is your daughter? She would be nearly twenty now, right?" Rhen asks. Leo sits straighter in his chair, his eyes darting between Thane and Rhen.

I, however, am trying to calculate how old Leo is because he looks so young. I know Alpha Packs age slower, but he looks to be in his mid-twenties. It also makes me wonder how old Corbin is.

"Your daughter is off-limits while you're part of his pack. I wonder if Corbin will stick to that deal once you're dead?" Thane says, looking at Rhen, who shrugs.

CHAPTER FOURTEEN

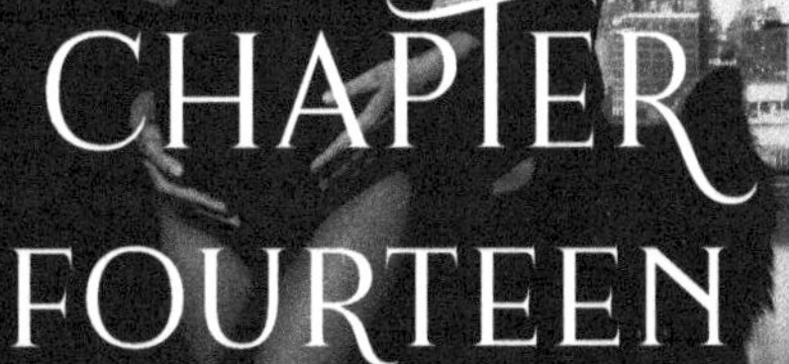

"She's not even registered. She has immunity since Corbin is part of the state parties."

"Maybe so, but I'm willing to bet, once you're out of the picture, Corbin will register her as his own," Thane tells him.

Leo's eyes widen, and he shakes his head. It appears this man does have a conscience after all. He swallows, considering Thane's words.

"Tell me what I need to know, and I will ensure she ends up in my city. She'll be safe here."

Leo scoffs. "Bullshit! No Omega is safe anywhere."

"She will be safe here. I am changing the laws in my city. Here, Omegas will be free to choose by the time I am finished with the council's board of directors."

"You're a fool. You won't get rid of those laws. They line the pockets of every government official. It's why your mother never succeeded. The only thing you'll accomplish is getting yourself killed, just like your mother," Leo snaps.

"Well, that tells me a different story," I say to Leo. He raises an eyebrow at me. "The only reason someone would try to kill her is if she actually stood a chance at changing those laws, or why bother over just one Omega?"

"Mom and Dad are on their way," Raidon says as he comes back in. If anyone can tell me if Harper is my mother, it should be Elaine. She knew her, so why didn't she recognize her from the picture in my wallet? Raidon moves toward Leo when he speaks.

"Wait!"

Raidon steps aside as Leo peers around him to look at Thane.

"I want your word you will get Emily," he says.

"You have my word," Thane tells him, but Leo shakes his head.

"Not yours, hers. If she is anything like her mother or yours, she won't stop fighting for their rights," Leo tells Thane, and I swallow when he turns to me. "He'll listen to you; he'll fight for you. I want your word that you'll get my daughter from Corbin's pack."

"If you tell us what you know, I will give you my word," I say, though I probably would have pestered Thane about saving her, anyway. No woman should be subjected to living in Corbin's pack. It is clear he is a different sort of monster, and by the look on Leo's face, he knows it, too.

"Fine—what do you want to know?" Leo asks.

"Start from the beginning," Thane tells him while I shift uncomfortably on his lap. His hand rubs my belly, and Leo sighs.

"I want to know about Harper. You said Hana belonged to you, and so did Harper, when you…" I stop, knowing Thane is beneath me, yet Leo doesn't need me to elaborate.

"Yes. Hana was the Omega Corbin initially bid on, but your fathers outbid him. Harper, on the other hand, was promised to Curtis," he spits the name, and I can tell he has a special dislike for the man.

"Corbin didn't like that, his father just giving Harper to him, while Corbin was forced to bid," he shakes his head.

"Why would that matter?" I ask.

"Because Waylen was changing his will. He hated that Corbin started an Alpha Pack. He was traditional, so he set a rule, whichever of his sons produced an heir first would inherit everything."

Thane leans forward in his chair, pushing me closer to his knees. "Wait, but Corbin did inherit everything," Thane says, and Leo nods.

"Yes, because he killed his father before he had a chance to change his last will and testament. He knew Curtis was set to inherit everything."

"Curtis has no kids," I tell him, and Leo shakes his head.

"Correct, but your mother was a rarity. Her scores were the highest recorded in over a decade, higher than even yours and Zara's. Her levels were 100%," Leo says.

"Well, then Harper can't be my mother. My mother had a Beta father."

Leo shakes his head.

"No, she was born from two Omegas. She was pure; your father wasn't. Corbin knew Curtis would inherit everything if Harper became his Omega, but if Corbin marked and mated her first, Curtis couldn't keep her. However, she was already gone by the time we came for her."

"So that's why Corbin had you kill my mother?" Thane asks.

Leo chews the side of his lip as I am forced to stand, my stomach cramping and tightening again. Only this time stronger, the pain radiating all through my belly.

"Is she alright?" Leo asks as I grit my teeth through the pain.

"I'm fine. Answer his question!" I growl. My claws slip into Thane's arm when I grip the armrest. Thane jumps, not expecting it. "I'm fine," I tell him.

"No, you need to lie down until Elaine gets here," he says, and I shake my head. I want to know—need to know.

"I will when she gets here," I tell him, and the pain eases off. I look at Leo. "Answer him."

"Harper was part of it, but not the only reason. Hana found proof of Corbin's involvement in his father's death. She was planning to release that information if Corbin didn't shut down his facilities and back her bid to change the laws. She needed one more signature, and Corbin's would have ensured the laws regarding Omegas were changed and the facilities shut down," Leo says, and I nod. Now that makes sense. So, my assumption was right, she was on the verge of winning.

"So how do Harlow and Zara fall into all this, then?" Rhen

asks. Leo looks to the ceiling and exhales.

"You make sure you get my daughter away from Corbin," he says, and I nod.

"I promise," I tell him.

Leo exhales and nods his head a few times, looking at the floor before sitting higher in his seat to look at Thane. "We found out about Harlow first, right after you bought her. We didn't know about Zara until recently. Curtis called Corbin and said he could fix the situation with Hana, but he wanted into the pack. Corbin agreed. Curtis told us he had Thane's Omega, and one way to get at Hana was to blackmail her back. We planned to take Harlow and demand the footage she had on Corbin."

"But that makes no sense. How would she even know I existed? How did Curtis plan that?" I ask him. Leo shrugs.

"No idea. All I know is Curtis called Corbin, told him he had Thane's Omega, and we could use her to get back at Hana. However, when we realized Hana was the one coming to collect you, Corbin changed the plan. He ordered me to kill her and take you. Kill two birds with one stone. We didn't even realize you were Harper's daughter until we tested your DNA. Even Curtis was shocked. He didn't realize until after we started looking for you. Your DNA from the car was added to the registry, and it struck a close match to Harper's, whose blood was still registered with the facility."

"That makes no sense, though. Elaine—" I look at Raidon.

"My mother told us Hana bid on Harlow, and Sophia convinced Jake to bid as well, to also bid on Harlow. The twins had switched places at that point," Raidon tells him.

"I don't have those answers. I only know what Corbin was told, so if she knew who the girls were, she didn't learn it from us. We didn't know until after the accident, and she was already dead."

"Well, someone is lying then because my mother told me once Hana was well aware of who she was bidding on," Raidon says, his brows pinching together.

"Curtis swore he didn't know," Leo says, looking confused.

A sharp pain makes me suddenly cry out. The terrible pain rips through my stomach. Raidon moves toward me, but Thane grabs me first as I double over. I try to breathe through the pain as the bending motion builds up pressure in my groin. I suddenly feel my legs become drenched. Thane jumps, his feet getting wet, and I know my water just broke, the floor becoming soaked along with my pajama shorts.

"I fucking knew it! Stubborn little Omega," Raidon growls, scooping me up. I moan as pain tears through my lower back and abdomen.

"Leon, call Mom and tell her to hurry up," Raidon calls over his shoulder as he heads for the Den. The moment I see where he is taking me, my eyes widen, and I claw at his back, trying to get out of his grip.

"No! No, I am not going down there!" I thrash. Raidon stops when Thane grabs my face in his hands.

Thane's bottom lip quivers, and his eyes dart to the door leading to the Den before coming back to mine. I know I am being irrational, but I hate that Den. It haunts me more than anything Thane has done in the past. There's a reason I haven't set foot in there.

"I'll remove the door, but you need your Den, Harlow. You won't be able to handle all the scents in the house. It's either the Den or the hospital, so pick," he says.

I shake my head as another contraction cripples me.

"I'm sorry. I'm so sorry. I promise I will stay with you, but you need to pick, love," he murmurs.

I shake my head. Omegas are primal creatures. Yes, there are

Dens at the hospital, but the idea of leaving home also frightens me. Thane presses his head against mine.

"I'll remove the door."

"You'll remove the door," I repeat, and he nods.

"I'll do it now," he says, backing away from me. Raidon sets me on my feet. I clutch onto him, liquid still running down my legs, drenching the tiles. It makes me wonder how much water is in there. It feels gross and smells funky. Yet, as the contractions return, my gross state is far from my mind.

"Leon!" I grit out, and he is beside me in an instant. He starts walking down the steps, but my vision tunnels as I stare down the stairs leading to the hell I lived in for months.

"I'm right here," he says, motioning for me to follow. Thane moves toward the door. The moment I take a step, pain tears through me, and I feel something hit my feet. I look down to see a massive blood clot, and my vision to blurs. I take another step, or I think I do, before everything briefly goes black.

I wake up to Thane screaming. I feel myself being placed on something hard and cold. I stare up at the ceiling, dazed, and wonder what happened. Leon is suddenly prying my mouth open before I choke on his blood. I cough and sputter, trying to sit up.

"Where the fuck is your mother?" Thane growls at Raidon as Leon pulls me back down.

"Rhen, call an ambulance!" he orders, and I begin fading. "Stay awake for me, Low," Thane tells me, ripping my shorts off. Thane gasps, and I turn my head, dazedly searching for someone. I don't care who, I just need someone's face to focus on.

"Is that—?" I hear Leon ask.

"The umbilical cord," I hear Thane murmur.

I blink, my mind foggy. Isn't that supposed to come out last? I think when I hear Leo's voice.

"I can help her. Let me out of this damn chair!" he shouts.

"You're the reason she is fucking like this!" Leon snarls.

CHAPTER SIXTEEN

RHEN

Harlow fades in and out of consciousness. Raidon is on the phone with his mother, and I am on the phone with emergency services, calling for an ambulance. The medic is trying to explain what to do, but we aren't doctors, and it is clear something has gone very wrong.

"Mom's here," Raidon shouts, opening the front door. Elaine rushes into the dining room, where Thane has placed Harlow on the table.

"How far away is the ambulance?" she panics, looking at me.

"Ten minutes out," I tell her.

She goes over to Harlow and checks her before staggering back. She shakes her head, and Thane grabs her, shaking her.

"Elaine?" he snarls.

Blood soaks the table, so much that it drips onto the floor.

"I think it's placental abruption," Elaine says.

"No, we had her checked earlier, when she was asleep, Doc said she was fine," Thane tells her. The pack doctor came out earlier. The baby was fine, so what she's saying makes no sense.

"Let me out of this chair. I can fucking help!" Leo snarls, and Thane glares at him. What can he possibly do to help?

"Where's Dad?" Raidon worries.

"Stuck in surgery. We need to get the baby out."

I can tell Elaine is freaking out. She is a pathologist and medical practitioner, but she hasn't actually practiced medicine in years, and she is definitely not a surgeon. She hushes us, waving her arms to shut us up. She tilts her head to the side, and I do the same. I can hear the baby's heartbeat, though it seems extremely fast.

"Baby is in distress, we… We need…" Her eyes dart around frantically.

Raidon grabs her arms, forcing her to look at him. "Mom! What do you need?"

"I have to get the baby out," she whispers, though her face is deathly pale at the thought.

"Oh, for fuck's sake, untie me! If her placenta detached, we need to get the baby out before you lose them both!" Leo snarls, banging his feet on the ground and tugging on the chains.

"Harlow, I need you to stay awake for me," Thane tells her, but her eyes flutter. Leon continues to pump her full of his blood.

"My baby," she murmurs.

"Elaine, you know I can help," Leo yells and Thane tells him to shut up. Leo is no doctor.

However, the moment Elaine's eyes fall on him, she looks relieved. "Leo?" she asks before taking off into the living room. "Whose got the fucking key? Now!"

Raidon rummages through his pocket, tossing it to her.

"What are you doing?" Thane demands.

"We haven't got time for this," Elaine says, frantically unlocking the chains while Leo unravels them.

"He was in medical school with me. He is a trained obstetric surgeon."

"Huh?" I blurt, and so does Raidon.

"He lost his medical license. He was caught selling drugs."

"Hurry up. I need towels and a scalpel," Leo says.

"We don't keep that shit here," Thane snaps.

"Claws it is, then," Leo says, shoving past us the moment Elaine undoes his hands.

"You're not touching my fucking mate or our baby!" Thane shouts.

"If you want them to live, I will be," Leo tells him as Elaine presses a hand to Thane's chest.

"He can help. He was top of all his classes, worked with Charles for three years," Elaine tells him, but Leo shoves past, not giving a care for permission. He tears Harlow's shirt open.

"Hold her down, she'll pass out quickly enough. And you," he says, looking at Leon. "You need to be ready to feed her your blood."

"Wait! You can't just cut into her. She's awake," Raidon protests.

"Barely, and she's fucking bleeding out. What she'll remember will be brief," Leo snarls at him. "Do you want them to die?"

Thane backs away, though he watches Leo like a hawk. I look away, unable to watch as he cuts into her with his claws. Instead, I focus on the baby's heartbeat, which is now starting to slow down and grow faint. I hear the sound of Harlow's flesh tearing, hear her brief scream. Leo is right, she passes out almost instantly.

I can hear Leon, continually biting his wrist, feeding her his blood. Seconds feel like hours as the smell of her blood fills the room.

"Stop, you're healing her around my hands," Leo says. I hear more flesh tearing. The sounds will forever haunt me, the sloshing and scraping. Raidon, I see, looks rather pale, like he may faint. "As soon as I pull her out, Elaine, you need to get the placenta out, then hold her skin together, so he can heal her fast enough," Leo says. I can hear sirens, but they are faint, so I know they are still a ways off.

"Now!" Leo snaps at Elaine. I look over at the table and instantly regret it. Elaine is clearing out the placenta frantically, while Leo holds our daughter in his hands, sticking his fingers in her mouth to clear out the gunk.

My heart stops when he starts rubbing her back. She is floppy and unresponsive in his hands when, suddenly, she lets out an ear-piercing scream.

I exhale before my eyes go back to Harlow, who is deathly pale. Her stomach is healing together, with the help of Leon's blood. I see Raidon is also feeding her his. She gasps, breathing hard, and she looks around frantically. Leo slashes the cord, tying it in a knot.

Elaine places the placenta in a bowl, wiping Harlow down with some towels she retrieved.

"Lucky girl. If you were both human, you would probably be dead," Leo says, wrapping our daughter in a towel.

Harlow whimpers, and we all kind of stand there, knowing the man Thane was about to kill is now holding our daughter in his hands. Harlow whimpers again, her skin still pale as her hands grasp at the air, trembling. Even looking half dead, her canines slip out. We all stand there in horror, knowing with one twist, Leo could kill her.

Harlow's eyes flicker. Shifting right now would be dangerous for her, but it is clear she is willing to risk it. He turns to look at her, and I see Thane tense and take a step toward him.

Our daughter screams, ear-piercing cries. Her little lips quiver, and her face screws up. Elaine, noticing us all frozen with our eyes on Leo, also tenses as she goes to move the bowl with the placenta and cord in it. Elaine turns to look at Leo. He rocks our daughter's toweled body in his hands, patting her bum.

"Shh, shh, it's okay. I will give you to your mother. Is my ugly mug scaring you?" he coos, passing her to Harlow. I nearly faint from relief when Harlow's shaking hands all but snatch her from him.

"Can I at least wash my hands before you kill me? I'd prefer not to die wearing your mate," Leo asks.

Thane nods, watching him follow Elaine to the kitchen. I turn back to Harlow, and I see Raidon follow his mother and Leo.

As I move closer, Harlow tucks the towel under our daughter's chin, gazing down at her.

"Hello, Scarlett," Harlow whispers, kissing our daughter's head. Thane gasps, and I choke at the name she gave her, knowing how much Thane's sister meant to him.

"Can someone please get me off this table?" Harlow groans, arching her back.

Thane doesn't move, staring in shock, like he can't believe both of them are still here. So I move, scooping my arms under her, and Harlow tucks baby Scarlett closer. Glancing down, I see bright silver eyes peering back at me, and a full head of light brown hair, matted in blood.

"I'll remove the door," Thane says, rushing off to the basement door. I hear the sirens grow louder and know they are coming up the driveway. That was the longest ten minutes of my life.

After the EMTs leave, I get Harlow settled in the Den and make my way up the stairs. I hear Leo speaking quietly to Elaine. "I suppose I should retake my seat and await my death upon my mighty throne," Leo gently chuckles. Raidon growls at him as I climb the last three steps.

"Why?" Elaine asks. "I know you are part of Corbin's pack and all, but after what you just did, I am sure all that can be forgotten."

"Somehow, Elaine, I doubt Thane will suddenly forget I murdered his mother," Leo tells her, just as I step into the hallway across from the kitchen. Leo turns his head toward me and moves to step past Elaine when he suddenly stops with a gasp. Raidon jumps. Leo's eyes peer down, and it takes me a second to process what I'm seeing.

Elaine gasps. I didn't even see her move. One second, she is drying her hands on the tea towel. The next, she's plunged a knife into Leo's ribs. I watch Elaine stagger back. She's shocked by what she's done, as if stabbing him was a knee-jerk reaction, one she had no control over. Leo coughs, glancing down. I stand rooted, stunned. I was supposed to kill him, but for some reason, I am struggling with the idea of him dying.

Raidon, sensing this, rushes over to him, grabbing tea towels and placing pressure on the wound. "Mom!" he growls, snapping Elaine out of her thoughts.

"He killed her," she says, stunned. She blinks, taking a step back, and nearly falling over her own feet. I spring into action to catch her, the movement pulling me out of my own stunned state.

Once Elaine is steady, I move to help Raidon, which is something that shocks both Raidon and myself. Leo killed my mother, brutally murdered her, yet he saved my mate and my daughter. He saved them, and now I suddenly can't bring myself to want him dead.

"Elaine, grab the first aid kit!" I snap at her. She rushes off while Leo clutches the countertop.

"Just rip the damn thing out. I'll heal. Pretty sure she missed anything important," he lets out with a pained wheeze.

"Help me get him to the chair," Raidon says.

Growling, I grab his arm, tossing it over my shoulder. Raidon gets the other as we both grab a handful of his pants, hauling him out to the living room and the chair he used to be chained to.

"Oh, for fuck's sake! At least pull the damn knife out before I take my royal throne of death," Leo hisses at me. With one quick yank, Raidon rips the knife out before replacing the pressure as Leo groans. Moments later Elaine rushes in, looking quite lost.

Raidon snatches the first aid kit from her, and she backs away while Raidon sets to work. Leo's wounds heal slower than they normally would because of all the fighting today.

"Harlow?" Leo asks, clearly needing a distraction.

"She's fine," I tell him. I may not want to kill him, but I haven't forgiven him enough to make small talk.

"Move, let me do it," Elaine snaps, seeing Raidon fumble. She pushes him aside.

"You don't have another knife, do you? I expected that from him, not you, Elaine. You should be about saving lives, not taking them. Playing grim reaper doesn't suit you."

"I could say the same thing about you, Leo. Hana was my best friend," Elaine says, clearly feeling just as torn as I am. Raidon restrains him again and stands back. I watch Elaine work for a few minutes before checking on my other mates. When I return, Elaine is still stitching Leo up and Raidon is questioning him.

"So, Bree is how Talon got involved with Corbin?" Raidon asks. They both look over at me as I move across the room, taking a seat in the armchair.

Harlow is in the Den. I still haven't held our daughter. I tried. Harlow even offered her to me, but I am terrified of breaking her. Breaking her like I broke her mother.

"You're looking rather conflicted there, Thane," Leo states.

My eyes flick to the bastard who murdered my mother. His hands are once again restrained as Elaine patches him up. She, too, looks conflicted.

"Because killing you doesn't seem right anymore," I growl, annoyed. I want nothing more than to destroy the person responsible for my mother's death, yet I know she would curse me for it after what he just did.

"We're even. Just get my daughter back from Corbin, okay?" Leo sighs heavily, clearly content to die. I shake my head. It is no longer that simple. Besides, I want to hear what he has to say about Bree and Talon.

Ignoring what he said, I ask, "What were you just telling Raidon?"

"How Talon got mixed up in this mess with Corbin," Raidon answers, making me look at him. I turn my attention back to Leo.

Leo groans before letting out a breath. "When Talon fell into some financial trouble, Bree introduced him to Corbin," Leo answers.

"But how does Corbin know Bree?" Raidon asks. "Did she meet him at Tal's?"

Leo shakes his head. "No, but damn did it cause some problems when her father caught her there a few months back. We were invited to this gig, a glory hole event. Bree said some Omega girl was going to be there. Anyway, I guess the Omega backed out. If it weren't for Bree's birthmark, her father wouldn't have recognized her. And that caused some conflict, let me tell you," Leo chuckles.

"What's that got to do with anything? You said Corbin didn't meet her at Talon's," I ask, confused at the contradictions he's making.

"No, Corbin knows Bree from the Omega Sanctuary," Leo says, and I look at Raidon, now more confused than ever.

"Bree is Beta," I tell him.

"What? No, she isn't. Bree is Omega. She just never bloomed. One of those oddities of nature, I suppose."

I lean forward in my chair, trying to take in what Leo is saying. None of it makes sense. Bree claims she is Beta. Not that Betas have an overly strong scent, and she constantly douses herself in pheromones for work. But still, surely Talon would know if his girlfriend is Omega or not?

"Wait …" Raidon looks at me confused, like he doesn't know what he is about to ask or needs confirmation that he heard correctly. I can offer him no help. I am just as confused.

"And let me tell you, the look of horror on her face when she realized her father attended the glory hole gig was priceless! He looked like he was going to kill her," Leo chuckles to himself.

"Who's her father?" I ask.

"This is why there's conflict between Curtis and Corbin now. We didn't know Bree was his daughter, not until he saw the birthmark on her hip and started freaking out."

"Whose daughter?" Raidon asks before I get a chance.

"Curtis's. Who else? Corbin doesn't have any kids. Girl needs therapy. I know Corbin isn't her real uncle, but damn that shit is still gross. And that's how we all found out about Curtis's dirty little secret."

"Wait, Bree is Curtis Black's daughter?" I ask, wondering if I heard that right.

"Yes. I just said that, didn't I? Are you listening to anything I'm saying? But don't worry, no one fucked her, thank the goddess." Leo shudders. I shudder, too, at the mere thought.

"But you bet your ass Curtis beat her from one end of the club to the other when he found her lying on that table. Poor girl. She didn't know she was offering herself up to her father and uncle. We didn't even know she was his!"

Raidon clutches his hair, and I sit back in my chair, absolutely blown away by the information Leo gives us. "I can't believe this,"

Raidon mutters.

"So Curtis never told Corbin he fathered a daughter?"

"Nope. We did ask why but never got an answer."

CHAPTER EIGHTEEN

"Untie him!" I order Raidon.

Leo's head turns to look at me as I rise from my seat. Confusion crosses his features as Raidon sets about freeing him. I reach for my jacket hanging over the back of the couch.

"What's going on?" Raidon asks, glancing at me over his shoulder while undoing Leo's legs.

"We're going to see Bree. Then Leo is going to help me break into the sanctuary," I announce, my gaze carefully following Raidon's movements.

As long as Leo was tied and restrained, I didn't have to worry about him. But now that he'll be free, there's no telling what kind of tricks he might try to pull in order to escape.

I can only hope he has some understanding of how dangerous it is to defy me, of how much he will risk if he tries anything, but no one can know how far he is willing to go.

Desperate times always call for desperate measures. Leo reminds me of a rat stuck in a trap. While others might admit defeat, this rat is stubborn. He would rather die trying to escape than give up. Yet I have one advantage, one I know he won't risk: his daughter.

"You wanna what?" Raidon's head snaps up, his hands still

clutching the chains.

My eyes focus on Raidon's back. The tension taking over his body is obvious as his muscles flex and relax. I knew he wouldn't like what I have planned, but he knows better than to question me.

The only thing I ever ask is for them to trust my judgment. Letting out a deep breath, I look up at the ceiling as I explain myself. "I want Curtis Black." Turning my attention to Leo, he chews his lip. "You know where the sanctuary is, right?" My words don't earn me a response, so I keep going. "Do you know how tight security is there?"

Raidon keeps oddly quiet as Leo gets up from the chair. "Yeah, it's guarded, but not from the pack," Leo announces as he rubs the reddened skin on his wrists. My eyes flicker between them as Raidon glances up at Leo. "I have the gate card, but I need to shower first. I can't walk in there like this," he says, staring down at the shorts Rhen gave him earlier.

I nod in agreement. It seems the tension has finally faded, and Raidon becomes visibly more relaxed, which allows the heavy tension to leave me, too. The last thing I need is unnecessary drama and possible arguments.

"So, what are we seeing Bree about?" Raidon asks, glancing between me and Leo.

I pinch the bridge of my nose and sigh. "To find out what she knows about her father and uncle's plans."

"Are you sure we should leave Harlow? She just gave birth to our daughter," Raidon asks.

He has a point. A very good point, but we have to act before this mess becomes something we can no longer handle. Sometimes, it is better to die trying than spending an entire lifetime on our knees praying shit doesn't go south.

"Corbin won't come back anytime soon. He'll wait for the heat to die down. Not only that, but corruption will be on the elders' radar now. He isn't stupid enough to draw more attention to himself. The State Council is one thing, but the Supernatural Parliament? Not even Corbin is stupid enough to try to bribe or blackmail one of them," Leo assures me.

Corbin may not be stupid enough—as Leo put it—to blackmail

the Supernatural Parliament, but I am. And I will, I think with a smug smile across my lips. One thing about owning a tech company is that my fathers had dirt on nearly every member. Dirt they left me along with the company.

That is exactly what I plan on using to get the laws surrounding Omegas changed. Something my fathers should have done to help my mother.

"Maybe you should organize for the city exits to be guarded. Especially since it is a six-hour drive," Leo adds.

Even though I can't stand the guy, I have to admit he has a point. It does annoy me, however, that he assumes I didn't think of that already. I'm clearly not as brainless as he might think.

"We aren't driving. We're flying. The guards are already posted. The city is in total lockdown. No one can enter or leave without my knowledge," I assure him.

Raidon leads Leo toward the stairs to shower and find him some clothes, but he stops halfway up as I grab my keys off the hook.

"Since we are heading back that way—"

I already know where this is going, so I raise my hand to stop him. "We'll get your daughter," I assure him. As soon as the words leave my lips, he lets out a breath of relief.

"We'll grab her first, then head to the sanctuary," I add, just to emphasize how serious I am about the decision.

"Thank you," Leo whispers.

I nod and wander down to my mates in the Den. I have to let them know what is going on. And once we find Curtis Black, I will speak with Jake and his mates.

We are about to have one hell of a manhunt on our hands. My plans are so grand, all of us might go down in history. I know Corbin's death will, that I can assure everyone. His death will be remembered and will be a warning to never fuck with my family.

As I get to the now empty door frame that leads to the Den, her scent smashes into me like a truck going a hundred miles an hour. My blood simmers in my veins as I stand frozen, relishing the moment.

I thought her heat was potent, but damn, does her scent stir up another need now, one I didn't realize could grow any stronger—an intense need to protect my pack, my Omega. That deep desire to covet and protect grows fiercer. Especially now that she's had our pup.

The stairs creak when I reach the last set, and I hesitate. She stirs before I step onto the concrete and walk over toward the sunken Den. I glance down at the red cushioned floor and the dozens of comforters and torn pillows.

Carefully, I jump down, trying not to jostle her too much. Her hand instantly moves to the small bassinet at her head. The feral snarl that leaves her makes me smirk. That's my girl.

Still bleary-eyed, I offer her my hand and watch as she sniffs the air before relaxing.

CHAPTER NINETEEN

Snuggled beneath the blankets, I feel the bed dip, and a feral snarl tears out of me. My hand instantly falls into the bassinet next to my face. I sit upright, and Thane holds his hand out to me. I blink the haze away and sigh after picking up his scent. I rub my eyes, trying to determine how long I was asleep for.

Tugging the blanket higher, I feel no tension on it and glance around to find Leon and Rhen gone. Their scents remain strong, however, so I know they are close. I turn my head, hearing the shower running, and I let out a breath of relief.

"Leo? You… you didn't…" I stop. I can't blame him if he did. He has wanted vengeance for years. I will not deprive him of it, but some part of me hopes he will have a change of heart.

Thane grips my chin, tilting my face up and forcing me to meet his darkened gaze. I swallow, seeing the thoughts swirl in his eyes.

"He's alive," Thane assures me. I chew my lip, and he lets me go. Thane kneels beside the small bassinet, and his hands pull the blanket down slightly, allowing him to see her face. He brushes Scarlett's cheek with the back of his finger.

"You can take her out. You still haven't held her," I remind him. Thane shakes his head.

"Let her sleep," he whispers, his brows pinching slightly. I can feel his anxiety through the bond, his worry bleeding into me. "I need to go speak with someone, but I will return home soon. I'm taking Leo with me," he tells me. I sigh, a little disappointed he isn't staying, yet also curious.

"Where are you going?" I ask, a little uneasy about him leaving us.

"Just to Tal's, and then we're going to retrieve Leo's daughter. I also need to look into something. Raidon—" he stops, and we listen as footsteps come down the stairs. Speak of him, and he shall appear. Raidon moves across the room before dropping into the Den.

"Go. She's fine with us," Raidon tells him. I don't get a chance to argue as Thane is already climbing out of the Den. I purse my lips, slightly annoyed as Raidon cuddles beside me.

He pulls me to him, digging into his pocket. My troubled thoughts about Thane are quickly forgotten as I snatch his phone. I want to call Zara to let her know about Scarlett. My fingers jab the screen before finding her number and dialing, just as Scarlett starts to squirm.

The phone rings a couple of times before Raidon moves, leaning around me and reaching for our daughter. He grabs her, cradling her close and rocking her while I wait for Zara to answer. When the video call connects, I see her beaming face, smiling brightly at me.

"I have a surprise for you," I quietly laugh.

"So do I," she giggles. I tilt the phone just as she does, nearly dropping it when I see not two, but three bundles, in Jake's arms.

"Wait, you had her?" Zara gushes, jerking the screen back to her face.

"And you had three?" I ask. "A litter!" I gasp, shocked.

"Yeah, my pack ain't shooting blanks, that's for sure. I tried to tell them the scans were wrong. You saw how huge I was. I was twice the size of you. Let me see. I want to see her," Zara says, peering into the phone as if she can stick her head through it. Raidon slides Scarlett into my free arm, and I tilt the screen, listening to her gush. Raidon pulls me back against him, watching Zara over my shoulder as she baby-talks to Scarlett.

"What did you name her?" Zara asks.

"Scarlett," I tell her, and she smiles softly, her face glowing. I suddenly realize I don't recognize the background behind her.

"Wait, where are you?" I question and Zara snickers.

"I was wondering when you would notice." She smiles softly. "I'm at the hospital. We had a few complications with our extra surprise."

"Wait, you left the property?"

Zara nods, and I nearly start crying at the thought of her leaving the house. I know it is the hormones, but still. Zara is agoraphobic, and this is an enormous achievement for her. We managed to get her into the yard while I was visiting, but that was it.

"Okay, I want to meet my nieces or nephews," I tell her, and she turns the camera to Jake.

"Two nieces and a nephew," she says. "Meet Sophie, Sabrina, and Samson."

I can't stop the huge grin on my face. At the same time, I can't wrap my head around the fact she had triplets inside her this whole time.

By the time I get off the phone with her, Rhen and Leon are out of the shower.

"Thane?" Leon asks, climbing into the Den.

"Wait, he went alone with Leo?" I ask, my head turning to glare at Raidon.

"Thane can handle himself. Besides, Leo has his own agenda. He won't risk his daughter, especially now that they're going to get her."

"Wait, but Leo's—" Leon starts to speak, only to be cut off by Raidon's growl.

"He'll be fine."

Rhen curses, also not happy about what is happening. "So, he already left?"

"We'll speak about it when he gets back," Raidon says, his voice threatening. I don't understand the need for secrecy. What's going on?

"You're hiding something. Either tell me, or I will go looking for Thane," I snap at him. Raidon reaches for me as I climb off his lap, but I slap his hands away. He grits his teeth, shooting a look at Rhen and Leon.

"He's gone to question Bree and pick up Leo's daughter."

"Why does he need to talk to Bree?"

"Because Bree is Curtis Black's daughter."

I blink at him. He could have told me she has tentacles and webbed feet. That would sound more plausible than what he just said.

The first place we go is Bree and Talon's apartment. Bree isn't there, however, so we go looking for her at the club. Pulling up in front of the seedy building, the music is pumping loudly and patrons are lined up, trying to get in. The moment I step out of the car, I groan, seeing the media are here reporting on Talon's abduction. I am only out of the car for a few seconds before they start snapping pictures of me with Leo.

Leo curses, and I know he's worried about those photos getting back to Corbin.

"It won't look good for you, having pictures of you in front of a strip joint splashed all over the front page," he says, closing his door. I shrug, uncaring. I would never cheat on Harlow. That is not something she ever needs to worry about.

"I would never hurt my mates like that," I tell him, moving to the front of the line. The bouncer instantly steps aside, recognizing me. "Bree?" I ask him.

"In the office. She seems quite upset," the bouncer tells me, and I nod, going inside. The strobing lights and heavy bass of the music give me an instant headache as people part, letting us through.

I make my way to the stairs and head straight for Talon's office.

The door is closed, and I twist the handle, finding it unlocked. Bree is bent in front of the safe, digging through it. She jumps when I close the door and spins to look at me. She looks like shit. Her mascara is running down her face, her lipstick is smeared, and she looks like she hasn't slept in days.

She clutches a hand to her chest and drops her head before Leo steps out from behind me. A furious growl tears out of her, and she lunges at him. I catch her around the middle, tossing her onto the couch. She moves to get up, but I growl.

"Sit down!" I order.

She grits her teeth, fighting my command before giving up and leaning back. She folds her arms across her chest and crosses her legs, glaring daggers at Leo, who moves toward Talon's desk and sits on the edge. Her eyes track his every move. I reach over, grabbing a chair and placing it in front of the couch before sitting. I motion toward the safe.

"What are you doing?"

"Trying to find enough money to buy Talon from this bastard's mate!" she spits angrily. I hear Leo sigh behind me.

"Ex-mate. The bastard abandoned me," Leo corrects her. She tilts her head to the side before muttering under her breath.

"Do you know where Talon is?" I ask her. She runs her fingers through her hair.

"No. I've tried calling Corbin, but he won't tell me where he took him. He won't respond to any of my messages," she says, clasping her hands in her lap.

"How do you know Corbin?" I ask her, wanting to see if she will tell me the truth. Bree looks down at her hands.

"He's my uncle, sort of. Not by blood, anyway." She lets out a breath. I sit back in my chair, watching her. At least now I know Leo didn't lie to me, not that I doubted him when his daughter's life is at risk.

"So, Curtis Black is your father?" I ask her, and she lifts her head.

"Yes. How did you know that?" she demands, her eyes shooting past me to glare at Leo.

"I told him," Leo tells her. She puffs out her cheeks and chews her lip.

"Of course you did."

"Was that supposed to be a secret?" I ask her, and she shrugs.

"No, not really, but it's not exactly something I like to tell people. No one wants to be known as a trafficker's daughter," she tells me, and she has a point. It is no secret that most Omegas in the facilities are there against their will.

"Did you know Harlow is from your father's Omega facility?" I ask, and her brows furrow.

"Not until recently. I haven't spoken to her since…" her face turns red, "since the glory hole incident."

I growl at the memory of it. Harlow came too close to the monster hunting her without even realizing it.

"Do you know where your uncle may be hiding out?"

"Ask him," she says, motioning to Leo. "It's his mate. He will have a better guess than I will. I just want to get Talon back, which is why I am looking for money, hoping to find enough. The bastard is my uncle and still won't let him go until his debt is settled."

"Money won't settle that debt. He wants Harlow, Bree. Money won't get Talon back," Leo snaps at her.

"Well, have you got a better idea? Because I won't let him die. I fucking love him!" Bree screams before trying to get herself under control. "Why Harlow?" she asks.

I look at Leo, and he nods, getting the message to keep his mouth shut and let me explain. "A vendetta against my mother," I tell her, and she sighs.

"Everything is so fucked up," she mutters.

"And your father won't help?"

Bree scoffs and shakes her head.

"Definitely not. He blames Tal for me working here, says I humiliated him. He wants Tal dead," she says, staring up at the ceiling, her eyes turning glassy.

"I have another question," I say. Bree tilts her head to the side, watching me. "Why did you book your uncle for—" I grit my teeth, not even wanting to say it, "the glory hole job."

"To be fair, we did not know who she was at the time!" Leo states.

She glares at him. "They booked online; I accepted it."

"But he's your family," I tell her, and she shakes her head.

"Not by blood. Don't make it gross. Talon got himself fucked over with the vamps who burned down that firm. He needed money, and I had cameras set up in the room," she admits, and my brows furrow.

CHAPTER TWENTY-ONE

"You had cameras? For what?" Leo asks, standing.

"Doesn't matter. Dad ruined those plans, didn't he?" she snarls at him.

"Thankfully," Leo shudders before pointing an accusing finger at her. "You were going to set us up?" he demands, and she glares at him.

"I needed the money. I couldn't ask Dad for it. He would have wanted to know why. And Corbin has connections with the vamps."

"You were going to use the footage to blackmail your own uncle to make Talon's debts go away?" I ask, and she hangs her head.

"Yeah, but I didn't expect my father to show up, so that didn't work." She cringes as if remembering something unpleasant.

"So, you've always known Corbin is your uncle?" I ask her and she nods.

"Yes," she says. I turn to glance at Leo questioningly. She continues. "Corbin didn't know, though. Dad told me he could never find out. He didn't want to risk Corbin using me as a weapon against him. It's why he sent me away to boarding school and then college. That's where he thought I was—at school, not here. He didn't know I dropped out and started working for Tal."

This entire situation is becoming more bizarre. Why would Curtis hide his own daughter from his brother? "Why did he think Corbin would use you against him?"

"Because one, I am Omega. I never bloomed," she says, dropping her head. Another confirmation of what Leo told me. "Dad didn't want me to get lost in the system, so he registered me as Beta. He made me promise to never tell Corbin who I am to him. Uncle Corbin used to visit the facility when I was a kid, and up until I left, Dad was worried Corbin would kill me. He believes Corbin killed their father to gain control over his assets. Dad didn't care about the money, he just wants me alive."

"And your mother?" I ask her.

Bree shrugs. "Dad never spoke of her. He says he found me on his doorstep and awoke to the sounds of my cries. A note in the basket claimed I was his. He did a DNA test to confirm it and kept me hidden. I was raised by Mrs. Yates. She was a warden at the facility."

"When was Harlow at the facility?" I ask, looking at Leo.

"Her paperwork says she was delivered there by the authorities when she was a teenager," he answers, and I look back at Bree.

"So, you didn't know Harlow?"

Bree shakes her head. "No, Dad sent me to a boarding school for Betas when I was ten. I only saw him on holidays when he would visit."

"How did he get you into a Beta boarding school?"

"He forged my documents, and the warden there owed him a favor. Dad helped him find a suitable Omega, so he helped cover up what I am. Not that it mattered. I am a defect Omega, anyway."

"Defect?"

"Yes, I am missing some chromosomes, the ones that force us to bloom. I have everything else, just not the essential bits," she explains.

I sigh, knowing we're at another dead-end. She told me nothing I don't already know, and I still have no idea where Corbin is hiding, so I get up.

"Wait, you're going? What about Talon?"

"Corbin is wanted in every state right now, Bree. The authorities are searching for him, and he'll be located soon enough," I tell her.

"But Talon could be dead by then!"

I shake my head. "What exactly do you expect me to do about it? You said yourself, you can't get a hold of Corbin, and you don't know his location, which is why I came here. I was hoping you had answers."

She nods, her lip quivering. "So, we just do nothing? You aren't even going to look for him?"

"No, I am going to visit your father, if you want to come?"

She quickly shakes her head. "Dad and I are not on good terms right now, and if he finds out Corbin has Talon, he will ask Corbin to kill him," she says, breaking down again.

I look at Leo, who is also looking away from Bree. One thing about Alpha genes is the instinct to protect and comfort lower ranking wolves, and Leo and I both have to fight that urge right now.

"If you love Talon so much, why haven't you let him mark you?" I ask her. It is no secret Talon is in love with her. She peers up, and a tear slips down her face.

"Because I can't give him the one thing Alphas want: an heir."

"Talon doesn't care about having an heir," I say, feeling bad for her.

"He says that now, but if I let him mark me, he will be tied to me. I don't want to take that from him." I shake my head at her words but she continues. "And if he marks me, changes his mind, and tosses me away, I'm forever tied to him," she whispers, and my stomach sinks for her.

"We'll get him back, Bree," I tell her, and she nods sadly.

"I hope so," she whispers, wiping away a stray tear. "Harlow?"

"At home with the others. She gave birth to our daughter," I say, and Bree perks up, smiling brightly.

"That's great news! I was worried when I heard Corbin went out there. I'm glad she's okay."

"I'll tell her to call you when she gets a chance. Just hold on and focus on this place. We'll get Talon back. You'll see, everything will be fine."

She nods. I leave, followed by Leo.

"So now where?" he asks.

"The airport to get your daughter. Then we are paying Curtis Black a visit."

CHAPTER TWENTY-TWO

Thane calls to check in on us before boarding the plane. Bree was a dead-end, but he was able to confirm everything Leo said. So they are now on their way to collect Leo's daughter. I learn her name is Emily.

Thane also tells me about his photo being taken at the strip club and to ignore the media. We already saw a report on the news, minutes after the photo was taken, trying to portray Thane poorly and stating there are problems at home with his Omega. My eyes rolled so hard while watching the news anchor. Anything to make headlines and grab attention.

Thane says he should be home early tomorrow morning. It makes me nervous, him being away, but we need information, and Curtis Black is the only person we can get it from. Thane says he will call us when he lands, and I once again curse myself for not marking him before he left. If I had, I could use the mind-link to talk to him.

I just finish eating when Leon crawls into bed beside me. He rests his head on my now squishy belly. I run my fingers through his hair and can feel his hunger through the bond. Scarlett stirs, waking up to eat. I've been expressing milk because they want to feed her, too, which is nice, because it gives me a chance to rest. Scarlett seems to only sleep for two-hour intervals.

"Do you want her, or should I go up and make her a bottle?" Rhen asks, plucking her out of her little bed. I hold my hands out for her, and Leon lifts his head so that I can feed her. My boobs start aching from just the sound of her cries. Her mouth opens like a fish, searching for my nipple, while I try to wrestle the damn thing out from my bra.

"Hang on. I gotta get the boob out." I gently chuckle at her face headbutting my breast impatiently. Rhen unclips my bra strap to help me. I've given up on wearing anything besides this sports bra because I'm constantly having to flop a breast out.

There's instant relief the moment she latches on. I never thought breastfeeding would be so damn hard, and painful! Her cries are an alarm for my titties to go haywire and start a tsunami of milk. I groan, feeling the other boob leak into the breast pad. I feel like a cow, and she has only been here for a few hours.

"Lucky baby," Raidon softly laughs.

"Feel free to drain the other one," I reply.

"Don't tempt him. He likes the taste," Rhen laughs before he shudders. I give Raidon a questioning look. He looks away guiltily.

"I may have tried some upstairs," he shrugs. "I was curious."

"Curious is taking a sip. You drank the entire bag," Rhen scolds him, and Raidon slaps his chest.

I shake my head at them as I feel Leon swipe my hair over my shoulder. I turn my head to look at him. His eyes are bright crimson, pupils dilated, and his fangs protrude from his lips, yet he makes no move to bite me. His eyes move to the pulse on my neck, and his hunger is almost rabid. I know the only reason he is currently frozen in place is because I have Scarlett in my arms.

"Leon!" Raidon snaps at him, making him jump and pull his gaze away from my neck. Leon mutters an apology, his embarrassment smashing into me through the bond. I glare at Raidon, who is glaring at him.

"Leave him. I can feel him, and he wasn't going to bite me," I scold Raidon. Glancing down, Scarlett is already falling back asleep. Her lips still suckle, but her gulps slow to a more comfortable pace.

Great, now I'm a pacifier.

I sigh and try to unlatch her, only for her to munch down harder, making my eyes water at the pain. Deciding to wait for her to completely fall asleep, I leave her be, turning my attention to Leon.

"Once she is done with the cafeteria, you can line up," I chuckle, reaching for him. His cheeks tinge darker, and I glare at Raidon for upsetting him. He's been fine, but they have been on edge with him since Scarlett was born. It is starting to grate on my nerves. I know it is mostly because Thane isn't here.

The moment she falls asleep, Rhen takes her from me. I expect Leon to pounce, but he just stares vacantly at the TV Rhen brought down earlier. Tucking everything away, I crawl over to him. He purrs, reaching for me and tugging me into his lap. He buries his face in my neck, and I feel the sharp points of his teeth sink into me, just as Raidon's phone starts ringing.

I gasp at the brief pain, and Leon's grip on me tightens as he tugs me flush against his chest, his tongue lapping at my neck.

"Hey, what's up?" Raidon says, answering the call. Silence follows, except for the muted voice coming from the other end.

"What? When? How bad is it?" Raidon asks. I turn my head to look at him. Raidon gets up, and Leon's teeth tug on my neck, making me hiss.

"Yeah, I'll be right there. What channel?" Raidon asks. He picks up the remote, flicks to another news station, and I gasp. Leon pulls his teeth from my neck before running his tongue over his bite mark.

"Fuck!" Rhen growls, getting up, but Raidon stops him.

"No, stay. I'll take Leon with me," Raidon says, causing Leon to lift his head to watch the TV, his lips smeared with my blood.

A fire has broken out at their office, and a good chunk of the building is ablaze. Leon kisses my cheek, before gently shoving me off his lap.

"Yeah, we're on our way," Raidon says, hanging up.

"What happened?" I ask.

"They aren't sure. They're trying to extinguish it first," Raidon says, nodding to Leon. Leon hastily gets up and climbs out of the Den. Raidon's phone starts ringing again. He sighs. "That's Thane," he tells me, leaning down and brushing his lips against mine.

"Keep in touch," Rhen tells him. Raidon nods before leaving with Leon.

"Thank god for insurance," Rhen says, staring down at Scarlett sleeping, as I chew my lip.

CHAPTER TWENTY-THREE

An hour passes. Raidon calls to tell us the fire started in the rear loading dock. They're still waiting to get clearance to enter the building, so they can check the security cameras to see what started it. All the fire department can tell us is that an accelerant was used.

We don't hear from them after that. I end up dozing off, only to be awoken by a loud knock at the front door. I see Rhen go to answer it, and my eyes flutter closed, until I hear a familiar voice. Bree. I instantly sit up, hearing her trot down the stairs.

"Bree, you can't just walk down there," Rhen scolds, and she stops on the stairs.

"Shit! Sorry, I forgot."

"She's fine," I call out. Although, I'm grateful I'm already awake because I nearly attacked Thane earlier when he crept up on me while I was sleeping.

"I'll wait here. Sorry, Harlow, I am not good with the whole Omega nesting thing," she calls out, sounding rather embarrassed.

Checking Scarlett, I quickly climb out of the Den and grab one of my mate's shirts, tugging it over my head. Peering up the stairs, I see Bree has stopped hesitantly at the top, and goosebumps rise on my arms when I catch a whiff of her scent.

I make my way up the stairs, her scent nagging at me as it filters into the Den. It makes me itchy. I need to get her away from the Den. Rationally, I know who she is, but this is my space. It makes me edgy, knowing her scent is mingling with my baby's and mates' scents.

By the time I climb the stairs, she is in the kitchen, leaning against the counter. She is wearing jeans, a white top and a black leather jacket. It's the most clothes I've seen on the girl since I met her. I can tell she's been crying. Her face is blotchy, and her hair is tied back in a messy bun.

"Sorry. I tried to go home, but I can't without Tal," she says, suddenly bursting into tears.

Rhen stares awkwardly, clearly not knowing what to do. He nods to her, wanting me to deal with the tears. I feel terrible for her, but I'm also angry at Tal for the mess he caused us.

"I'll make coffee," Rhen announces, grabbing some mugs. I take Bree to the living room. Rhen brings the coffee out just as Scarlett starts crying downstairs. "She's fine, I'll get her."

Rhen leaves, and Bree starts telling me about Thane and Leo's visit, her relationship with Corbin, and also about Curtis being her father. Then I tell her about the fire. Everything is a mess. I desperately want to go back to my Den with Scarlett, but I know I can't just kick her out. Eventually we both fall asleep on the couch, watching TV.

A couple hours later, I hear Scarlett crying. My breasts ache, and I yawn, jerking awake when I notice Bree is no longer on the couch with me. Getting up, I find her in the kitchen with Rhen, who is holding Scarlett and trying to heat up some breast milk. I wander over to him, take Scarlett and flop a boob out for her. I don't care that Bree is right here, my breasts are throbbing.

"I just made some," Rhen says, holding up her bottle. I wave him off, and he sighs, dumping the wasted breast milk down the sink. "Coffee?" he asks Bree, and she nods.

"Tea," I tell him before I ask if he's heard from Raidon and Leon.

He nods, and Bree nudges him out of the way to make the tea and coffee. Rhen leans on the counter, watching me as I sit on the stool next to the kitchen island.

"Yeah, they found the servers on the top floor intact and are combing through the footage now. They hope to be home soon," he tells me. I nod as Bree sets our cups down.

"Are you staying the rest of the night? If not, I can have Raidon give you a ride home when he gets back. Save you from calling another cab," Rhen tells her.

"Yeah, if he doesn't mind. I don't know if a cab will come out here this late," she says, and he nods, sipping his coffee. "I'm thinking of messaging Tammy to stay with me. She'll be off work in an hour," Bree tells me, glancing at her phone screen. I nod. As much as I like Bree, I want my house back.

Rhen asks a few more questions about Tal and what she knows about Corbin. Her story remains the same, matching what Thane already told us. I start to feel sluggish, and I can tell Rhen is also exhausted. He keeps shaking himself awake and yawning, which makes me yawn, too.

I'm fighting sleep as Scarlett unlatches, and I tuck my boob away. Rhen holds his hands out for her, and I give her to him, nearly busting with my need to pee.

I race to the bathroom downstairs and empty my bladder. As I wash my hands, I feel an intense wave of vertigo. I can't stop yawning as I trudge back up the stairs. Extreme fatigue washes over me. When I get to the top, I blink, wondering why Rhen is on the ground. My mind feels sluggish, and it takes me a few seconds to catch up.

"Scarlett?" I call, like I expect her to answer me. I blink, trying to work out what's wrong. Confusion smashes into me.

"Rhen? Rhen!" I screech, running over to him in panic. I push at him, thinking he's crushing our daughter. When I roll him over, however, I find his arms empty. I see feet walk up next to me, and I look up to find Bree, standing there with my daughter in her arms.

"I could have been you, you know," she says, looking around the room. "I could have had this. A family. A pack. But nope, I had to be born a defect," she says, smiling down at Scarlett. My eyes lock onto my daughter in her arms as Bree's eyes flit to mine.

"He's not dead. I drugged his coffee. He's just taking a nap," she says so casually. My heart races in my chest at the sight of my daughter in her arms. I stand, my mate at my feet.

"Bree?" I hold my arms out for Scarlett, my hands trembling, but Bree pulls away from me.

"Alphas. You just gotta pull out the tears, bat your lashes, and smile and their instincts kick in. And they think Omegas are weak," she laughs.

CHAPTER TWENTY-FOUR

ONE HOUR EARLIER

The security at the facility thinks nothing of it as Leo buzzes us in. They don't question him about the purpose of his sudden visit or the unexpected company he brings with him.

It feels a little weird to me. Personally, I wouldn't let shit like this slide, but it isn't my place to voice opinions. At this point, I'm just glad we get in without raising any suspicions.

Getting out of the car, I glance around the underground parking lot. I have a strange feeling in my gut, as if someone is watching us, so I want to ensure our surroundings are clear.

It's dark down here, without much lighting. Not that I would expect there to be a lot of lights on this late at night, but perhaps one or two extra lights wouldn't hurt them. If they have any security cameras down here, I bet the video quality is shit.

Leo's door opens, and I peer over the roof of the car as he leans in. He's talking to Emily, his daughter, who is trying to get out of the car.

She did not appreciate being ripped from her bed in the middle of the night. I understand. She's frightened and wants to stay near her father. Any child, especially one her age who's already bloomed, would act the same. We should be thankful she didn't throw a fit about us taking her to an Omega 'Sanctuary.' These places are far from what I would call 'sanctuary.'

I wait for Leo, who is scolding her as she tries to open the door. He slams it on her, giving me an apologetic look. Yeah, never mind my previous statement. This behavior very much reminds me of a temper tantrum.

"Stay in the car and lock the damn doors. We won't be long," he says, trying to sound stern. The sigh that leaves his lips makes it sound like he is at the end of his rope. He shakes his head as his shoulders slump. "Just try to sleep. We'll be back soon."

The girl must notice how defeated her father appears because she finally gives in. She nods and lays down in the back of the car. At least the little Omega understands that we have to keep a low profile.

"This way," Leo nods to the doors opposite where I think the main entrance is.

I follow him to the reinforced glass door, which I never would have guessed can be used to get inside. My gaze follows him as he unlocks the door with a set of keys and pushes it open.

As soon as we're in, Leo quickly clears the alarm that had started going off.

He closes the panel and glances over his shoulder at me. At least this is more proof that he didn't lie to me. He seems to know this place, as if he spent his entire childhood here.

Leo leads me through the huge corridors. I would have gotten lost very quickly if I had to find my way around here without any help.

The place reminds me of a school. We pass a lot of classrooms, yet they don't look like the classrooms I remember. The more I see, the more clearly I recall what Harlow told me about growing up here. She didn't exaggerate. In fact, it is much worse than what she described.

We stop at one of the doors, and I feel sick to my stomach. Like I will actually purge my previous meal all over the dirty floor.

The walls inside the room are covered in various posters, each worse than the last. It's every sick dream of the worst degenerate. There are pictures of sex, with various poses, suggestions of vile acts, and even diagrams.

I almost laugh at one that describes how to give the best blowjobs. It's so damn laughable, but I can't find it in me to even chuckle at the fucking irony. How goddamn sick does someone have to be to stick these things all over the walls?

As my eyes take in more of the room, I barely hold back the anger that is slowly filling my veins. It burns through me with such vigor that I'm not sure if I can keep quiet any longer.

I count dozens of various sex toys left out on the desks. If this were any other scenario, it would look fucking hilarious, but it's so damn sick that this is what they teach here. Suction cup dildos stamp each desk surface. I want to get away from here before I lose it, so I urge Leo to move forward.

My relief doesn't last for long. Leo stops at the door to the next room. This one has racks of skimpy clothing and ridiculous make-up stands. I can't understand how anyone can think this is even close to normal.

They must find natural beauty useless, so they force young Omegas to paint themselves as clowns, just to follow insane beauty standards. And what should be a room for sex education looks more fitting as a place to train high-end prostitutes.

We keep walking and stop at another door. This room is such a polar opposite to what we've already seen that it almost feels as if we have entered a different dimension.

This has to be some sort of etiquette class. It's all I can assume based on the picture on the wall — a tall woman balancing a book on her head.

No one should be able to call these classrooms. Hell, none of them have anything a normal classroom should have. I definitely don't remember ever seeing them in my school.

As much as I can recall, my classroom walls mostly held maps and graphs — the classes focused on geography, history, math, languages, science, and so on.

Everything I see is obscene, utterly disgusting, and fucking disturbing. It's inappropriate for children who are supposed to learn life skills here. Instead, they are taught how to please Alphas and to keep their mouth shut to avoid being beaten by the very men they are sold to.

Growling, I turn to Leo to find him watching me. He takes a step aside, clearly fishing for a reaction to the things he's showing me.

My face must be burning bright red as he spits out, "I may be an Alpha, but I never agreed with the curriculum in these places. Sit, obey, fuck. It's one of the reasons I refused to let my daughter attend the sanctuary."

I nod in agreement. Seeing this place with my own eyes and listening to Leo's observations makes me even more certain about the need to change the laws. If my daughter turns out to be Omega, I will kill anyone who dares to put her into one of these places.

Leo leads me to the back of the huge facility and blocks off the area. Surprisingly, he turns out to be a master lockpick. I watch as he easily unlocks the door with the small tool kit he brought with him.

When I first noticed his kit, I stared at him as if he just grew a second head. It proves you can't judge someone based on first impressions. I assumed he was planning on using his claws or something. Leo seems to be a jack of all trades. No wonder Corbin made him pack.

Stepping inside, I find what looks like an office, but there's a door at the back that leads into a small apartment. It's clean and neat. Not a single thing is out of place. It's too quiet for my liking.

CHAPTER TWENTY-FIVE

Thane

eo walks around, clearly having been here before. He moves around with such confidence, I'm sure he knows where to find every secret nook and hideout in this place.

I follow Leo to a bedroom, stopping at the door. My eyes take in Curtis, asleep in his bed.

I can't understand how he thinks it's appropriate to have his own apartment here. This place is vile and disturbing. Not to mention it gives me the actual creeps.

Striding over to him, I rip the blue and white comforter back. His eyes shoot open at the sudden loss of warmth and comfort it provides.

Curtis jumps awake, startled. Before he has a chance to realize what's happening, I grab the front of his shirt and drag his sorry ass out of bed. He's too shocked to even recognize me.

While I grab Curtis, Leo races into the small dining area. I'm suddenly grateful he's here. The anger burning inside me is taking er my senses, so having him here is sort of a blessing. As long as Leo is around, I won't think about killing this piece of trash. At least for now.

Leo pulls out a chair, and I toss Curtis into it. The chair flies backward, but I catch it by gripping the arms before it tips all the way back.

Curtis, the worm he is, raises his hands to protect his face. It's funny how he thinks that's where he'll be hit first. I can think of a million things more painful than a punch in the face.

He looks petrified as his gaze jumps between me and Leo. When Curtis finally returns to his senses, he drops his hands and gasps. "Leo? Thane?" he asks, finally recognizing us.

His mouth remains open in shock until Leo tosses a glass of water in his face. Curtis chokes on the liquid. He coughs as most of the water goes into his mouth. That's what he gets for acting like an idiot and forgetting to shut his damn trap. Not to mention the list of other vile shit he's done, but that topic is still ahead of us.

"Good, it looks like you're finally awake. Took your damn time," I growl at him. Curtis rubs a hand down his face, wiping the water off so it now drenches his shirt.

"What is this about? Why are you here?" he barks at us.

I find it funny that Curtis thinks he has the right to demand answers from us. If anything, it's time for him to shut the fuck up and comply with our demands. I didn't come here to play games or joke.

Gripping the arms of the chair, I lean in close to his face and sneer. "We're looking for your brother. He killed my maid and gardener. More importantly, he attacked my Omega," I snap at him. He should understand now that this isn't a matter of silly pride or dominance games.

"He did what?" Curtis chokes out. He blinks at me like an idiot. I'm not completely sure, but he appears shocked at the information. As if my words confuse him.

"Harlow! My Omega!" I emphasize each word. "Where is that no good piece of shit hiding?" My grip on the arms of the chair becomes so tight that the wood cracks.

Curtis shakes his head as he raises his hands in a defensive gesture. "I... I... don't..." he stutters, glancing at Leo. "Don't you know?" Curtis asks him.

To anyone else, his behavior may seem normal, but I know what he is trying to do. He's shifting the attention, the blame, to someone else rather than coming clean.

"Would I be here if I did?" Leo deadpans, rolling his eyes.

Curtis's brows furrow. The worst part is that he really does look confused. I hate it—I want him to say he knows where I can find his brother and what that bastard has done.

"Last I heard, he was picking up some girls from the vamps," Curtis stammers out, glancing between Leo and me again.

I want him to face me. To look me in the eyes while he tries to lie to me. I let out a loud roar, grabbing his attention. "Yes, Harlow! He came after my Omega and nearly killed two of my other mates. So you need to tell us where he is!"

Curtis seems to think. I'm beginning to wonder if this is yet another dead-end.

"Your daughter, Bree, has caused me quite the headache. She's been cutting deals with Corbin for Talon, which put my mate Leon's head on the fucking chopping block."

"Wait! Who told you Bree's my daughter? And what has she got to do with any of this?" he snaps, eyes wide.

I should have seen this coming. I really should have. How can Curtis be so smart and so dumb at the same time? Does he really have no idea who told me these things when Leo is standing right beside me?

I point to Leo, and Curtis shakes his head in denial. I smile widely as I lean in even closer to add, "Plus, I spoke to her at Talon's club before we came here. I'm quite impressed. She helped me learn a few interesting things."

"Leave my girl out of this. It has nothing to do with her! That Talon has been pimping her out for god knows how long! He has her fucking brainwashed!" Curtis spits at me.

"And my mother?" I snap at him.

He blanches, mouth opening and shutting again as he glares at Leo. I turn to grab a knife from the block on the counter. Just as quickly, I turn back and plunge it into his leg. His scream is loud and visceral, but quickly cut off by Leo's hand.

"Now, I have questions, and you will answer," I smile at him, twisting the blade in his thigh.

Curtis grips the arms of the chair and stiffens as muffled screams try to escape past Leo's hand. Tears roll down his cheeks as he nods. I let go of the blade, and Leo uncovers Curtis's mouth.

"Corbin is going to kill you for betraying him! I tried to tell him you were a weasel!" Curtis spits at Leo.

I backhand him. His head whips to the side, blood spraying out of his mouth as his teeth cut through his lip. He growls, pinning me with a glare so pathetic a child could imitate it before spitting out more blood.

"Your mother was trying to shut us down. What did you expect us to do? And she stole my Omega!"

"You alerted Corbin that she would be the one picking up Harlow," I snarl at him.

"That bitch had it coming. She almost did it, you know. She almost got the laws changed. One signature was all she needed, just one. I warned her. She just had to walk away, leave it be. I would have left the past behind, but she had to try to blackmail me instead."

"I thought she tried to blackmail Corbin?" I say, and he nods.

"Corbin laughed her off, told her no one would believe her. So, she came after me. I couldn't risk Bree. She wanted me to convince Corbin to sign the petition, which would have shut us down."

CHAPTER TWENTY-SIX

I rock back on my heels, wanting nothing more than to kill the man in front of me. My hands literally itch, and my mind keeps picturing how great it would look to have this fool's blood coating my hands. But I can't act on instinct, at least not yet. We need him alive because he has information. He worried about my mother taking down his vile industry. By the time I'm done with him, he'll be the one responsible for shutting it down. That's if I don't kill him first.

"So, you told Corbin?" I ask.

"She left me no choice!" Curtis screams. I barely hold back my grin, knowing I've got him.

Curtis is an easy clown to break, but I'm not sure if saying more will work to my advantage or the opposite — force me into a corner. Sometimes, low-life scums like Curtis and Corbin can't accept anyone looking down on them, thinking of them as less. Adding a little fuel to that flame isn't the worst idea. If I'm lucky, he will lay out everything, to the last detail.

"What did she have on Corbin?" I ask. He just shrugs at my question.

"Some proof about him killing our father," Curtis mutters as if it isn't a big deal. You would think such information would affect him, but clearly, Curtis doesn't care. Rats never do.

"But that would help you. So why not give her what she wanted?" I ask, arching an eyebrow as if I'm genuinely interested in his side of the story. My interest isn't entirely fake; I need information, but to get it, I have to listen to the unimportant bits. Right now, the only thing that matters is finding Corbin.

Curtis's face turns deep red as he glares at me. "This place is all I have. She was trying to shut the sanctuaries down! That does not help me. It would only have put Bree in danger! She would have just become another target for Corbin to wipe out," he barks the words.

Am I the only one who finds it ironic how protective Curtis is of his own daughter, while he doesn't give a flying fuck for other Omega girls? He would watch his monster of a brother take Harlow and possibly harm our daughter, and he wouldn't bat an eyelash.

Curtis is more than willing to sacrifice countless innocent lives, as long as it doesn't put him or his daughter in danger.

"So, what did she have on you?" I hum, bringing my hand to my chin as if deep in thought.

Curtis huffs and looks away. "It doesn't matter. She crossed too many people. If it wasn't Corbin, it would have been someone else."

I can't believe this shit. He's trapped, looking right into the face of death, and he's still refusing to give up the information.

I grab the knife, rip it out of his leg, and plunge it into his other leg. I make sure to use enough force to stab the knife all the way through his thigh and into the chair.

"A little warning next time?" Leo scolds me as he jumps to cover Curtis's mouth with his hand, silencing the screams of pain.

I shrug and turn around to rummage through the drawers. A silent gasp leaves my lips as I find a spoon, and an idea pops into my head.

I smile sinisterly as I turn to face them. "Gag him and hold his eyelids open," I tell Leo. Curtis tries to stand, but Leo elbows him in the face, breaking his ugly nose and making him fall back into the chair.

Leo grabs his head and pries an eyelid open. He doesn't question my intentions for even a second. Curtis grips Leo's arm and struggles against his hold. Slowly, I bring the spoon closer to his face, pressing it into the white of his eye, more than ready to scoop it out like ice cream.

"Wait, wait!" Curtis squeals. I stop, raising an eyebrow, and give him a second to catch his breath. It seems Curtis is only just now realizing he could lose more than his precious sanctuary.

"She had footage of the night Bree was dropped on my doorstep. She had your fathers break into our servers and steal it," Curtis pants.

"And why is that an issue?" I ask. I'm curious what could be on the footage besides the obvious—surely whoever Bree's biological mother is wouldn't damage his reputation.

"It's not the only footage she had," Curtis admits, glancing at the spoon in my hand. "She also had video testimony from Bree's mother and DNA swabs. And the tape from the night it happened," he explains as Leo steps back.

"You were worried about Corbin finding out who the mother is?" Leo asks, but Curtis shakes his head.

"No, that was just part of it. It proved her claims that the system is rigged and the Omegas are held against their will," Curtis states.

"But that's common knowledge," I say. Does he take us for fools? Why does he think it's a good idea to share old news in a situation where he is about to lose his eyes? Perhaps I should change my approach? Go for his testicles first and then scoop out his eyes.

"It is now, yes. But before Bree was born, sanctuaries were painted as safe havens for Omegas. A fair system that women joined willingly to find the best packs. Your mother was the biggest whistleblower on what my father spent years trying to cover up. Most girls were too scared to speak up, for fear they would end up back here. But not your mother. She wanted to take us all down. Her videos would have done that."

That makes more sense. I hum and scratch my chin. "So, you told Corbin I bought an Omega to get back at her?"

"Yes, and when I found out she was the one picking up your Omega, I saw an opportunity to make all her threats disappear. So, I told him she was coming and placed a tracker on her car before she left," he mutters.

I take a step closer. "And the footage?"

"No idea, but it was never released," he shrugs. I glance at Leo, who has a dark look on his face.

"What's on the footage, Curtis?" Leo asks, his voice ice-cold. His tone is laced with so much power and dominance, I'm sure Curtis feels cold shivers of fear run down his snakey spine.

Curtis swallows and looks away, appearing ashamed about what he is about to share with us. As if someone as vile as him can feel shame at all. Leo and I exchange looks and focus back on Curtis right as the worm speaks up.

"My father was going to change his will. The first of us to produce an heir would inherit everything, but then Corbin killed him. It was too late, though, and I was desperate. I couldn't lose this place, and it's no secret Corbin hates me. He felt I deserved nothing. It's why I convinced my father to let me pick one of the girls here. I didn't have the money to win an auction. Dad was pissed Corbin made an Alpha Pack, so he agreed."

CHAPTER TWENTY-SEVEN

THANE

"We already know this!" Leo snaps, sounding very close to the end of his rope. "What is on the fucking footage?" he snarls, getting closer to an already trembling Curtis.

If this worm has ever made even one good decision, this has to be it. He can go around and act like a tough guy all he wants, but Leo isn't one to mess with, not now. The aura that surrounds him is dangerous and threatening.

"She refused me! She wouldn't let me mark her and said she wouldn't give me a child. I offered her freedom if she helped me. I loved her, but she only loved that fucking guard!" Curtis spits out, still dancing around the subject.

"Who?" Leo barks. I'm not entirely sure where this is going, but I'm eager to learn more.

Curtis grits his teeth and his eyes return to mine. He locks his gaze with me, as if this sudden burst of confidence will help him. I didn't mind. The guy can use his eyes however he wants, while he still has them.

"Harper. She was mine. He promised she would be mine. But once I got the chance, she refused me. She fucking rejected me. I would have taken care of her. I would have given her the world and the fucking sky if she damn well asked, but she kept refusing me. She wanted him, not me! Why? Why didn't she want me?" he screams at the top of his lungs.

Leo unfolds his arms as our gazes meet. I think we both know where this is going.

"Wait, Harper escaped. She ran," I say. Curtis nods, averting his gaze to the floor as if ashamed by his outburst.

"Eight months later," Curtis whispers, and I hold my breath, waiting for him to admit what I think he is about to, "Bree turned up on my doorstep. I found her in a basket," Curtis adds.

"Is that what's on the video? It was Harper, wasn't it? The video is of Harper dropping Bree off. Harper is—" I glance at Leo, who is glaring at Curtis. If looks could kill, Curtis would already be six feet under.

Slowly, I turn my gaze back to Curtis. He curses and shakes his head again, as if he thinks the reality of the situation might fade, if he only keeps shaking his head. It has to be the most ridiculous attempt of a person forcing themselves into denial that I have ever witnessed.

"Harper, she… she's Bree's mother. And Bree is Harlow's and Zara's half-sister." Curtis swallows loudly. His eyes flicker up to me, only to look away in guilt once he notices the contempt on my face. He is kidding himself if he thinks I am going to let him drop the subject after the bomb he just dropped.

"Keep going. Talk!" I snarl at him. My body shakes in rage. Every part of me: my muscles, body, and mind have one intention engraved in them—to kill him.

He says nothing more. In fact, he forces his lips in a thin line, as if demonstrating that I can't get any more out of him. Ha, we will see about that.

I grab the knife and rip it out of his leg. I press the blade against his throat and snarl in his face. "What did you do?"

As adrenaline and rage boil my blood, my canines start protruding and fur grows along my arms. Curtis nods eagerly, obviously aware of how fucked he is.

"Hana had the footage from the laundry rooms!" Curtis cries

out, trying to get further from the blade that is millimeters away from ending his pathetic life.

"Is that where she broke back in?" I growl the question. I can't let him think he's off the hook that easily.

Curtis shakes his head again. God, doesn't this guy have any other way to deny something? He looks like a stupid old one-trick toy. I need fucking verbal answers, not this.

"She refused me. I couldn't lose this place. I needed an heir."

My stomach sinks as I realize what he refuses to say out loud. His words are pieces of a puzzle that have finally fallen into place.

"You raped her." I stagger back, no longer caring about how much I want to slit his throat. "Bree is a product of rape?"

"I would have done anything for her! I offered her the world! Money, power, social status—everything could have been hers! I would have looked after her like no other man ever could! I loved her!" Curtis screams as I blink at him, unable to believe he is this delusional. "But she didn't want me. She didn't want anything I offered. No matter what I did, it wasn't enough for her. She left me no choice. She pushed me to do it. That's what your mother had on me. Harper still had her clothes from that night, so Hana and Sophia convinced your fathers to hack into our surveillance cameras for the video."

I want to show Curtis exactly what a rapist like him deserves. I want to kill him in the most painful ways I can imagine, but I have to hold back. I still need more information from him, and unfortunately, I also need him alive if I'm going to shut down these sanctuaries for good.

"Wait, how old is Bree?" I ask him.

"Five years older than Harlow and Zara." Curtis hangs his head as the answer leaves his lips.

"Did you know? Did you have any idea who Zara and Harlow were when they came here?" I press.

Curtis shakes his head vehemently. "No, I didn't know until their DNA results came back. We didn't add either of their DNA to the registry until after Harlow ran and it dinged."

"So how did they end up here?" I ask, starting to pace. I have to do something so I don't snap this moron's neck.

"There was a car accident, and the authorities said they received an anonymous tip about it. That two Omega girls were trapped inside a car, their parents dead. We were the closest sanctuary, so they were brought here," he explains.

"And you didn't recognize Harper from the accident?" I ask.

Curtis shakes his head. What is with him and all this shaking? "No, there was nothing left of her. The car was completely burnt out. They found Zara and Harlow injured and unconscious on the side of the road. The authorities said it was a miracle they survived because they shouldn't have been able to get out of the car. Half of Zara's face was hanging off, and both of them were pretty banged up. Harlow had an arm and both legs broken. They thought Zara was dead when they found them."

"So, the authorities never looked into their parents?" The question leaves my lips before I can think of it.

"No, they took statements from the girls but didn't investigate any further. I swear I didn't know who they were. They told us their parents' names, but Harper was using an alias. There was nothing left of their parents' bodies to prove anything different. No leads, nothing." Curtis is clearly trying to make it seem like he didn't have anything to do with the accident or Harlow and Zara ending up here.

I press my lips in a line, trying to make sense of everything when my phone starts ringing. It's the security team at work. I leave Leo with Curtis as I take the call. "What's up?"

"Ah, boss, there's a fire, and it's bad. Merl is calling Raidon now, and the fire department is on the way. I think it was set deliberately," he tells me. Cursing, I hang up and call Raidon.

CHAPTER TWENTY-EIGHT

RAIDON

Thane is finally heading back from the sanctuary. He surprises me by saying he is bringing Curtis back with him. Here I am, thinking that monster would be dead already.

On the bright side, the authorities will be waiting when their plane lands to take him into custody. Perhaps that is better than letting Thane kill him.

I completely understand my mate's need for vengeance, but ridding the world of a piece of shit like Curtis would only be a fleeting pleasure. The guy would be gone, but that's it. He doesn't get to take the easy way out of the shit he's created.

Now, Curtis will have to face the consequences of his actions, even if we won't be the ones to deliver said consequences. He is also necessary if we're going to shut down the sanctuaries. His testimony will be front page news and cause an uproar. Corbin won't be able to keep it quiet, and it will be even more damaging that the son and brother of the biggest sanctuary owners acts as their whistleblower.

"Rhen must be asleep already. I can't reach him," Leon announces, pulling me out of my thoughts. My eyes are still focused on the surveillance screen.

I'm about to say something, but out of nowhere, I smell

something that reeks of burning plastic. The stench is so strong I can taste it in the back of my throat.

Half of the building, if not more, was destroyed. Everything is covered in soot, and the contents in the rooms on the lower floors is completely gone. Yet structurally, the building appears sound.

Moving the mouse, I click on the next video. We had a rough time when the fire first broke out, but now that I search the security footage, I'm realizing the angles for some of our cameras are terrible. We can't see anything. There are too many blind spots. As I fast-forward to the correct time, Leon peers at the screen, noticing something I missed.

"Wait! Go back. Who's that?" He points a finger at the screen and I grab the mouse again.

The rear loading dock takes up most of the image as I rewind the video a few minutes back. I furrow my eyebrows, wondering what Leon might have seen. I can barely make out the footage, but in the background, I notice the smoke shop on the street behind our building. The light flicks off as the owner and key cutter opens the door to leave the shop.

"Ah, it's just Vadum," I mutter, about to fast-forward again when Leon asks me to rewind more. As I reach for the mouse, I notice a movement on the screen. I pull back my hand and keep watching the video.

Vadum starts walking across the road. He then stops to talk with someone I can't quite make out because they are wearing a leather jacket and a beanie.

However, as my eyes carefully look them both over, I notice an important detail. The person Vadum is talking to is wearing thigh-high boots. That, and with what I can see of their silhouette, is enough to tell it is a woman.

My eyes follow the scene with newfound interest. What on earth is happening here? And why is Vadum acting like he's sneaking around? I guess Leon did notice something important.

Vadum unlocks his car, and the woman hops in the passenger seat. She looks like she is in a hurry, while Vadum cautiously continues to cross the road. I furrow my brows as Vadum leans down, checks his surroundings, and pulls a hood over his head.

I hold my breath as I watch him approach the back of our building. I see security come into frame. They are doing their rounds, checking the doors and the perimeter. Vadum hides in some shrubs when he notices them.

Yeah, this is definitely suspicious behavior. Vadum waits for the security guards to finish their rounds and leave before he walks over to the huge roller door. He then pulls a bottle out from the pocket of his hoodie.

A part of me can't believe I'm actually seeing what is happening on the screen, but I keep watching regardless of my doubts.

Vadum sets the bottle down before he starts rummaging in his back pocket, finally pulling out what looks like a key.

"Motherfucker!" Leon growls at the screen when we watch Vadum unlock the door. He then pulls a lighter out of his pocket, sets the accelerant on fire, and tosses the burning bottle onto the packing boxes and travel blankets behind the door.

Vadum shuts the door casually, as if he hadn't just set anything on fire or committed a crime. He quickly turns around, drops his head, and jogs back to his car. He doesn't bother to glance over his shoulder, completely carefree about everything happening behind him. Hell, he didn't even bother to check if anyone was inside the damn building; people he would have left to burn alive.

Then Vadum hops inside his car and takes off with the mysterious woman. It takes a couple minutes before the safety alarm goes off, alerting everyone to the fire.

"I bet you that's where Harlow got the key cut when she was sleeping in the loading docks. That bastard must have cut himself a copy, too," Leon groans, clutching his hair in frustration.

"But why would he?" I ask. What motive could Vadum have to set the fire? We've known him for years and never had any issues. "This makes no sense."

Before he can say anything, I grab my phone to call Thane. But as soon as I pull up his number, I remember he is probably still on the plane. For now, the safest option is to use the mind-link. At least he isn't driving, so I won't distract him from the road.

As I open the mind-link, Thane answers instantly, as if someone already alerted him that I am about to dump the news before I opened the link.

'What's up? Any news on the culprit?' he asks.

'Leon noticed something on the security tape. It was Vadum. He was with some woman, but neither of us can identify her,' I growl.

Thane's confusion comes through the bond loud and clear. The feeling is way louder than a thousand words he might have shouted.

'Vadum?' He repeats the name as if he thinks he misunderstood me. *'Have we ever had any issues with him before?'*

I try to think of literally any reason why Vadum would try to sabotage us. *'None that I know of. What do you want us to do besides report it?'*

Thane hums. *'First, find Vadum. And then find out who the woman is. Are you sure she isn't anyone you or Leon recognize?'*

Leon pulls his phone from his pocket. I know he tried to mind-link Rhen earlier and didn't get an answer. I watch as he calls the house phone. Still getting no answer, he tries Rhen's cell.

I focus back on Thane. *'No idea. The woman was too far away, and she was wearing a beanie. It did look like she was purposefully disguising herself, though. She jumped in the car, Vadum set the fire, and then they drove off together.*

'Call Rhen, too. I can't get a hold of him,' Thane tells me.

CHAPTER TWENTY-NINE

"Shit. I still can't get a hold of Rhen. No one is answering the home phone, and he isn't picking up his cell. He's not responding to the mind-link either," Leon announces just as Thane tells me to check on Rhen.

Thane is the Alpha-of-Alphas for our pack. He is the only one with the ability to wake Rhen using the mind-link. None of us can defy his command or get away with ignoring his attempts to reach out.

A sinking feeling settles in my gut as I suck in a breath. 'Wait. You can't reach him either?' I ask Thane, dumbfounded by his words.

'No...' Thane drags out the word as if he is thinking. 'It feels like he is asleep. I tried the house phone but got no answer, so I thought maybe he reached out to you guys.'

The sinking feeling in my gut grows, and I start to fear the worst. I don't want to raise panic if it isn't necessary yet, though, so I try my best to sound as calm as possible.

'Maybe you should try to force him awake? We have been trying to get a hold of him for the last twenty minutes,' I suggest as I nod for Leon to follow me.

Leon pulls the memory card of the video footage for us to give to the police, and we make our way out of the building using the fire exit. I feel Thane trying to force the mind-link, but he gets nothing, and my stomach sinks once again. Now, I definitely know something is wrong.

Thane groans after a few more attempts. *'When was the last time you or Leon heard from him?'* Thane asks. Leon and I exchange glances as we feel his frustration and a slight hint of fear reach us through the bond.

As I glance at Leon, he raises one finger. *'I don't know, a little over an hour ago?'* My answer sounds more like a question. I can't think clearly as the panic slowly takes over.

If anything happens to my mates, I know I won't forgive myself for not being there when they need me.

'I see. That's roughly when I last spoke to him, too. Something doesn't feel right. Go home and check on them first. I just landed and will get there as soon as I can,' Thane tells me.

He cuts off the mind-link before I can say anything else. A loud, frustrated sigh leaves my lips as Leon rummages in his pockets for the car keys. He tosses me the keys, and I snatch them from the air. We both ignore the police officers as they step in our path.

"We would have been told if anyone crossed into the city. Thane has the place on the lockdown. No one can enter or leave without us being notified," Leon reminds me, but his attempt to reassure me doesn't work as planned.

The nagging feeling in my gut doesn't settle. Quite the opposite, it gets way worse. I need to get back home, back to my mates.

It takes a quarter of the time it usually would for us to get back home, all thanks to my maniacal driving. As soon as I pull into the driveway, we hear Scarlett crying.

Even this far from the door, I can hear our daughter screaming her head off, and Leon is out of the car long before I even manage to unclip my damn seatbelt. Her crying stops just as I enter the house through the garage door.

I barely take one step inside before I freeze in my tracks. My eyes focus on the blood all over the floor. It's Harlow's blood, and I can't see or sense her anywhere, so I race to the kitchen.

As soon as the door opens, I find Leon, clutching Scarlett to his chest. His eyes snap to mine, full of panic. I scan the room, my gaze falling on Rhen, who is face down on the floor.

"Where's Harlow?" I gasp out. Leon peers down at Scarlett, rocking and trying to calm her.

"I found her next to Rhen," he says as Scarlett starts screaming again.

I frantically look around before taking off. I race to the Den, screaming out for Harlow. But I don't receive an answer, no matter how loudly I keep calling out. My heart races as I run upstairs. Leon meets me back in the kitchen, having already checked the upstairs rooms.

Rhen groans from the floor, finally seeming to return to his senses and regaining consciousness. I grab his shoulders once he jerks awake. His eyes shoot open in confusion.

"Scarlett!" he shouts as he jumps to his feet. A second later, dizziness sends him crashing into me.

"Scarlett is fine. She's fine, Rhen. Tell us where Harlow is!" I clutch his arms, both to hold him up and to attempt to wake him up more. I need him to hear my questions and answer them before anything else can happen.

Rhen's eyes roll slightly as Leon comes back. Scarlett is settled now, already asleep in his arms. Rhen attempts to reach for her.

"How? I was…?" Rhen cuts himself off. He seems out of it, very confused. He's extremely disoriented and acting as if he can't control his body or thoughts.

"Rhen, listen to me! Harlow! Where is she?" I snap at him, unable to hide my frustration, anger, and fear.

"Huh? Oh, she went to the bathroom. She must be with…" Rhen mumbles under his breath as he gets out of my hold and tries to stagger toward Leon.

"I think he's been drugged. He isn't acting like himself. Not quite present, you know? On top of the weird behavior, his blood smells off," Leon warns me as I grab Rhen again.

I tighten my hold on Rhen's upper arms and spin him around to face me. "Rhen, who is here?" I yell in his face as I shake his body.

"Why are you yelling? They're watching TV," Rhen groans as he tries to force his hand over my mouth to shut me up.

My eyes widen at his words. "Who is they?" I scream at him. I'm barely holding myself back from slapping my mate back to his senses.

"Harlow and Bree," Rhen slurs.

I am freaking out at this point, losing my goddamn mind, but also wondering what the fuck he was drugged with. I have never seen anyone react to drugs like this before, and Rhen isn't one to be taken down easily either.

"Bree?" Leon gasps out the name just as Thane smashes inside and slides into the kitchen.

"Did you find them?"

Thane snarls before his eyes focus on Rhen, who can hardly stand upright, still completely out of it.

"No!" Thane gasps. His voice is laced with panic as he races over to him, grabbing him from me and shaking him the same way I did a moment ago. "Rhen, where is she? Where is Harlow?" He screams the question with such desperation, I can feel the ping in my heart.

"He said Bree was here," I say over Thane's voice. Thane lifts his head right as Leo walks inside, just as naked as Thane. So that's how they got here so fast — they ran from the airport. Wait, where's Leo's daughter?

CHAPTER THIRTY

"I can't help but wonder… I wonder if our mother felt any guilt when she set me in that basket and left me on Dad's doorstep. How could she walk away from her own child like that?"

Those are the last words I hear from Bree as I desperately plead for her to set Scarlett down next to Rhen. My heart is beating so violently that it feels dangerous, but I am ready to do anything to protect my daughter. If something happens to Scarlett, I will lose the very reason for my heart to continue beating.

My body is suddenly slammed against something hard. My eyes shoot open, and a loud gasp leaves my lips. The last thing I remember is trying to convince Bree to set Scarlett down and her strange words.

Bree had placed my daughter on the floor next to an unconscious Rhen. I had never felt such an intense and raw fear before that moment. I felt something crack against the back of my head, and the tiles rushed at my face before I finally saw Bree walk away from my daughter. I didn't care that she was coming toward me. As long as Scarlett was safe, I didn't care what happened to me.

When I manage to pry my eyes open, I can hear two people talking.

"You're revolting. She just had a baby for fuck's sake! Did you forget that already?" Bree growls angrily.

Clearly, they are discussing me. Yet, in this state, I can't understand why or what is happening. My head is pounding to its own beat.

"Yeah? Well, let me give you a damn news flash. You have no idea what it's like being a vamp. I never asked for this, but at the end of the day, blood is blood, like it or not. She, however… She smells fucking divine. Not that you can tell a gem from a stone or anything. Pull this piece of shit over. I just want a quick taste."

I blink a couple of times, struggling to get back to my senses. As if this confused state isn't bad enough, I also can't remember where I've heard that voice before. I know I recognize it, but I can't tell from where. Nothing makes sense.

"Climb over the seat, then. I am not stopping or pulling over until we get to Corbin. Especially not for you and your sudden, sick needs," Bree snaps at the strange man.

Now that I know Bree is near, I find the energy to sit up. I finally register that I am in a car, and I have bled through my pants. I peer out the blackened windows, and I can barely make out the trees and the highway. Where is Bree going?

The car suddenly hits a bump, and a groan escapes me as my head smashes against the window. I touch the aching spot, only to discover my wrists are tied together.

Disoriented and absolutely lost, I blink a couple of times to clear my vision. I pull my fingers away from my head, and I notice my fingertips are stained with blood.

"Well, well, well, aren't I lucky? Look who's wide awake and ready to play? Just in time, too." The sultry purr startles me, and I barely hold in the scream that threatens to escape me.

My head rolls back to hit the headrest as I try to recognize that voice. My gaze settles on a man I have met only a few times before. Vadum, the keyman from the smoke shop.

"How are you feeling, sugar?" he speaks up, offering me a sickening smile. He tilts his head and, somehow, manages to smile even wider. "Want some company back there? I would be more than happy to help you out," he growls.

Cold shivers run down my spine as I watch his eyes oddly flicker. The fact Vadum actually licks his lips as he stares at me makes the situation much worse. I know exactly what sort of creep he is. This is the same bastard who asked me to flash my tits for a ride and then snapped a picture.

While I think of that vile memory, Vadum keeps licking his lips. The action makes my gaze dart to them. I can see the sharp points of his protruding fangs almost piercing his bottom lip.

My heart starts beating a little faster as I finally remember that Vadum is more than just the key guy: he's a vamp. He uses my momentary confusion and suddenly climbs between the front seats.

Realization crashes over me like a ton of bricks. I try to thrash to get out of the restraints, but all he does is laugh and climb into the back, grabbing my knee. I quickly turn in my seat and kick my tied-together legs out. My feet hit his chest, shoving him against the other door.

"Someone woke up cranky," he mutters under his breath. His eyes set on my feet and slowly travel up my body. "You should have warned me you're not a morning person," Vadum growls as he traps my feet against the leather seats.

"Let go of me! Don't touch me!" I try to scream, but the sound of my own voice makes my head pound even harder. Vadum unclips my seatbelt and drags me toward him. I thrash and try to fight, but he presses his weight on top of me. I act on instinct and headbutt him.

Pain explodes through my skull, while all he does is release a barely-audible grunt. His hands wrap around my throat and cut off my oxygen. I struggle and gasp for air, yet despite my attempts, I am unable to do anything or fight back. After all, I am restrained, and he is holding me down. My eyes hurt, tears sting them, and my face feels swollen.

"You stupid bitch! Do you have any idea what you did? That fucking hurt!" he screams in my face as he adds more pressure to my neck.

"Hey! Hey!" Bree yells as her hand slaps my attacker's shoulder from the driver's seat.

He responds with a growl. He's too busy with me, apparently

intent on ripping my shirt apart.

"I need her alive, damn it! Don't you dare fuck this up for me, you moron!" Bree snarls. His grip around my neck tightens again before he slams my head into the car door.

For a brief moment, all I can see is black. My eyes roll back while I feel him rip my shirt to pieces. To my surprise, he lets go of my throat, and I instantly take the opportunity to gasp in a breath. Somehow, I manage to choke on air when I feel him bite into my breast.

His fangs sink into me painfully. The scream of agony that tears out of me is deafening. Tears escape my eyes, and once again, I start thrashing against him. My attempts to fight him off do nothing but make him laugh. He pulls his fangs out, just to bite my other breast.

A weak whimper escapes me. I feel disgusted when I finally understand what he is doing. This creep is feeding on me.

"Please. Please, stop. I'm begging you. Stop this," I croak out as he sinks his fangs into my neck.

CHAPTER THIRTY-ONE

"Fuck! You taste so fucking good! So much better than you smell. I had no idea anyone could taste this fucking divine!" he groans as his body shakes in pleasure.

I gasp for breath. I'm already starting to feel lightheaded, and my limbs begin to tingle. I can barely feel them. Tears flood my eyes, and I fight to stay awake. Too much, he is taking too much. Leon fed on me earlier, and god knows how much blood I lost from the gaping head wound Vadum gave me. The longer he feeds, the weaker I get, and the colder I feel.

"Vadum! That's enough, you creep. Let her go!" Bree roars at him.

I don't for a moment believe he will listen to her. Men like him don't know when to stop and don't bother to listen to others. Even when they are wrong, they keep insisting they are the only ones who can be right.

But to my surprise, Vadum pulls his teeth from my flesh. My vision is blurry, but I can still see my blood run down this disgusting man's chin.

"Spoiling all my fun. You're such a buzzkill, Bree," he purrs as his hands return to my breasts. He squeezes them before trailing his hands down the rest of my body. I feel him fiddling with the restraints on my feet for a bit, but he groans and gives up. Instead of trying to get them off, Vadum flips me over onto my stomach.

Realizing his intentions, my fight or flight instincts kick in. Of course, I choose to fight, but even if I want to, there is nowhere I can run or hide. I lash out, trying my best to fight against him, even when he yanks my pajama bottoms to my knees and tries to pull my hips in the air.

"No!" I scream at the top of my lungs, to his displeasure. I keep thrashing and moving until I fall headfirst into the foot well of the backseat. The blood from my head and neck wounds runs into my eyes, partially blinding me.

Vadum's hand comes down on my ass as he struggles to pull my underwear down. He jerks them past my hips when Bree suddenly slams on the brakes, sending the creep flying forward.

"I thought I said that was fucking enough! You already fed on her. Now get off her! I won't watch you fucking rape her!" Bree screams furiously as she smacks the shit out of him.

I wish she could smack some sense into the man, but it is clear he is too far gone in his creep ways to ever become a normal person.

I hear a grunt from Vadum before I catch onto the sounds of choking. He's now putting his hands on Bree, too.

"Touch me again, and it will be your ass I fuck!" Vadum snarls at Bree. "I never asked you to watch. Now do your fucking job and drive!"

Bree gasps for air, and I almost feel sorry for her. Almost. She deserves this, and honestly way more, for pulling me into her shit.

"I said drive!" Vadum growls again. The sudden sound of his voice startles me.

"No!" Bree screams back with just as much anger as Vadum. "You fucking drive. If you fucking rape her, I will tell Corbin. You might get away with your sudden need to feed, but why don't we see how he reacts when he finds out you forced yourself onto his property?" Bree shouts, and a moment later, I hear the driver door open.

Vadum curses under his breath as I hear the rear door open. I notice a brief movement, but I'm stuck in the precarious position of my head in the foot well and my ass in the air, so I can't say who is where.

A cold breeze rushes over me as I listen to more movement before I feel hands grip my hips tightly. A whimper escapes me when I feel fingernails dig into my skin.

It doesn't take me long to realize it is Bree. She pulls my pants back up, and I hear two car doors slam before the car starts moving forward again. Vadum must be driving as Bree is still in the back seat with me.

"God, you're so stupid, Bree. Someone might think you actually like the whore if they saw how you just protected and helped her," Vadum snarls at Bree while she helps me sit up.

She wraps my seatbelt around me and leans me against the door. Bree is surprisingly gentle as she checks my restraints.

"You have no fucking right to an opinion! And don't call her that!" Bree snaps at him as she smacks his seat with her palm. "Just shut up and fucking drive!" she growls. I try to catch my breath as I watch her.

"I can't believe you. I really can't," Vadum whines, making me wonder what he means by those words. I don't have to wonder for long as he speaks up again. "You never cared when I had my way with those other bitches. Are you sweet on this one, Bree? Wait, are you into pussy now? Dicks no good for you, anymore? Did Tal make you switch sides?" he mocks.

Bree snarls at him again while I try to understand what he's talking about. His rant doesn't make much sense, and I'm too weak to process the information, barely catching the words.

"No, fuck face. She's my sister! Now do your damn job and fucking drive!" Bree says as she kicks the back of his seat.

I stare at her, completely shocked. Bree glances at me before quickly averting her gaze. Suddenly, the words she spat back at the house make sense now. But how is it possible? Could it be the truth, or did she just say that to trick Vadum?

"Scarlett?" I murmur my daughter's name. My tongue feels so thick in my mouth, I'm surprised I manage to push out even one word.

"I wrapped her in her blanket and left her next to Rhen. I didn't hurt my niece," Bree says as she keeps her gaze fixated straight ahead. She doesn't bother to so much as glance at me, let alone look at me as she speaks. I suck in a breath just as Bree mutters, "I'm not a monster."

Funny. Her actions so far prove otherwise.

"What did I ever do to you?" I whisper the question, followed by a violent coughing fit. Blood fills my mouth from where I bit my tongue earlier.

"This has nothing to do with you, believe it or not," Bree whispers as her gaze travels to her hands. She sucks in a deep breath and shakes her head. "I just need Talon back. I'm not asking for much. That's all I need, and Corbin wants you. I never intended for this to happen. I know I sound sick, but I really didn't plan this." Bree tries to explain herself, but nothing she says can convince me that there aren't other hidden agendas.

I struggle to keep my eyes open. I am pretty sure I have a concussion. Fighting the insane exhaustion, I want to question her about the claim she made earlier. She said I am her sister. I want answers. I need them, but when I feel the cold seep in and my body start to ache, I know I can't stay awake for much longer. I'm fighting against time before my body gives out.

Thanks to that creep, Vadum, I've lost too much blood, and my head is pounding even harder than before. Against everything, I try to remain awake, yet as the car sways in a comforting motion, I am sucked into oblivion.

CHAPTER THIRTY-TWO

lap… Slap
The sound echoes somewhere deep in my mind until silence overtakes wherever I am. Now, I feel like I can keep sleeping. I deserve this rest.

…Slap…

Apparently rest is only for the fucking wicked. I don't want to wake up. I want to keep drifting in nothingness, drifting in peace.

…Slap…

Yet, at the same time, I feel the urge to return, or more accurately, feel something forcing me to return.

"Wake up!" someone shouts from what seems like miles away. "Wake up!" The distant voice invades not only my hearing, but also my senses. My cheek feels warm as my eyes barely flutter. I don't want to open them.

"Wake up!" I hear the distant shout again. It's somewhat annoying, and I almost keep my eyes closed out of spite, until I feel panic through the bond. The fear is so strong I fight the urge to drift back to sleep, but the pull sucking me under is strong. Almost too strong.

That is until I feel my head whip to the side. My cheek starts burning furiously from the force of someone's hand connecting with my face again after who knows how many times they've already slapped me. I hear the voice again, and this time I can recognize it as Bree's.

"Come on, you useless piece of shit. Give her your blood! You know as well as I do she is no good to either of us dead!" I hear Bree snap.

A loud, pained groan leaves my lips as I force my eyes open. My vision blurs, and relief flits through the bond from my mates. I don't have time to examine it before I am thrust back into the nightmare I thought I escaped from. I'm still in the car with my tormentors. A man who stole my blood and tried to rape me, and a woman who claims she isn't a monster but kidnapped me from my home and tore me away from my newborn daughter and mates.

Sadly, this isn't just a bad dream. A whimper escapes me as I'm forced to abandon the hope that this was never real.

The car stops suddenly, and Bree leans closer to pry my eyelids open.

"Why isn't she healing? Aren't werewolves fast healers or is that just bullshit? Is it only Alphas that heal fast?" I hear Vadum's disgusting voice echo around me.

I feel like I am floating. Like my body is about to lift into the sky and settle on a fluffy cloud.

"Oh, so smart to think of that! Maybe it's because you took too much blood, you imbecile! You said you just wanted a taste, but no, you had to go overboard and forget there's this thing called limits. She isn't a never-ending fucking blood bag! She just had a baby, you idiot. She wouldn't have shifted yet. Not while she's breastfeeding!" Bree screams at Vadum.

I don't hear his voice or any stupid remarks, and despite the throbbing pain, I'm pretty sure my body jolts when I hear a ripping sound.

My lips are suddenly pried open, and instinct takes over. Despite how weak I feel, I thrash as Vadum presses his bleeding wrist to my lips. I cough and sputter, refusing his blood and spitting it out. I don't want it. I refuse to accept any part of that vile man inside me, even if it ends up costing me my life.

"Stop being so stubborn, Harlow! Do you want to die? You just stopped breathing a few seconds ago! Think about your daughter and drink his fucking blood!" Bree snaps at me.

She pinches my nose as Vadum forces his blood down my throat. I can feel the wound on my head closing. The pounding slowly fades, leaving behind nothing but a dull ache as my vision clears.

Bree finally lets go of me and lets out a breath of relief. How can she think it is okay to act relieved when she is the one who fucking did this to me?

Well, technically, it was Vadum, but it isn't like she tried to stop him from sucking on me until he nearly drained me.

"She's fine now," Bree mutters to him. "Keep going. Corbin said he will be waiting for us near the service station. He just needs to figure out how to get off the mountain, then we can follow him from there."

Vadum gets back in the driver's seat and starts the car.

I wiggle, sitting up higher and flexing my wrists in an attempt to loosen the ropes. Bree slowly leans back in her seat. As her eyes meet mine, she notices me watching her and shakes her head.

"Don't look at me like that. Don't pretend you're better than me. As if you wouldn't do the same thing for one of your mates!" she snaps.

I both understand her and don't at the same time. I know I would do anything for my mates, that's just a fact, but I never asked her to justify her actions. All I can do is look at the woman who kidnapped me and claims to be my sister. There is no way I would hurt a sister like this, even one I just learned about.

"I'm not claiming I'm better, but I would never do this," I shake my head to emphasize my words. "I would find another way to help them," I tell her, certain I would never stoop so low.

Bree presses her lips in a thin line and focuses her gaze out the window. As much as I want this conversation to end, I need to know more.

"What did you mean when you said that thing back at the house?" I ask her, letting my gaze focus on my own window as I try to figure out where we are. To my great disappointment, I don't recognize my surroundings at all.

"'I can't help but wonder… I wonder if our mother felt any guilt when she set me in that basket and left me on Dad's doorstep. How could she walk away from her own child like that?'" I repeat Bree's words. I don't struggle to quote them because they are burned into my memory. Without thinking, I turn my head to look at her right as she purses her lips.

"I never understood why my father never spoke of her," Bree says. I tilt my head to the side, watching as her strange statement slowly sinks in. "She left me in a basket on his doorstep and walked away. But she kept both of you," Bree adds, and my brows furrow. I squint my eyes as I try to read her facial expression, but she doesn't give anything away.

"That makes no sense. Thane told me you are Curtis Black's daughter, but I don't remember ever seeing you at his facility," I hum once the words leave my mouth, still raking through my memories, just in case I had seen someone resembling Bree.

She rolls her eyes at me and scoffs, crossing her arms in front of her chest.

"Yeah, that's because I was sent away to boarding school. Besides, I'm five years older than you," she pauses. "Our mother told me she couldn't bear to look at me. Her own daughter. Her flesh and blood. All because I resemble my father. Her rapist," Bree says, gazing out of the window. Her last words come out as just a whisper, and I barely catch them.

I suck in a breath. "Harper?"

Bree closes her eyes and exhales. "Yes Harper. Your mother… She was supposed to be mine, but instead, she abandoned me… Not you two, though. She loved both of you. More than you could ever imagine… But she couldn't love me. She couldn't even look at me."

A tear rolls down her cheek, and all I can do is stare at her. I don't know what to say, but Bree doesn't need my words as she keeps talking. "I just wanted to know her… To get to know both of you."

CHAPTER THIRTY-THREE

A lump forms in my throat, and a jolt of pain hits my chest as I watch and listen to Bree lay out her pain for me.

I hold my breath as I notice her bottom lip start to quiver.

"It took me weeks to track her down, and I had to steal Mrs. Yates's car. Boy, did I get my ass beat for that. I watched you all for days before I finally caught her alone. You were all at some fair, and I followed her into the bathrooms. But she told me to go home… I didn't ask for much. Just a chance to get to know my mother and my little sisters, but she told me to leave." Bree looks over at me, focusing her gaze on mine.

I feel like she's staring straight into my soul; as if she's trying to show me a glimpse of the pain she experienced when she was younger, and how it felt when our mother rejected her. I can only imagine how heartbreaking it was.

"You know, when she told me to leave, she also said I wasn't her daughter, only his. That she wanted nothing to do with me. I followed all of you for four weeks. Four weeks. Only for her to tell me to go home because she couldn't stand to look at me."

I understand why our mom did it. Bree is the product of her rape. All Bree wanted was to be loved and accepted by our mother, but not every woman can love the physical representation of the trauma they went through. In this case, they are both victims.

I don't understand what's happening now, though. Bree sounds devastated, and her eyes are filled with tears. She looks sad, but the corners of her lips keep twitching, as if she is barely holding back a grin.

"You were there that day, weren't you? The day of the accident?" My eyes widen as the realization hits me. Was it even an accident? Bree has already crossed a line by stealing me away from my mates, but who knows how far she was willing to go back then, after our mother hurt her so badly.

Bree nods. "Not my proudest moment, but I had watched for weeks as she doted over the two of you. I watched her act like the mother I always wanted, the mother I wished she would have been to me…" She stops and stares down at her hands.

For some reason, it feels like she is checking her hands to see if they are covered in blood. Is she about to confess that she had something to do with our mother's death?

"After the months I spent pestering her, Mrs. Yates finally told me who my mother was. Dad had always refused. He said I was better off not knowing. And he was right." Bree pauses, sucking in a deep breath. "Mrs. Yates gave me her name and an old picture of her, so I slept with the Dean's son at my school to use their photo recognition program to track her down. Her face popped up on a security camera at some hotel, and it wasn't hard to find her from there. I knocked on some doors, and a woman told me she saw her car at a camp ground. So, I went there, watched you all leave, and I followed you."

"Is that why you're doing this?" I question Bree, unsure if I even want to know. I'm terrified of what else she might have in store for me.

"What?" Her eyes snap up to me. "No, I just want Talon back. He's the only person who has ever wanted me. Ever loved me. I was just too blind to see it."

No matter how much Bree denies it, I don't think I can believe her. Her actions don't align with her words.

"Ah, girl hug!" Vadum taunts from the driver's seat.

Bree snarls and kicks his seat again. "Shut up, fuckwit!"

Vadum snickers, but I pay him no mind. He is the least important person in this situation, no matter how annoying or dangerous he might be. Instead of giving him the attention he obviously wants, I focus on getting as much information as I can from Bree. Once the car stops, I'm more than ready to run for my life. I will force the shift to break these restraints and get away from these sickos.

A sudden question pops into my mind. I don't bother to consider if asking it will be a good idea, I just voice it. "And you think Talon will be okay with this? That he'll just leave with you after he finds out the price of his freedom?"

"I'm doing this for him!" Bree screams as if I just insulted her in the worst possible way.

"Are you, though?" I press. It might cost me to anger her, but I'm willing to keep pushing her buttons. "Or are you doing this to get back at our mother? To get back at me for receiving the love she never gave you?"

Bree's eyes widen in shock as she frantically shakes her head and raises her hands in denial. "What? No! I would never! I have nothing against you, Harlow. Or Zara. Nothing! I just wanted to get to know you! Why do you think I pulled you both from that car?"

I blink at her, utterly shocked at the sudden confession. I was mentally prepared for Bree to say something about causing the accident, but I never would have guessed that she saved Zara and me from dying with our parents.

As the wheels in my mind start turning, another, somewhat unexpected realization hits me. "It was you. You were the one who drove us off the road. You were the one who forced us into that ditch!"

Bree looks away and presses her lips together. My mind takes me back to that awful day. The smell of gas. The sound of my mother's screams as the car caught fire, and she was engulfed in the flames.

Zara and I were hanging upside down in the backseat. My father, who was driving, died on impact. Yet, I heard my mother's screams as she burned alive before my eyes. I can still smell the scent of their burning flesh. My father's seat was pushed back against my legs, trapping me in the car. I thought Zara was dead. Half of her face was hanging off.

I passed out before the flames reached us. I can remember waking up and peering around, wondering how we got out of the car. The next thing I remember is waking up again to the paramedics working on us. I kept falling in and out of consciousness, and I spent the next few days drugged up on painkillers before we were taken to the facility.

"When I hit the back of your car, I was just hoping you'd have to pull over, and she would explain to you both who I was. But your car spun out of control. It smashed through the barrier and down the hill before rolling into that ditch," Bree whispers, pulling me out of my dreadful memories.

"By the time I drove down there, the car was already on fire. I tried to get to her, but… there was nothing I could do, so I pulled Zara out first. I was barely able to get you out after her because your legs were trapped. I dragged you both up to the road and called for help."

"Then you ran. You killed my family, destroyed my life, and then fled the scene," I spit at her. She might have saved our lives, but she is the one responsible for all of it. Bree is the one who took everything from us.

"And she destroyed mine!" Bree snarls.

Tears prick my eyes as I recall the small fragments I have of the accident. Zara remembers the day at the fair, but she doesn't remember anything from the accident. I never told her that Mom was alive. That I watched her burn. Her screams haunted me until, eventually, they became a distant memory. Until I was able to pretend the screams that woke me every night for months weren't my mother's.

I can't stand to look at Bree anymore, so I turn my gaze back out the window. So much for her claim of not being a monster. She is worse than that.

CHAPTER THIRTY-FOUR

We have all our friends, every person who works for us—and even their friends—out scouting the city. No one was seen leaving, so they have to be here somewhere, hiding right under our noses.

However, as hours pass with still no sign of Harlow, I start to lose my mind. I'm not alone on that. My mates are going just as crazy as I am. I'm about to go knock on every door in the entire city when we get a hit on Vadum's car from a speeding camera, one town over. Then another lead from a gas station where Vadum is caught on the CCTV, filling his car up.

We retrace his steps and find his car, but it was abandoned as a ploy to make it look like they haven't left the city. They used the tunnels, and another car was waiting out near the old mine shafts, right outside the city border. That car was stolen, and we manage to track how they made it out of the city via cameras.

Now, we have the make and model of the stolen car, but that only gets us so far. No doubt, he already changed the plates, making it more difficult to trace.

"Thane? Where are you going?" Raidon perks up and asks as I walk outside to stand on the front porch.

We're at Elaine's house. We came here to drop off Emily and Scarlett, so they will have a safe place to stay while we go look for Harlow. Also, I am planning to do bad, bad things to that asshole, Vadum, once I get my hands on him, and that definitely isn't something the kids should be around to see.

We all know where Bree is heading. She is taking Harlow to Corbin in exchange for Tal. However, we are facing a major obstacle. We have no clue, not even a hint, about Corbin's location. We aren't even completely sure which direction Bree and Vadum went because there's a few major highways not far from the gas station where Vadum's last picture was taken, and there is no footage on any of those highways.

"Thane!" Raidon raises his voice as he calls out my name.

"Just let him be, Raidon. He has a lot on his mind. Leave him alone to think!" I hear Rhen snap at Raidon from a distance.

While my mates keep bickering in the background, I accept that we are still too short on people. We will need more help if we want to check out all the highways.

But I'm not too keen on trusting the authorities right now. Since there is no one else I can think of on such short notice, I pull my phone from my pocket and call Jake. I'll tell him to create a search party while we check the most obvious place—the Mountain Pack's home.

Although, I doubt Corbin would be stupid enough to return home. He is well aware that his entire town is currently under government surveillance.

I grip my phone and press it tightly to my ear. It rings a few times before Jake groggily answers. I stare out at the gardens as the sun slowly comes up over the horizon and casts the sky in pink and orange hues.

"Hello?" he grunts.

"Jake, it's Thane. I need your help," I say, getting straight to the point. This isn't the time to beat around the bush or exchange pleasantries—every minute counts.

Jake perks up, and it sounds like he jumps out of bed as he asks, "What do you need?"

"It's Harlow. She's missing. We believe she is being taken to Corbin, but we have no idea where he's hiding out." I lay out everything. It isn't like I have more information to share.

We don't want Bree and Vadum to get Harlow anywhere near Corbin. We hope our assumption of where Bree is taking her is correct, because then we have at least one lead to follow to get our mate back.

"Whatever you need," Jake says as I hear him move around. I let out a breath of relief once I hear him start to wake his mates. He has no idea how much we need them.

"So, where do you want us?" Jake says, getting straight to business. I appreciate that he doesn't want to waste any time and keeps with the no-bullshit policy.

"I have no idea—the highways might be a good start. I will send you some photos of the car we are looking for. But that's all we have. We know who they are taking her to but no idea where he could be hiding," I explain the most important details.

I don't even consider lying to Jake. I trust him and his mates' abilities to track down anyone, so misleading him is the greatest mistake I could make in this situation.

"Yep, but I can't leave Zara unprotected. I will leave three of my mates here with her, and the rest of us will help," Jake says.

"Thanks. I will send you the details and locations we need checked out."

"I'll let you know as soon as we get on the road," he replies.

I suck in a breath, and turn back toward the doors, where Elaine is trying to calm Scarlett. She holds my daughter out to me, but I shake my head.

"Let Rhen take her," I say, trying to step back, but she follows me.

"They are all talking to detectives. Just hold her while I make her a bottle," Elaine pleads, giving me no other option but to take my bundled-up daughter as she thrusts her toward me.

"Elaine!" I snap at her.

"Hold your daughter, Thane. She'll help you think more clearly," Elaine says, trotting off.

I shake my head before peering down at Scarlett, who is screaming her lungs out. "Shh, shh," I tuck her closer, her head moving from side to side as she searches for her mother's scent and breasts, neither of which I have.

I rock her, walking back inside while I wait for Elaine to come back. Scarlett starts crying louder. I adjust her and sit on the couch. I lay her on my chest, glancing around for Elaine.

I need to be out looking for Harlow. Scarlett rubs her face, and I instantly notice her little nails dig into the delicate skin as she scratches her face up. She is missing one of her mittens. It has to have fallen off somewhere. But I can't focus on the lost mitten saga as Scarlett's screams grow louder.

"Elaine?" I call out for help but get no answer. I'm slowly losing my mind over my useless attempts at consoling the small bundle in my arms.

I fear I will break her as I hold her in my giant hands. "Hold on, Scar," I whisper as I kiss her little head. "Shh, shh," I try to hush her before I begin purring.

Scarlett instantly stops crying, as if I'm working some sort of magic on her. Her tiny little brows furrow as she yawns. Once I understand how the approach works, I continue to purr until she finally falls asleep. I manage to stop one disaster, just to face another. I am now too scared to move in case I wake her up and she starts screaming all over again. Fuck, where is Rhen when I need him.

CHAPTER THIRTY-FIVE

I must have dozed off at some point because I wake to the sounds of Bree talking on the phone. She sounds frustrated. I hear Corbin's voice on the other end, and my blood runs cold.

"The entire mountain is being watched. I can't meet you at the gas station. It's too risky. You need to use the tunnels," Corbin tells her. Bree growls angrily. I sit up to see Vadum light a smoke.

"Someone better be at the tunnels to unlock the gates," Bree says, hanging up. Seconds later, the door I am leaning against is ripped open, and I nearly fall out. Vadum catches me easily, tossing me over his shoulder. As soon as the breeze hits me, my canines elongate. I try to force the shift, only to feel a sharp pinch in my neck.

Vadum smacks my ass, and my entire body tenses and spasms painfully as I see Bree pull a needle from my neck. "Did you think we weren't prepared, Sis?" she chuckles as I feel my limbs become heavy.

My body turns slack. Tears prick my eyes as the feeling wraps around my limbs. I am officially powerless. She even stole my ability to run. My tongue feels thick in my mouth, and my body sways as Bree and Vadum start trudging through the forest. All I can do is stare at Vadum's back, completely paralyzed by whatever Bree injected me with.

It feels like hours pass as they trudge through the forest, yet I know that can't be right because the sun is only just starting to come up. The little light it offers allows me to see my surroundings. I hear the creak of something metal, just as Vadum jumps down. The air in my lungs leaves in a puff as he lands in what appears to be some sort of storm drain.

"Finally! Take her. She's making my back ache," Vadum snaps at someone.

"I swear, Corbin. If you've hurt him—"

"You'll what, Bree? Don't fucking threaten me," Corbin snarls. A whimper escapes me when I feel Corbin's menacing aura envelop me as he takes me from Vadum and cradles me in his arms.

"Hello, there, beautiful," he says, bringing his face to my neck. "Now, we just gotta take care of these marks," he purrs, and a feral snarl erupts out of me. Corbin chuckles to himself, paying me no mind and stepping back into the tunnels. Darkness swallows us. I hear the gate close and lock. His footsteps echo, and it feels like he's walking up an incline. The deeper we go, the colder it gets. Finally, I see a glimmer of light up ahead.

As he steps into what appears to be a huge library, I wonder if we've entered a haunted manor. The door we come out of is not a door at all, but a sliding bookshelf. The bright lights make my head hurt, and I take in my surroundings. I hear someone groan as I'm unceremoniously dropped onto a chaise. My breath hitches when my eyes land on Talon.

Bree shrieks as she comes in behind us and rushes over to him. Talon is handcuffed to a chair, his face so bloody, I can barely recognize him. He has slash marks down his chest, and one arm is broken. The bone juts out of his skin in a gruesome display.

"You fucking bastard. You promised me, Corbin!" Bree screams, turning on her uncle. He backhands her before she manages to even lay a finger on him. At the sound of her voice, Tal tries to lift his head.

"I said I would let him leave. I never promised anything about the state he'd be in!" Corbin snarls at her. Bree glares at him while Vadum walks in, closing the bookcase and wandering around like he owns the joint. He makes it all of two steps before Corbin suddenly snatches a stake off the desk behind him, plunging it into his heart. Vadum's shock is evident as he gasps.

"Why can I smell you all over her?" Corbin asks, twisting the stake. Vadum's eyes go wide. He shakes his head, but Corbin plunges the stake in deeper. Vadum goes completely immobile, and his features go slack. Corbin growls menacingly, letting him go, and I watch as Vadum hits the floor in a heap.

"Chuck him in the incinerator. Make sure he is dead," Corbin snaps. Only then do I see the other man in the room as he steps away from the door. He is much more menacing than Corbin because of the horrid burns that cover an entire side of his face.

He smirks, his face looking crooked as he moves toward Vadum. He grabs his arm and starts dragging him away.

"Oh, and Sawyer, tell the rest of our mates to come meet their new toy," Corbin tells him, making my breath hitch. Corbin slowly turns to me with a sadistic grin on his face. "You, my pretty, are about to meet your Alphas," he laughs.

Bree whimpers as she lifts Tal's head, forcing my attention back to her.

"Bree?" Tal chokes out, his voice raspy.

"I'm right here. I'm so sorry," Bree murmurs to him.

"How?" Tal coughs out. He repeats the word before his head snaps up, as if jolted with electricity.

"What have you done, Bree? What did you trade?" Tal demands.

"I had no choice," she whispers. "It's either her or you." I watch their exchange as Bree fusses over him. She turns slightly and Tal's eyes slip to mine. He sucks in a shuddering breath and shakes his head.

"No!" he screams in her face, making her jump.

"Well, the deal is done. Your debt is paid, Tal. Feel free to take your leave," Corbin laughs. "Besides, I have an Omega to mark," he states, wandering over to me. I try to wiggle back in the chair, but my limbs are still too heavy.

"Now, let's get you cleaned up, Omega. I'm not fucking you while you still reek of that leech," Corbin purrs. Tears prick my eyes as he scoops me into his arms, lifting me from the chaise.

Tal goes manic trying to get out of his restraints. "Corbin, you piece of shit, let her go! Let her go, you fucking bastard!"

Corbin only laughs, strolling away when Bree speaks up.

"The keys?" she asks.

"Lost them!" Corbin chuckles, not bothering to stop as he saunters out of the library.

CHAPTER THIRTY-SIX

TALON

At first, I think I'm hallucinating when I see Harlow on the chaise across from me. I pray I am. I'm willing to die for my mistakes, but there's no way I am letting her suffer for them. I yank on my restraints as Bree clutches my face in her hands. Baring my teeth at her, I growl. How could she do such a thing? How could she drag Harlow into this? "Don't touch me!"

"Baby, you don't mean that," she purrs at me as I watch Corbin get further away with Harlow. I need to get her out of here. "It's fine. It was the only way to get you back," she says as I blink at her.

"They are planning on marking her!" I scream in her face. She flinches. Adrenaline and panic surge through my veins. Gritting my teeth through the bloody torture, I force the shift. My body is deformed as I try to force the Wolfsbane out of my system. Bree shrieks, but it works. I feel my bones snapping back into place, and my hands slip out of the restraints. Shoving Bree aside, she screams as I rush after Corbin.

Before I reach him, he spins, and I collide with Harlow. Her body is tossed across the floor. Corbin also shifts, and we start tearing into each other before three of his seven mates rush into the room. Slater and Kingsley rip into me as they shift, and Corbin shifts back.

Eventually, I am left naked and limp on the floor as Bree wails loudly. I gasp, watching as Corbin moves toward Harlow. She is exactly where he tossed her, unable to move. Teeth sink into my neck, and I cough on my own blood as Kingsley shifts back in front of me. Yet I can't tear my eyes from Harlow as she whimpers and pleads with Corbin to let her go.

Kingsley, the prick, grabs my foot and starts dragging me back to the library. They don't bother restraining me this time, almost like they're taunting me. The adrenaline is gone, and I am struggling to heal. Bree fusses over me, screaming her outrage at them. Her hands clutch my shoulders, and all I can do is stare at her in disgust. It's the first time I truly see her, and the depths she is willing to fall to.

When I started having money problems with the club, and I couldn't bear asking Thane for help again, she said she had a solution. I never dreamed it was trafficking Omegas. It's why I couldn't go through with it. I thought I could, but I'm not that sort of predator.

When I found out Bree had been luring them, building their trust, only for Vadum to traffic them, it disgusted me. But I was already in too deep, so I figured I would do just the one job. Yet when I got the Omega, I realized she wasn't a woman but a young girl. So, I gave her all the money I was given for the job and told her to run. Now Bree has shown me she truly has no limits because she dragged my family into this mess now, too.

Bree helps me sit up, which opens my airway. "Get me your first aid kit, asshole," she snarls at Kingsley. He stares down at her and smirks. Using his fingertips, he flicks his ash blond hair from his eyes before wandering off. Slater stands guard by the door as Bree stands. She retrieves the whiskey from the desk and sips on it before wandering back over to me. She tries to pour some in my mouth, but I turn my head away from her.

Tears well in her eyes and she growls. Her canines protrude as anger takes over. Bree has always had a short temper. She's beat on me many times, whenever she doesn't get her way. For years I took it, knowing how frustrating our line of work can be. Now I'm beginning to wonder if it is just one of her many faults.

"It will help," she states. Still, I refuse. I want her away from me. Bree snarls, and I recognize the unhinged glint in her eyes. It's the one she gets when she is on the verge of losing it. And she does, smashing the bottle against the wall in a fit of rage.

"After what I just did for you, Tal? After everything I've done!" she screams. Slater growls, moving toward her when she grabs a glass and throws it at the wall beside my head. She reaches for something else, only for him to catch her hand before she gets the chance to lob the paperweight at me. They tussle, and Slater drags her away as she lashes out, kicking and screaming.

"Let go of me!" she barks, as if he will listen to her. She kicks off the desk, and he snarls, backhanding her. I watch as she flies forward, barely catching herself on the desk. She instantly turns and attacks him, claws out, going straight for his face. Slater kicks her legs out from under her, and she hits the floor as something hits my foot. Her phone.

She doesn't seem to notice it fall. With what little strength I have left, I use my toes to drag it closer. Bree unknowingly acts as the distraction I need to quickly snatch it. I place it under my ass, leaning back just as Slater knocks her out.

"Crazy bitch!" he spits at her while she lays face down on the ground. Kingsley returns a few moments later, stopping in the doorway. He groans when he sees her on the floor. "Well, I'm not cleaning him up," he snaps, thrusting the first aid kit at Slater. Slater waves him off.

"Fuck him. She can do it when she wakes. Hopefully in a better mood, too," Slater says, snatching the first aid kit and tossing it on the desk.

"What about him?" Kingsley nods toward me.

"He ain't going anywhere. Come on. We need to mark the Omega. Corbin is convinced it will be the only thing that stops Thane from killing us," Slater says, nudging him toward the door. I watch them both leave.

Slater is right. If they mark Harlow and force her to mark them, Thane can't kill them. If she marks Corbin, it will override Thane's mark on her and make a complete bond. If Thane kills Corbin after that, he kills Harlow.

Once I'm sure they're gone, I quickly grab the phone. It's password protected, but Bree always uses her birth date for her passwords. For once, I'm glad she does. I dial Leon's number, but before I get the chance to lift the phone to my ear, I see Bree move. She groans, and I tuck the phone away, praying Leon picks up.

CHAPTER THIRTY-SEVEN

Thane

After setting Scarlett down, I get ready to meet Jake as Leon comes busting into the room. Elaine hushes him, and I move toward him, feeling the urgency and worry running through the bond.

He shows me his phone screen, and I see an unrecognized number. I go to take it from him, but he pulls it back, covering the speaker.

"It's Tal and Bree," Leon whisper-yells at me. "Rhen's getting ready to trace the call."

I snatch the phone, putting it to my ear. They seem to be arguing, but their voices are muffled.

"The bastard took my fucking phone!" she yells, but I can only just make it out. Rushing through the house, I wave for Leo and Raidon as they come through the front door. Rhen also comes in from the kitchen. He's typing away on his laptop as Leon tosses him a cord. Rhen snatches it. I mute the phone and set it on speaker, holding a finger to my lips.

Raidon and Leo automatically shut their mouths before they can voice any questions. We listen while Rhen races to get his laptop set up, plugging the cord in before jamming the other end into the phone. He presses more keys while we listen to Tal and Bree argue.

"Don't touch me," Tal snaps. "I can barely look at you after what you've done."

"What did you expect me to do, let you fucking die?" Bree says as I glance at Leon.

"Yes! Better that than her being trapped here. They are going to fucking mark her, Bree! Force her into a fucking bond," Tal snarls.

I stagger back at his words. My stomach drops as rage sets my blood on fire. My hands tremble and fur grows along my arms when Raidon suddenly stands.

"So what? It's what she's made for."

Tal growls at Bree's words, and I become even more enraged. 'It's what she's made for'? Harlow is mine. She belongs in my pack.

It is cruel and inhumane of Bree to force this fate on her own sister and rip a baby away from her mother. Harlow will be powerless to stop Corbin, unable to resist if he commands her. She never took my serum. We found it in the Den, between the cushions.

"Calm down, Thane!" Raidon warns, feeling my uncontrollable rage through the bond.

"They have her," I snarl at him, stating the obvious.

"You'll get her back. Give Rhen a minute to locate her," Leo speaks calmly. Their heads will fucking roll for touching my Omega, my mate, my Luna.

"Got it!" Rhen snaps as Leo moves to glance over his shoulder. "Raidon, get the plane ready. We found her," Rhen tells him.

"Where is she?" I ask, barely finding the words. Rhen and Leon stare at me. I can feel their fear loud and clear as my aura slips out. I'm on the verge of snapping, and I can't rein it in.

"Mountain Pack. He went home," Leo whimpers as my aura crushes him.

"Get the authorities there now!" Rhen snaps at Leon as he chucks his phone to him.

"They can't," Leo grits out.

Rhen glares at me. "Get yourself under control, Thane!" he snaps as my vision tunnels.

I fight the violent urge to kill something, but it isn't enough. The fury burns hotter, and I feel the shift start to take over before I feel a pinch in my neck.

"Fuck!" Leon curses.

I feel wolfsbane burn through my veins. It won't stay in my system for long, a few minutes at most, but it's enough to act as a sedative and dull my senses. I see Raidon pull the needle from my neck, a phone propped between his ear and shoulder.

"Sorry, no choice. We don't have time to fight your beast right now," Raidon says before returning to the pilot on the phone. He tosses the needle onto the table beside us. Rhen catches me as my legs give out. Then everything goes black.

I wake up in the car. Jerking upright, Rhen slaps a hand on my chest.

"We are on our way to the airport," he tells me.

Peering over my shoulder, I see Leon, Raidon, and Leo jammed in the backseat. "Authorities get there?" I ask.

"We called them off. Leo says the place is booby trapped. There's explosives at every entrance, in case he's caught. If we send them in, they'll trip the sensors," Rhen explains.

"So, what, we let him mark her?" I yell.

"She can resist him, Thane. It will hurt, but she will resist. I know Harlow," Leon says with confidence.

Yes, but an Alpha-of-Alpha aura can be deadly. I see the vial of my serum sitting under the stereo. I grab it and shake my head before dropping it back into the little compartment. Why didn't she take it? She would be stronger than Corbin if she took it. Leo reaches between the seats, grabbing the vial and examining the contents.

"I think I have a plan," Leo says before I snatch my serum back from him.

"What is it?" I ask.

"There's a way through the tunnels. If I can get in, I'll be able to switch off the alarms and detonators."

"No. He'll question you, and since you're his mate, he'll be able to tell if you're lying to him," Rhen says.

"And I don't trust you to not go in there and mark my mate!" I growl. Raidon's hand falls on my shoulder from the backseat. I exhale, turning my face to kiss his hand. He gives my shoulder a squeeze, which is enough to somewhat settle me.

"Well, have you got a better plan?" Leo demands as we pull up beside the plane. I growl because I don't, and I know that waiting for an explosives removal expert to come in will take too long. The pilot is waiting for us as we climb out of the car. I'm about to board when I stop, racing back to the car to grab my serum. As soon as I get Harlow back, I'm forcing her to take it and mark me. I won't have her vulnerable ever again.

"What did you forget?" Leo calls from the top step. I hold up the vial. His brows pinch as if he's thinking before he nods, and we board.

Despite the flight only lasting thirty minutes, it seems to drag on much longer. Every passing second feels like an hour. What irks me the most is that Leo and I were just in the Mountain Pack's territory grabbing Curtis. Corbin's probably been there this whole time. He went home, back to the most obvious place we could have looked, but we didn't because I didn't think he was stupid enough to do it. Learning about the tunnels to the pack house through the mountain just infuriates me more.

Even Leo is shocked by his brazenness. He believed Corbin would try to flee the country. Thankfully he didn't because there's no way we could save Harlow if he escaped the country with her.

A car is waiting for us the moment we touch down. My phone rings as we exit the plane. Some authorities have arrived on the scene and are going to send in drones to see what they can pick up before we raid the place.

Leo was quiet the entire flight, and that doesn't change as we climb into the car. He jumps in the passenger seat, and I drive.

Heading up the mountain, we stop at a local gas station to get more fuel. As I fill up the car, everyone else gets out to stretch and walk around a bit.

"How much further up the mountain?" I ask Leo, having never been to Corbin's pack house before.

"Pardon?" he asks, looking at me over the car's roof.

"Your pack?"

"Another twenty minutes. It's built half into the mountain."

"Are you okay?" I ask. It must be hard for him, knowing we are about to rip his mates and pack apart. The bond, despite how much he hates Corbin right now, would make it difficult for him to not feel anything about what we are going to do.

"I'm fine. I just want to get your mate back," he says, and I swallow. That's the same thing I want.

"I'll pay," Rhen says, wandering into the service station. I nod to him and finish filling the car.

We know Corbin hasn't marked her yet. We would have felt the bond stretch if he had. We will also feel the tethers on our bond break if she marks him back.

Leo remains quiet as we head up the mountain. When we get close, I glance at him. "If you can't go in there, tell me now, Leo. I won't make this any more dangerous for my mate," I snap at him. He's making me very uneasy.

"It's not that. I know you don't fully trust me, but I can get in there. I can get to Harlow!" he snaps.

I glance in the rearview mirror to see that my mates share my worries. I know he will be able to get in there. I just don't trust how Corbin will react.

CHAPTER THIRTY-EIGHT

Tears burn my eyes as Corbin sits me on his lap while he draws a bath. His mates slowly trickle in, and I am soon surrounded as they start stripping me of my clothes. Corbin climbs into the bathtub first, before I'm placed between his legs.

The water is hot and stings my skin. I can do nothing except endure the torment of them washing me like I'm some prized jewel. Corbin purrs, using his Calling. I fight against it, refusing to give into the sensation as it rolls over me. Pain slivers up my spine, causing me to sweat.

"Such a stubborn little Omega. Don't fight it, Harlow," he coos while dragging a loofah across my skin. I feel like a rag doll as they pull and tug on me, yet the longer I am in the bath, the more I begin to feel my limbs and the stronger I get.

When he's done, he passes me to the man they keep calling Slater. Surprisingly, they are all very gentle, treating me like I am made of glass. I'm compliant, letting them believe the drugs are still in effect while they dress me in a chemise, as if I'm their personal doll.

"Are we sure this will work? What if Thane still kills us?" Kingsley asks Corbin as he pulls me into his lap. My heart skips a beat at the thought of them marking me and the thought of being forced to mark them.

"Thane won't risk her life. He'll be forced to let her go. The councils won't allow him to kill me if an Omega's life is at stake. They are too rare these days," Corbin says confidently. "Come, let's get her to the Den so we can prepare her. I want her marked and mated as soon as possible," Corbin states, taking me from Kingsley, who seems reluctant to let me go.

"Get my serum from the fridge," Corbin calls over his shoulder as we step out of the bathroom. Heading back the way we came, we pass the library, and I see Bree. She rushes to her uncle, clutching at his arm.

"Bree, I haven't got time for this!" he growls at her.

"Just help me get him to a car and we'll leave."

Corbin laughs and shakes his head.

"Stupid, naive girl. There's no leaving here. The authorities have the mountain surrounded. The only way in or out is the tunnels," he tells her, turning away.

"But we had a deal!" she yells angrily. I avert my gaze, looking for Talon. He gives me a slight nod when I spot him, and my brows furrow.

"You were the one stupid enough to take it! And for that prick?" Corbin growls. "Kingsley, get my serum. Just ignore her," Corbin yells over his shoulder making him refocus his attention. My lip quivers as I try to figure a way out of this mess.

Kingsley wanders off with Slater and another man whose name I don't know. Panic raises goosebumps on my arms. When Corbin turns toward a door that is being held open by another of his mates, I start to fight.

My claws slip from my fingers and rake down Corbin's face, forcing him to drop me. I run for the bookshelf with the secret door behind it. Arms lock around my waist before I reach it, but only momentarily. Whoever grabbed me is tackled by someone else. Bree screams her head off, and I'm tossed into a nearby shelf when I notice Talon is no longer where he was.

I look up to see him fighting Corbin and his mates, once again trying to protect me. Only this time, he doesn't have the ability to shift. I know Talon needs blood. He's a hybrid like Leon, and who knows how long it's been since he fed, muting his ability to heal. He looks over his shoulder briefly.

"Run!" he screams at me. My breath hitches as I get to my feet. I scramble for the bookshelves, looking for the right one and yanking it open. The moment I do, a gust of cold air smashes into me. I look over my shoulder one last time. Bree is screaming, trying to get Kingsley off Tal, who is holding Corbin down.

A whimper escapes me. I know this is my only chance, so I force my jelly-like legs to run down the steps. My feet echo loudly in the tunnel as I run, and I can hear them giving chase. I briefly wonder if Tal is alright, knowing he isn't.

I am on the verge of passing out when I finally get to the bottom, but I fight it back as I reach the gate blocking the exit. I yank on it, trying to open it, before scanning my surroundings. My hands brush the walls, hitting a box. I hear them closing in.

My fingertips feel numb as I fumble to pry the lid off and grab the key inside. I twist it and the gate swings open. I slam it shut behind me, hoping to buy a little time as I figure out which way to go. The simplest would be downhill, so that is the direction I run.

I run for at least five minutes before I suddenly stumble. My feet hit nothing but air, and I fly forward, landing on my stomach in the dirt. I try to get to my feet, but a growl stops me in my tracks.

Lifting my head, I instantly notice my mistake. Not that it is my fault, the woods are dense, and I was more focused on running than paying attention to my surroundings. However, I'm now nose to nose with a shifted rogue. There's another growl to my left, telling me I'm surrounded. I've fallen into a Den of sorts.

I crawl back while the rogue stalks forward. I dig my nails into the dirt wanting to shift, but the drugs still burning in my system prevent it. The rogue sniffs the air and cocks his head to the side, recognizing me as Omega. A loud whine leaves his mouth, and his tongue lolls out.

This can't be fucking happening. What did I do in a past life to have this much fucking karmic debt and suffer this much bad luck?

I hear running and yelling further up the hill. I grit my teeth, knowing my chances are better with Corbin than the rogues. They will both rape me, but at least Corbin won't kill me immediately afterward. I scramble back on my hands and knees while the rogue prowls toward me. I pivot, peering around to find there are at least five of them.

Knowing I'll probably regret it, and cursing the Moon Goddess, I scream, alerting Corbin and his mates to my location. I don't have any other choice, but the moment I do, the rogue lunges at me. I roll out of his way and narrowly miss his teeth sinking into me.

My fingers find a branch, and I grab it. Getting to my feet, I clutch the branch as the rogues circle me. A murky gray one suddenly lunges forward. I swing the branch, connecting with his head as a feral growl echoes behind me. I turn just as another one attacks.

My breath lodges in my throat. I think I am about to die when I am suddenly thrust forward. A heavy weight lands on me and crushes me to the ground. Only, instead of teeth and claws ripping into my soft flesh, warm fur covers me.

A menacing growl sounds from above me, and I realize Corbin's huge wolf is covering my body with his. He snarls, gnashing his teeth at the rogues. His aura rips out, making me whimper, and so do the rogues. They can't take the weight of it, and before long they scamper off, leaving me beneath his beast.

"It's not that. I know you don't fully trust me, but I can get in there. I can get to Harlow!" Leo snaps.

I glance in the rearview mirror to see that my mates share my worries. I know he will be able to get in there. I just don't trust how Corbin will react. Not only that, but what if Leo betrays us. Corbin is his mate, after all.

My hands tighten on the steering wheel. "And what exactly are you going to tell him? That we just let you go? That we had a fucking change of heart?" I demand. There's no way Corbin will believe that. Leo sighs and I glance at him before my eyes return to the road.

"I'll tell the truth, that I escaped." Leo shrugs as we drive around a winding bend.

"Escaped?" Rhen snaps, knowing it sounds just as ridiculous. Leo picks up my serum, twirling it in his fingers and examining it.

"I can mind-link him, tell him I escaped, and I'm coming in through the tunnels. He'll send someone to make sure I'm alone, and as long as it's the truth, he won't question me. I can tell him I came to warn him that we need to leave the mountain. He will already be aware of the authorities watching the place."

I shake my head, knowing his plan has a flaw other than the possibility of him getting caught in a lie. "He will mark her. I know he hasn't yet. I'd feel it through the bond," I growl.

"As long as she doesn't mark him, you can always remark her. It's the only way I can get to the control room, shut everything down, and let you in." He looks at the serum again. I want to snatch it from him, not liking the way he keeps eyeing it. He turns slightly in his seat, looking at all of us. "Why didn't she take this?" he asks as if he thinks she's insane.

"I don't know, but she's fucking taking it the moment we get her back. And marking me," I tell him. He nods in agreement, turning the vial in his fingers.

"She'd be able to resist his command if she took this," Leo says, as if I don't already know.

"Yeah, fat lot of good that is now." I shake my head.

"She'll resist, Thane. Your Omega is stubborn," Leo tells me.

"I'm not worried about whether or not she fights it. I'm worried that when she does, his command will kill her," I mumble, knowing it is a possibility. It rarely happens because normally no one would risk their lives when it comes to an Alpha Command, but he's right, she's stubborn enough to resist.

"So, I'll tell him I escaped, get Harlow to take your serum, and you four sweep in to save the day. You'll get your Omega back, and after, you'll keep my daughter safe. I'll keep my promise, but you need to keep yours, Thane. I'm placing a lot of trust in you to protect my girl," Leo says with confidence.

"Which is exactly why I don't trust you. You know Harlow won't let anything happen to your daughter, even if you do betray us. Harlow won't let me kill her or throw her in rotation."

"I won't betray you," he assures me, but I still don't believe him.

"So, you're fine with us killing your mate? Knowing full well you'll die not too long after."

"For my daughter? Yes. Wouldn't you die for yours?" Leo asks me. I press my lips in a line, nodding once at his words. I would give my last breath if it meant Scarlett got to take another.

"So—" he starts, but I shake my head, cutting him off.

"You're forgetting that Corbin will know you're lying," I growl.

"Not if I tell the truth," Leo says, and I scoff. He pockets my serum and suddenly throws his door open as we go around the next bend. I snarl, and Raidon screams, reaching for him. Leo throws his body out the door as I hit the brakes. The car screeches to a stop thirty feet from where he jumped out.

Tossing the doors open, we all jump out. The car was going too fast, and he'll be like a skinned rabbit. His body lays motionless as we move toward him. I curse under my breath when I hear him groan. He rummages in his pocket, and I scream as I watch him grab my serum, popping the whole vial into his mouth.

"No!" Rhen shouts. Leo turns his head and smiles before he shifts. We chase after him, but he darts into the woods long before we reach the spot he originally landed.

"Fuck!" I curse, turning back toward the car. Leon is leaning against the trunk with a cigarette between his lips.

"Thanks for your fucking help," I snarl at him, knowing he could have easily outrun Leo. He just shakes his head and draws back on his cigarette.

"I don't like Leo. Don't hate him, either, but I gotta give him credit. He is smart," Leon says.

"He is going to mark our fucking Omega! Our mate!" I snarl at him. Leon just sighs heavily. "He just took my serum!"

"Corbin will kill him when he realizes Leo is lying to him," Raidon snaps.

"Or he's lying to us! He took my fucking serum," I repeat.

"No," Rhen speaks, and we all turn to look at him. "Leon's right. Leo said he just had to tell the truth for Corbin to believe him. He did escape. He won't be lying."

Leon softly chuckles, and I can feel his smug satisfaction through the bond. He flicks his cigarette before walking back to the car. I scoff, then blink. Worry still laces me. Corbin could order him to mark Harlow, or he might feel differently once he's home with his mates.

"Come on, now we have to wait to see if he is telling the truth," Leon says.

"And if he is lying to us?" I ask.

Rhen shrugs. "We kill him."

CHAPTER FORTY

A whimper escapes me when I feel Corbin shift above me. "That was very stupid of you," he sneers, pressing the weight of his naked body against me. He bares his teeth and uses his hand to sweep my hair away from my neck.

I press closer to the dirt, not liking the feel of his naked body crushing mine, feeling every outline of muscle against me. His cock thrusts against my ass as he scrapes his teeth down my shoulder.

"Is this what you want, Harlow? To be fucked in the dirt, on display for the rogues to see?" he asks, rocking his hips against my ass. I grit my teeth and shake my head.

Corbin flips me onto my back, pressing himself flush against me. His tongue slides up my cheek and across my lips. "I'm going to make you bleed, make you scream. And you're going to love it," he purrs, using his Calling on me. It makes my skin crawl, yet my body still reacts to the sound, turning languid beneath him. Tears burn my eyes. He is not my mate. He is not them. I will never complain about them using their Calling on me again if the Moon Goddess gets me out of this mess.

Corbin nips at my neck and chin. I grit my teeth, refusing to give into his Calling, no matter how much it makes every part of me throb. Corbin licks my lips, and I press them more tightly closed. He grips my chin, making me whimper and forcing my jaw open. He shoves his tongue in my mouth, tasting every inch, brutally assaulting it. Tears prick my eyes, and I do the only thing I can think of. I bite down hard.

Corbin jerks back. His hand fists my hair, making me squeal as he viciously jerks my head to the side. "I was planning on being gentle, just marking and fucking you. But now I will let all seven of my mates run a train on you. In every fucking hole you've got." He snarls and spits his blood in my face. I glare at him despite the pain as he tugs the hair from my scalp.

"There are two things you need to learn, Omega: you are nothing but a toy, here to satiate my needs and those of my mates, and two, I own every inch of you."

"Wrong," I growl defiantly. He fists my hair tighter, but I continue through the pain. "You own nothing, not even your own life. Because Thane is gonna take it," I snarl at him. He laughs. I hear more laughter above me and realize his mates have arrived, surrounding us.

"Is that so, Harlow? I don't see Thane here," he says, motioning around us and laughing.

"You're right. He isn't here… yet." Corbin's laugh cuts off at my words. "He'll come for me. And you know it. When he does, he'll show you exactly what happens when someone touches his property. I am Thane's. And you… you are dead," I spit at him.

His eyes darken, and he growls, pulling me up by my hair and throwing me to his mates. I am shoved back toward the tunnels as one of them grips my arm tightly, his hold bruising.

I find myself back in the library as Corbin shoves me through the door. A shiver runs up my spine as a draft from the tunnels wafts over me, and I squint at the bright lights. Talon's head and shoulders drop when I walk back into the room, just as Corbin's phone rings.

"Watch her!" he snarls to his mates as he walks off to take the call. Slater shuts the bookcase behind us and nudges me toward Talon. I sit on the floor next to him, our shoulders touching as he tries to remain upright, clutching his stomach. Talon needs blood, I lift my wrist, draping it over his shoulder. Talon shakes his head as Kingsley growls at me.

"Move your arm. Try to feed him, and I kill him," he snarls. I let my arm fall and grip his knee.

Lifting my gaze, I see Bree glaring at me from across the room. She's sitting in an armchair, her clothes drenched in blood. I blink at her, wondering what her issue is, besides being a sadistic bitch. I don't have to wait long before she voices them, shooting a glare at Talon.

"I can't believe you would risk everything for her," Bree snarls at him.

Staring down at Talon, I see he is bleeding profusely. I reach over, moving the cloth he is clutching against his stomach. I gasp when I see the bone knife handle protruding from him.

"I'll be fine," he chokes out, dropping his head to my shoulder. He doesn't seem fine to me.

"Fine? You nearly got yourself killed. I did not risk everything for you to throw it away for her," Bree snarls.

"Enough, Bree," Talon coughs.

"No! I am your mate!" she screams. She leans forward in her seat, lips parting to yell at him some more. Can she not see he is fucking dying beside me? All she wants is to berate him.

"Oh, just shut the fuck up!" I snap, sick of her whining. Bree stands in a fury, baring her teeth at me. "That shade of jealousy you're wearing really doesn't suit you. It's a little off-putting," I tell her.

Bree quickly stalks across the room. Slater moves from his post by the wall, but he is too late. Her hand connects with my face, and my head snaps to the side, but I am too angry and too wired to feel it right now.

Her slap splits my lip. I wipe a hand across my mouth and shake my head as Slater rips her back by her shirt. Bree ignores him, pointing an accusing finger at me.

"I was good to you. I gave you a job. I was your friend. And you dare speak to me like that!" She curses. I scoff at her words and turn my attention back to Talon just as Corbin returns. He opens the door to the tunnels again.

CHAPTER FORTY-ONE

"What's going on?" Kingsley asks. Corbin's brows furrow and he nods toward the tunnel.

"Leo escaped. He called off the hidden Sat phone. Go let him in."

"He escaped?" Slater says. My stomach sinks, knowing exactly what Leo is capable of. "Oh, thank god," Slater murmurs with a spring in his step as he rushes off into the tunnels.

Corbin turns back to Kingsley. "Once he gets here, we need to proceed. Go get the others," he tells him.

"Why? Has something happened?" Kingsley asks.

"Yes. Thane is on his way. Leo came to warn us. Grab the first aid kit. He said he had to jump from their car. I'm not sure what condition he'll be in." Kingsley nods his head before darting off. Corbin actually looks concerned that Thane is near, and he should be.

Thane petrifies me and I'm his mate. I would hate to be one of the enemies on his hit list. My heart races when Corbin stalks toward me. I shuffle back before I hit one of the bookshelves.

"Either come willingly, love, or I will command you," Corbin purrs, reaching for me. I shake my head, and Talon growls at him.

"Just give up, Corbin. You're screwed. Leave her be," Talon growls, but Corbin smirks, bending down to grip my arms. Yet the moment he does, he chokes, sputters, and staggers back. I press against the bookcase when he stands upright, a brown handle protruding from his stomach. The same brown handle I saw protruding from Talon. I blink as his shirt turns red, stained with his blood. Corbin growls, pulling the blade out. I feel what he does before I see it. Blood sprays across my face, and Bree roars as Corbin slashes Talon's throat.

I scream, moving to grip his neck, but Corbin plunges the knife into his chest, making me jump.

"No!" I cry when Corbin rips the knife out before stabbing him again in a frenzy. Blood sprays everywhere, drenching and coating me. Talon's eyes bulge from his head as his hand knocks mine. I grip it, staring into his eyes. I can hardly see his face; my vision is too blurred through my tears.

I flinch each time Corbin plunges the knife into him. Talon chokes and I jump, my hands shaking. I close my eyes when I see the light fade from Talon's. Bree attacks Corbin, but I am too stunned to care, completely frozen. I let Talon's hand go, tucking my knees into my chest, wishing I could unsee what I just witnessed. Talon's blood is everywhere. It coats Corbin's arms, chest, and face, pooling on the floor in a huge puddle. Blood spatter covers me, and I hug my knees, trying to calm myself down.

Corbin turns and glares at Bree, fed up with trying to restrain her. She's attacking him, punching on his back and shoulders, but it has no effect on him. She might as well be a small child for all the reaction she gets from him. One punch from Corbin though, and she is down like a sack of potatoes.

"Well, well. What have we got here?" Leo asks as he enters the library.

Corbin spins, and a huge grin splits his face at seeing Leo, who is completely naked and covered in blood. Corbin embraces Leo before kissing him.

Tears fall down my cheeks as Talon's blood coats my hands and legs while I sit frozen in shock. He killed him. Talon died trying to save me. He's dead. How am I going to tell Leon that his cousin died for me? I jerk my hands away as his blood covers my fingers. A whimper escapes me, grabbing everyone's attention.

"How did you escape?" Corbin questions, turning to Leo and ignoring me.

"They left the door unlocked. They didn't realize I'm crazy enough to jump from the car. Fucking hurt. Damn near skinned me alive, too," Leo tells him, looking down at his body. Whatever injuries he had are now healed. Corbin cocks his head to the side.

"Where?" Corbin questions.

"On one of the bends at the bottom of the mountain. I shifted and ran the rest of the way here. I came across a few rogues, too," Leo shrugs.

"They didn't chase you? Try to catch you?" Corbin presses. His aura slips out, testing Leo.

"Yes. Thane, Rhen, and Raidon gave chase but quickly gave up as soon as I made it into the forest. Corbin, we need to get out of here. The authorities are everywhere. They have the whole place surrounded. They're even sending drones in to watch for us. We can't stay here. We need to take her and run," Leo informs him. Tears prick my eyes at his betrayal.

Corbin exhales but shakes his head. "No. We need to get this over with. Grab her," he tells Leo. Leo glances at me, a smile moving onto his face, and his eyes flicker.

"My pleasure," Leo purrs, stalking toward me. I shake my head and slap his hands away.

"Don't touch me!" I snap at him.

"Oh, baby, don't be like that. We're about to rock your fucking world," he taunts, before he grips my arms. I thrash, but he presses me against the bookcase.

"Watch it. She bites!" Corbin warns him.

Leo glances at him over his shoulder before looking back at me and gnashing his teeth in my face. "So do I, and I can't wait to take a bite out of you," he purrs, pressing his body against mine.

"Bite her in the room. Bite every part of her for all I care. I just want her marked, then you can have your fun with her," Corbin tells him.

"Den?" Leo asks, and I see Corbin nod his head. Leo's grip tightens on my arms, and I thrash, kicking and trying to rip out of his grip. He tosses me over his shoulder and smacks my ass before rubbing it with his palm.

"Oh, I can't wait to fuck this sweet pussy," Leo chuckles, and I sink my teeth into his back. He groans and slaps my ass again, making me whimper.

"You can have her pussy. She'll be taking my knot in her ass," Corbin laughs.

CHAPTER FORTY-TWO

Leo laughs, squeezing my ass again as he stops next to Corbin. "Thank god you're back. I was so worried they'd kill you," Corbin tells him, gripping the back of Leo's neck.

"We have another issue. Thane kidnapped my daughter," Leo says as I thump my hands against his back. I claw him, ripping at his skin, but he ignores my attempts to get down.

"We'll find a way to get her back. I promise," Corbin assures him.

I struggle harder, but Leo seems unperturbed by my attacks. Corbin kisses him, and it's so forceful that it seems like an assault. Leo is still squeezing my ass as Corbin's hand comes down so hard, it instantly makes a welt. I cry out as the pain shoots up my backside. Leo pulls away with a groan, but he hisses as I jam my claws into his ribs, trying to get him to drop me.

Corbin moves to see my hand in his mate's ribs. He grips it, pulling my claws out of Leo. He then squeezes my hand so tightly, I feel a couple fingers break, and I scream out in agony.

"Don't hurt your mates, Omega," Corbin orders me. His command rolls over me painfully. I scream as I try to fight it. He grips my chin, lifting my head. "Are we understood?" he snarls, pinching my cheeks so hard I think he will break my jaw. I spit in his face and lash out with my other hand. He grabs my wrist and squeezes so tightly I hear more bones break. I scream at the pressure and pain shooting up my arm.

"Are we understood, Omega?"

I nod, tears running down my face as he lets go of my jaw.

"Answer me!" he demands, shoving the full weight of his command on me.

"It's fine, Corbin. I'm already healing," Leo tells him.

"She needs to learn. Now, answer me, or I'll break your other wrist, too," Corbin says as I try to fight his command. Sweat beads on my skin. My teeth clench and my entire body tenses as it spasms.

"Yes. Yes!" I scream at him. Anything to make the pain stop.

"Good girl," Corbin says.

I slump over Leo's shoulder as Corbin's aura drops, leaving me breathless. Leo's hand strokes up my thigh, almost as if he's trying to comfort me.

"Chuck her in the Den while I get my serum," Corbin says, wandering off as Kingsley returns with the rest of them.

Leo takes me into a room that is completely red. I gasp as I take in my surroundings. Chains hang from the ceiling. The bed's headboard has chains, too. There's restraints everywhere. Kingsley smirks at my obvious horror. It's some kind of rape dungeon. There are no toys or anything for pleasure like Thane has. This is purely for holding someone down.

I shake my head as Leo drops me into a chair, though I'm thankful to not be on the huge bed. I go to move, but he stops me.

"You don't want me chasing you, love," he growls, gripping the arms of the chair. I lean away from him, my eyes flicking to Kingsley, Slater, and another man. They all smirk as they watch him tower over me.

Leo grips my chin, stroking his thumb across my lips before forcing them apart and grazing his thumb over my bottom teeth. "I can't wait to watch you choke on my cock," he purrs, using his Calling. I tense, pushing back. "That's it, little Omega, fight it. It'll be so much sweeter when I break you, and you will break. Then you'll beg me to put you together again," he whispers, pinching my chin. Leo kisses me, and I try to pull away when he bites my lip, making my eyes water as I try to shove him off. He laughs, letting me go and stepping back.

Two of them move toward the bed, fiddling with the chains and cuffs. The rattling sound makes my eyes burn furiously as someone places their hands on my shoulders. I look up to see Kingsley smiling down at me.

His hands move down my shoulders, gripping both my breasts. He squeezes them, making me yelp. They are already swollen and overfull. He twists my nipples, spraying milk everywhere. He laughs before ripping my shirt open further and swirling his fingers around my areolas. I grip his wrists, digging my nails in when he sinks his claws into my breasts. My scream resonates around the room, echoing off the walls.

I let his wrists go, and he retracts his claws. He leans down and runs his nose across my shoulder. His hands trail down my sides, and he suddenly grips my thighs, pulling them apart.

"Ah, ah," Leo tsks. "Best to wait for Corbin. You know he always likes to have the first taste."

Kingsley huffs, pressing his lips to my shoulder. "Soon, little Omega," he promises.

CHAPTER FORTY-THREE

LEON

We finally arrive at the property's west gate. The authorities have the place surrounded. They even have a helicopter flying above, taking aerial shots. One of the local news stations also has a chopper circling nearby, keeping far enough away from the official one. I shake my head, disgusted at how they're just here for the next big headline.

"Fucking vultures," I curse. No doubt, they are live streaming this entire thing. Law enforcement cars line the entire road, having blocked any traffic coming up or down the mountain. State and local officials scour the entire place.

Thane is out of the car first, followed by Rhen. We are all feeling antsy, made worse because the bond offers us little in the way of Harlow's wellbeing. We know she is alive, and that's all we care about right now. Once we get her out, we can deal with the aftermath. Yet her mental state will be another thing entirely.

Corbin has seven mates, like Jake does. Harlow just had a baby and will struggle to shift. She is also Omega and powerless against mands since she hasn't taken Thane's serum or marked us yet. I know Thane will ensure both those things happen the moment we get her back.

I follow Thane and Rhen as I climb out of the car, while Raidon checks the fences. I peer at the drone viewscreen the authorities show us. Heat projections show some of them deep inside the mansion. The others aren't visible, likely somewhere too deep for the heat vision to penetrate as half the house is embedded inside the mountain.

State officers have scoured the perimeter, trying to find a way in. "How long until the federal officials arrive?" Rhen asks. The man gulps, glancing at Thane nervously.

"Still two hours out," he explains.

Thane looks at the reinforced gates. "That's too long," he mutters. His emotions are all over the place. He feels like he's failed us all, but mostly he feels like he failed to protect Harlow.

"The explosives team sent in drones and equipment earlier. The entire fence line is wired underground. Even the tunnels leading in."

"There has to be some way in," Rhen snaps, snatching the man's tablet as he takes control of the drones.

"We searched everywhere," the man tells him.

"You can't have. Corbin wouldn't lock himself in with no way out. He will expect us to barge in, so there has to be an exit, some type of escape route," Rhen argues.

"The only way in, other than through these gates, is the tunnels, and they are all wired with explosives. We aren't even sure if there are explosives waiting for us inside the mansion."

"Can't we drop in?" Thane asks, pointing to the helicopter above.

The man sighs and shakes his head. "Not unless you want to fry. Those nets covering the top, they aren't for keeping the birds out."

Thane and I look up.

"They can't cover the entire place," Thane mutters.

Rhen steps closer, using the drone to show us they do, in fact, have the entire place completely covered in nets.

"If you drop in from above, you'll be barbecued. They're covered with barbed and razor wire. And see here?" Rhen shows him a huge panel on the wall as the drone hovers just above the netting. "Electrically charged."

"Yeah, we lost two drones in the nets before we figured that out," the man states as Thane growls.

"So, what? We wait for the federal authorities to arrive? That will be too late," Thane snarls, eyeing the high fences.

"We have no choice. We have to wait," Rhen says.

"Maybe Leo—" Thane cuts me off before I can finish.

"For all we know, Leo's getting ready to fucking mark her. He is Corbin's mate, Leon! Would you go against me? Kill me?"

I clench my jaw and look away, knowing that would be impossible for me, but Thane hasn't done the things Corbin has.

"We have his daughter," I tell Thane.

"Yes, but he knows I won't kill her! And the council would never allow for her to be killed. So, basically, we're sitting ducks while they do god knows fucking what with our mate!"

"Leo had to have a way in. He said so himself, he could get in through the tunnels. Send the fucking drones back out."

The man quickly nods, taking the tablet from Rhen and using his radio to talk to the other men as Thane starts taking his clothes off.

"What are you doing?" Rhen asks him.

"Finding a way in!" Thane snarls before shifting, and I see Raidon rush over.

"For fuck sake," Raidon says, ripping his shirt off and tossing it to me before shedding his pants. "Fool will get himself killed," he snaps, shifting into his huge bear-like wolf and taking off after Thane. Rhen shakes his head, snatches the man's radio, and walks back to the car when Thane's phone rings. I pull it from his discarded pants to see that it's Jake calling.

"Hey, Jake," I answer, knowing it's up to me to tell him what's going on. Somehow Zara found out what happened and wants to come help Harlow, despite having just given birth to three babies. I know Jake has his hands full with her, and this is not going to help matters. I quickly explain everything before I hang up and call Elaine to check on Scarlett.

Elaine answers after only two rings, as if she was waiting by the phone for one of us to call.

"Hey, Ma. How's Scarlett?" I ask.

"She's asleep on Pop's chest. Any news? Have you got her back?"

I sigh. "No, and now we're stuck waiting. Leo escaped to try to help, but Thane has his doubts."

"As he should. Leo is Corbin's mate, and mate bonds are hard enough to go against, let alone your Alpha's command." I nod, falling silent. "Harlow will be alright, Leon. You'll get her back, and she'll be fine. She's durable. All Omegas are. We have to be," Elaine says.

"Yeah, I know. I just worry about the state she'll be in when we find her," I admit, glancing back up at the mountain mansion.

"Where's my son?" Elaine asks.

"Chasing Thane. He's trying to find the tunnel Leo used to get inside."

"Is that about my dad?" I hear Emily ask in the background.

"No, it's Leon. He's checking on Scarlett," Elaine says. She must have pulled the phone away from her ear since her voice is not as loud.

"And my father?" she asks, and Elaine sighs.

"He escaped and went back to Corbin," Elaine tells her, and I hear the girl whimper.

"No, no! My father wouldn't abandon me. Dad only agreed to be Corbin's mate to protect me, so he could get me out of rotation and away from my mother. He wouldn't run back to him, knowing Thane would get rid of me for betraying him."

"Thane would never put you in rotation, and even if he tries, Harlow and I won't allow it. Your father knows this!" Elaine tells her.

"He also knows I don't stand a chance without him. He wouldn't risk it," Emily tells her.

"What does she mean?" I ask Elaine.

"Leon wants to know what you mean," Elaine says.

"He knows Mom would come for me." My brows furrow in confusion. I don't even have to ask Elaine to question her, she just does.

"So? She is your mother."

"Doesn't mean she's a good one. I've been her pawn since she realized I'm Omega. Dad raised me. Tried to convince her I'm

Alpha blood, not Omega. Why do you think he got fired for stealing those drugs from the practice? They were pheromone blockers. He was never selling them. She got me back after that, though, and she offered me up as a feeder as soon as I came of age."

"Your mother sold you to the vamps?" I hear Elaine ask.

"Yes, Omega blood is addictive. When Mom found out I'm Omega, she offered me to the vamps. Mom was a rotation Omega and had three other children before me, but with regular Alphas. Since they were all born Omega, too, the Alphas didn't want them. Dad intended to keep her as his mate when I was born, but she refused to give up the lifestyle."

"And where are your siblings?" Elaine questions.

"I don't know. Mom sold off my two sisters to be raised by other Alphas for breeding. My brother was sold to the vamps. Dad tried to find them for me. It's one of the reasons he met Corbin, because of his links to the vampire community. So, when he found out I'm Omega, he tried to hide it with the blockers, but Mom found out. Then Dad bought me off her. He borrowed the money from Corbin. In exchange Dad had to become his mate."

"My god," Elaine gasps. Her story is absolutely horrifying. No wonder Leo asked Thane to take her. But it reassures me that Leo will come through for us. You don't join an Alpha Pack for your kid to turn around and risk her life, especially knowing she is Omega.

CHAPTER FORTY-FOUR

LEO

I can smell Harlow's fear as I drop her into the chair. She looks so tiny as she stares around the room. I am not a good man, yet not even I like seeing the fear on her face. She knows what this room is for, what happens in here. It is not a regular playroom.

No, Corbin doesn't like his girls willing. It doesn't matter that a few of us hate this room, he is our Alpha, and it is impossible to go against his command. Corbin comes into the room with a black leather pouch in his hand. It contains his serum.

Luckily, I was able to avoid lying to Corbin, so he believes my deception. Nothing I said wasn't true. Unfortunately, I can tell Harlow believes I'm exactly like him. A monster. In some ways, she may be correct.

"Get her on the bed. She is no use to me in the chair. Tie her down," Corbin orders, and both Kingsley and I go about the task. I need to find another way. I need that serum bag. The bond won't be complete if she doesn't mark us. But she will if Corbin commands her.

I reach to grab her, but Kingsley gets her first. Harlow fights, as expected, and I turn my gaze away, suddenly sickened. I don't know if it is because I know Harlow or because she is around the same age as my daughter.

Corbin pulls a syringe from the leather pouch. Harlow sees it and thrashes. I try to figure a way to avoid this but see no options. Kingsley starts tying her down, with Slater's help, while Corbin climbs on the bed. She kicks out, and Corbin barks at me to grab her legs as she attempts to kick him.

I move quickly, gripping her ankles as he goes to jab the needle in her thigh. I let one of her legs go as she thrashes, and her knee hits him in the chest. She thrashes more frantically, seeing his serum about to be plunged into her. She screams in rage, thrashing and bucking like a crazed animal. Her eyes even flicker to her wolf form.

Corbin growls. I can tell he is two seconds away from commanding her. I grab her legs again while Kingsley moves to restrain them, having finished her hands. I time her movements while Corbin tries not to get kicked. When I feel her muscles tense, I throw myself at Corbin, pretending her momentum pushed me into him, and we both topple off the bed.

The syringe goes flying, and three of our other mates move to hold her down.

"Fucking pin the bitch! How hard is it? She is fucking tiny," Corbin snarls as I snatch the needle, quickly breaking the tip off while Corbin gets to his feet. I pass it to him just as they finish restraining her. Harlow breaks down. Tears streak her face as Corbin grabs her thigh for his serum.

"Oh, for fuck's sake! Leo, see if there is another syringe," he tells me. I move to grab the little black bag off the table, knowing full well Corbin only keeps one in each bag.

"None left."

"Go grab another bag from the fridge," he dismisses me, tossing the broken syringe into the trash bin by the door.

Harlow's eyes meet mine in panic. I swallow, pulling my gaze away, and leave to retrieve what he asked for. I hate leaving her alone with them, but this is my chance.

I race through the house in a hurry. I stop at the front door and quickly punch in the code to disarm the alarms and detonators. I also unlock the front gate.

It will take them at least ten minutes to get up the driveway. I race to the kitchen and rip open the fridge, grabbing another bag with Corbin's serum. I then grab a knife and slash it down my bicep, where I hid Thane's vial. I hiss as the blade digs into my muscle before jamming my fingers into the wound to pull it out. I quickly rinse it and empty one of the syringes, not having time to hunt for a new one. Glancing at my arm, I see the wound closing over.

I try to clean the syringe as best I can, using boiling water and the hand sanitizer we keep on the counter. I break out in a sweat and glance over my shoulder. Each passing second feels like an hour, when I hear Harlow's scream ring out through the mansion.

My hands shake as I fill the syringe with Thane's serum. Tossing the vial, I put the syringe back in the bag. Before racing back to the room, I check the driveway camera by the front door. I see the cars coming up the driveway. All their headlights are off. There's a huge black wolf on the roof of one of the cars. It jumps off and starts running up here.

Getting back to the rape room, as I call it, I stop in my tracks. Corbin has already marked her. So has Slater and a few others. Harlow screams as Kingsley bends down to bite her.

"Just in time. Give her the serum and mark her," Corbin tells me. I fiddle with the zipper on the bag, trying not to let my hands shake. I pull the syringe out and move toward the bed as Kingsley steps back. Tears leave tracks down her face as they start undressing her.

"Please! Please, don't," Harlow begs me. Her neck is a bloody mess after my seven mates marked her, and I'm not about to make it any better.

I crawl onto the bed. "Hang tight, sweetie. Leo will take care of you," I purr, knowing Corbin is watching me. Harlow cries and sobs when I kiss her. Thane is going to kill me for this. I want to kill me, seeing Harlow fight against this. I lick a line across her jaw, down to her neck where the skin is marred. Yet, I can still smell Thane in her blood. That bond won't be broken until she marks us. This is reversible, I tell myself as I sink my teeth into her neck, trying to be as gentle as possible. Harlow shrieks, her voice raspy from all her screaming.

Harlow suddenly starts laughing, her fear turning her hysterical. "I'm going to watch you fucking bleed out. I will bathe in all your fucking blood!" she screams furiously.

I run my tongue over her neck. Her breathing is heavy with rage. "I'll get you out of here," I whisper so low that only she hears. Harlow gasps, and I pull away. I see the question in her eyes. As if she's wondering if she heard right.

The look on her face is giving too much away. *Damn Harlow, you're no actor*, I think. I pull back, cupping her cheek before kissing her. She whimpers as my tongue forces its way between her lips. I grope her, putting on a show for Corbin. He laughs, tapping my shoulder.

"Serum. Then you can fuck that sweet pussy," Corbin tells me. I growl, pecking her lips before climbing off her. I inject her with the serum.

Harlow hisses, and her eyes go wide before she suddenly stills. She blinks, realizing that it's not Corbin's serum. Her eyes flicker. Her entire demeanor changes as Thane's DNA burns through her veins, strengthening her. My heart rate slows, knowing in two seconds, Corbin's command will no longer work on her.

"Okay, sweetheart. Your turn," Corbin says, sliding in next to her. His hand trails over her body, and she grits her teeth when he squeezes her breast. I clench mine, too, as I watch him fondle her. Harlow shakes her head. Thane better hurry up. I can't take on all my mates.

I feel Corbin's aura rush out. She tenses, then quickly relaxes. "Mark me," he commands her. She grits her teeth before tilting her head. She regards him like some failed science experiment, not a man trying to force himself on her.

Corbin grips the back of her neck as he leans closer. Her eyes meet mine. I can feel his aura violently holding her, but she appears to be unaffected. I smile, my lips tugging at the corners, and her eyes narrow in realization as she looks at me. I incline my head. Her eyes flicker and sparkle deviously.

"Mark me!" Corbin snarls at her. Her lips open, and for a

second, I think he managed it.

"Go… fuck… yourself," she says, speaking slowly and clearly. The venom in her words drips off her tongue. Corbin jerks back, staring at her.

"I said mark me!" he snaps, gripping her hair. She hisses at his grip but smiles and sucks in a deep breath. I think she'll scream, but instead, she spits in his face. Corbin shoves her back, slamming her head against the headboard.

Corbin wipes her spit from his face before backhanding her. Harlow's head whips to the side, and she laughs, her lip bleeding. Her tongue darts out, sweeping over the cut.

"I can feel him, you know, feel him creeping closer." Harlow smiles and shudders as the power of Thane's Alpha-of-Alphas serum morphs her DNA. Morphs her. "Do you know what it feels like to die?" she asks Corbin. He grips her neck, and she cackles like a madwoman. "It feels cold. You can feel the life drain from your body. Literally feel the blood in your veins cool with your breath. Nothing is colder than death," she says, and Corbin slaps her.

"You're about to find out just how cold death feels. And as your heart beats frantically, trying to stop the cold, know that's death's knock you hear. Thump, thump… thump."

"Shut up!" Corbin screams in her face.

"You're a dead man."

Corbin grips her shoulders and slams her back against the headboard. I get to my feet, cursing at how long the driveway is because I know I'm going to have to intervene.

"Mark me!" he screams in her face.

"I'm gonna enjoy watching him break you. You fucked with the wrong Omega. His Omega!" she giggles. Corbin raises his hand to slap her again just as windows start shattering all over the house, causing him to stop and look up.

"Run, Corbin. Thane is coming for you," Harlow snickers. His head whips in her direction. A few of my mates run off to fight the incursion, but I can't leave her here. Not while she's still tied down, and not with him.

"Oh, you'll mark me, little Omega," Corbin snarls. She shakes her head.

"Nope. Thane already marked you. Only, he marked you for death." She smiles as we hear all hell break loose upstairs.

"Help me untie her!" Corbin panics, and I move to remove her restraints.

CHAPTER FORTY-FIVE

I knew the moment the needle pierced my skin it wasn't Corbin's serum. My skin tingles with a familiar sensation that I only get from my mates. I can taste him on the tip of my tongue. Thane, not Corbin.

Leo moves to undo my restraints. His hands move quickly, but not quickly enough because Corbin impatiently pulls me off the bed while one of my ankles is still cuffed. Leo yells at him to stop.

Leo makes quick work of the last cuff before Corbin takes off, running for the stairs. My surroundings blur as I try to adjust my new vision. My eyes catch everything and nothing. I find it quite distracting, as if I'm on drugs.

Are Thane's senses like this? Mine are so much more heightened than I ever imagined they could be. My eyesight from before seems almost dull as I pick up everything now, even the dust motes in the air.

Corbin pauses as he reaches the top of the stairs, peering out. "We'll head for the tunnels. Here, take her." Corbin turns, thrusting me at Leo before peering back out the door. It sounds like utter chaos outside. Yet I can feel them, all of them, moving closer.

Corbin darts toward the library and waves for Leo to follow

him. Leo ignores him, however, placing me on my feet. He grips my arm as I wobble from vertigo. Yeah, this is a strange feeling. Almost like walking with no gravity. I have to calculate each step I take. I will never complain about being Omega again if this is what it's always like for Alphas.

"Quick!" Corbin orders.

I step out the door and hear a growl. My head whips in Corbin's direction. His eyes are on me, standing beside Leo instead of in his arms.

"What are you doing?" Corbin snarls while I try to sense which direction my mates are.

"It's over, Corbin," Leo growls threateningly. Corbin's aura rushes out, and I know he is about to command Leo. But Leo rushes him before he can, tackling him to the ground.

"Harlow, run!" Leo shouts at me just as Corbin kicks him off. Leo goes flying into the wall. I back up, stumbling slightly as Corbin gets to his feet. Instinct kicks in, and I turn, running to where all the noise is coming from, knowing that's where I'll find my mates.

My bare feet slap against the cold tile floors as I try to navigate through the mansion without falling on my face. Corbin is hot on my heels as I slip and slide right into a statue. My vision blurs as I try to get used to my new senses. Seeing a set of stairs that leads down, I take them. Skipping some, I trip on the runner in my haste, face planting on the floor and finding myself in some sort of kitchen area.

I push up on my hands when Corbin jumps from the landing above. I scramble to my feet just as another explosion goes off, making me duck as the windows shatter. Before I can race for one, Corbin grips my hair, jerking me backward. I land flat on my back, my head bouncing off the tiles with a sickening crack.

"I'm going to fucking kill you!" Corbin growls as my claws slip from my fingertips. They rake down his face, and I roll as he rears back, escaping from his grip. I get to my knees as Corbin clutches his face. I hear the cracking and snapping of bones, and my eyes widen. He lunges at me in wolf form, only to be tackled by another huge wolf.

My scream is loud and visceral as the two wolves clash. The

other wolf must be Leo because I know it isn't one of my mates. I run for the huge bay windows, willing to go straight through the broken, jagged glass that covers the floor. There's only one thing on my mind, and that is to get outside.

Rushing through the kitchen, I don't see the frying pan until it's too late, just before it hits me square in the face and knocks me on my ass. All I see is black, and my ears ring as the thud rattles through my skull. There's a clang of metal hitting the floor, which makes my eyes fly open to see Bree.

She's standing over me with a crazed smile on her lips. I snarl as I hear a whimper behind me, yet I keep my focus on Bree as she stalks closer, smiling wickedly. I lift my foot at the last second, kicking her in her nasty vagina. She grunts but doesn't drop as a man would. It's enough for me to get to my feet, though, only to hear a threatening growl from behind me.

Turning to the side, I realize I'm trapped with Corbin on one side and Bree on the other. Leo is naked on the floor by the stairs, trying to get up. Bree snatches a blade from the knife rack as Corbin's claws click on the floor. Drool and blood drip from him onto the tiles. He stalks at me just as Bree slashes me with the knife. I twist, catching the blade in my arm instead of across my chest, only for Corbin's jaws to rip into my thigh, making me scream.

He shakes his head just as Bree plunges the blade into my side. I gasp. Corbin suddenly lets go when he's tackled, smashing into the kitchen island. I am also tossed, hitting the fridge from the momentum.

Blinking and groaning, I try to get to my feet, only for Bree to kick me in the face. My head snaps back, and I fleetingly see Thane's wolf ripping into Corbin's. My nose is bleeding, and my eyes sting as Bree goes to kick me again.

My newly heightened senses catch the movement, and time suddenly stills. I move my hands without thinking, grabbing her ankle. She shrieks as I twist, and she loses her balance, falling backward. I pull the blade from my side, gasping at the horrendous pain as she rises to her feet. With one foot off the ground, she shifts and lunges at me.

I try to shift, but my injuries prevent it, and she collides with me. I slam against the counter as she tears into my neck. A gasp leaves my lips as I choke. Her attack suddenly halts, and she wheezes. She is forced to shift back as I continue to choke on my own blood.

Blinking, my vision dulls and flicks to Bree. She's naked and on top of me, blood spilling from her lips and dribbling down her chin. Her eyes are wide as she gasps and chokes for air, each breath stuttered. Her hands feebly clutch at mine, and my eyes fall to see the knife sticking out of her chest.

With whatever strength I have left to muster, I shove her off me. My bleeding doesn't slow, even as I clutch my neck. I stagger to my feet, but my surroundings turn on their axis as I fall into the island. I feel like I am walking on the moon. My vision doubles as I make my way over to Thane. His wolf has torn Corbin's intestines out and spilled them onto the floor, unraveling like spaghetti. One of his legs is completely torn off and lying next to Leo, who is clutching his chest, pale as a ghost while his Alpha dies.

My heartbeat sounds loud in my ears, each beat louder than the last. I pull my hand back from my neck, and it's covered in blood. Out of the corner of my eye, I see the blood spurt from my neck. I clamp my hand back over the wound and feel my eyes roll into my head, just as Thane's huge wolf turns to me.

The roar that leaves him will be forever ingrained in my memory, my soul, and every aspect of my being, as death takes me. "Scarlett…" I murmur, wanting my daughter to see her face just once more. As the coldness seeps into my bones, I feel the life drain from my body. I almost see the motion of me falling, but I don't feel the impact.

I blink up at the ceiling, my eyelids growing heavy as exhaustion wraps around my limbs. Thane's face appears in my line of vision. His lips move, yet I am deaf to the world around me. But he is here. Thane came for me like I knew he would, knew they all would. His lips move as he tries to talk to me before I see him scream.

His hands try to hold my neck together. I want to tell him it's ok, that it doesn't hurt. I don't know if I speak the words or only think them as I peer up at him. My eyes lose focus just as Leon's face comes into view, then everything goes dark.

That familiar cold sensation slivers up my spine, entangles my nerves, and stiffens my bones. I only hear one sound, and I manage to focus on it.

Thump… thump… thump.

CHAPTER FORTY-SIX

THANE

My heart nearly stops as I turn to see Harlow staggering toward me. She's drenched in blood. It's spurting out of her as she clutches her neck. Her lips part, and she tries to speak as I watch her body go limp. Her hand drops from her neck, and I see the huge gaping wound. My eyes widen, and I feel the blood drain from my body as I force myself to shift back. Her blood spills across the floor as she hits the ground with a thud.

I run toward her collapsed body. Her neck spurts blood, and I clamp my hand down on the wound, trying to stem the bleeding. She stares up at me, almost dazedly. Her blinking slows as I try to get her to stay awake. The light slowly fades from her eyes as she continues to stare at me. She tries to speak, yet her words are lost over the frantic beating of my heart. Fear moves through every atom in my body. "I'm right here. Stay with me, Low," I plead with her before shouting for my other mates.

"Leon!" I scream, sounding broken as she begins to gasp, her eyes widening. Each thud of her heart sounds thick and forced. The length between each one stretches out further. "Leon!" I scream, seeing her face drain of life. She is dying in my arms when Leon finally smashes through one of the few remaining windows, along with the others.

"No!" Rhen gasps.

My gaze darts to him. He collapses to his knees just as her heartbeat stops. The silence is deafening as I wait for the next beat to come, but it doesn't. I start CPR. How can she die on us again? What are our chances when fate seems relentless in trying to take her from us?

A snarl rips out from somewhere behind me. I can't force my attention away from Harlow, but I see Rhen and Raidon take off to finish whoever it is. Leon is forcing his blood down Harlow's throat while I try to keep what little blood she has left pumping through her veins. The wounds on her neck start closing, painfully slowly. She feels dead beneath my hands, yet my mark isn't burning. I'm not in agony, so I know she is still here.

She has to be. I can't lose her. I need her. Scarlett needs her. We all do. This can't be the end for us. I won't accept it. Leon slaps her face gently.

"Come on, baby. Wake up for me," he murmurs. His pain courses through me, as if he blames himself. But this is all my fault. We're here because I failed to keep her safe from everyone, including myself.

A loud howl rips through the air, the sound soul-crushing. I know it's Leo. He made the same sound when I killed Corbin. It sounds exactly like what it feels like to lose a mate. It screams of the despair, agony, and coldness that floods through you. I refuse to let that feeling settle in me. Harlow will not die, for if she does, I know I will lay down and die right beside her.

Leon's mouth covers hers as he breathes for her between my sets. We wait a few half seconds each time, listening for signs of life before I continue. Raidon drops down next to me. His shoulders sag, and he's drenched in blood. Not seeing Rhen, I glance over my shoulder to spot him sitting next to Slater's dead body. His head is in his hands as he rocks back and forth, wailing for our mate. It was all for nothing. We're too late, and they all feel it.

Yet my hands refuse to stop, and I refuse to give up hope. If anyone can defeat fate, refuse it twice in a single lifetime, it's Harlow.

Leon slaps my hands away, his ear tilting toward her chest, listening intently. I go to shove him away and continue compressions when I feel it. The zing of the bond through my bloodstream. Then one soft thud.

Thump…

Thump …

Thump … Thump … Thump.

My heart jolts in my chest as hers picks up tempo, gradually growing stronger, and I break. My body collapses onto hers as I clutch her to me, smoothing her hair back. I crush her limp body to my chest as I pull her into my lap. I sink my teeth into her neck, rocking her as I feel my bond fall back into place, strengthening her, and her heartbeat picks up more.

Rhen collides with me as he tugs her head back. Her eyes flutter and roll into the back of her skull. She mumbles but crashes again as her body absorbs the bond, letting it heal her. She takes all the strength it can give her. The others are eager to mark her, too, but we have to wait. We can't risk her losing more blood while her body tries to heal.

"Good girl," I whisper. I rock her and clutch her tighter. My heartbeat syncs with hers as the warmth returns to her body. "We've got you. You're safe," I tell her. My fingers tangle in her hair as I kiss the side of her head. I can smell Corbin and his mates all over her. I want to get rid of their scents, reclaim what's mine, and show her how much we need and love her.

Ambulance sirens sound in the distance as they come up the driveway. Leon darts out to flag them down. Within minutes, the entire mansion is flooded with officials and law enforcement. Paramedics tend to Harlow and Leo, who has been staring off vacantly since Corbin died.

He must feel my gaze on him because his eyes slowly move from Corbin's corpse to mine. I nod my head to him, and he nods back. The movement looks like it takes every ounce of energy he has left as he clutches his chest. How he's still alive is beyond me. It must be torture, feeling the pain he is going through, but he kept his promise, so for that, I owe him.

I will do as I promised and keep his daughter safe, knowing I will never be able to truly make it up to him. He sacrificed his life for Harlow's and saved my daughter while trying to save his own from a horrible fate. He knew he couldn't protect her if she was left in Corbin's hands.

I want to mark him, but I won't. As much as he's done for us, and despite the fact I forgive him for killing my mother, he is old enough to be my father, not my mate. He also doesn't seem like the type of person who is willing to submit, especially to someone younger than him. Corbin was one thing. That was a deal made out of desperation. I know he will not make another, even to save his life.

I will also never share Harlow with anyone else. She is ours. He knows that and knows what he signed up for when he gave her my serum. I can smell it on her, smell it over all the other scents I want to rid her of.

CHAPTER FORTY-SEVEN

Warmth surrounds me. And the smell of safety. I inhale it with each breath I take. It's a scent I thought I would never smell again. It's the scent of my mates. There's a distant beeping noise that grows louder, along with the feeling of someone moving me. There's a cuff around my arm, and it grows tighter as it squeezes. The surrounding murmuring also grows louder.

I groan, not wanting to move. Every part of me feels like dead weight. I ache everywhere, but it is so painfully delicious because it means I am alive. Pain proves my heart is still beating, and it's in time with Thane's. I am lying on his chest and I turn my face into his neck. I feel the paramedic remove the blood pressure cuff and open my eyes to Thane's.

"Hey," he whispers, brushing his nose across my cheek before kissing it. "We thought we lost you."

"Leon?" I ask, suspecting he's the reason I'm alive. Nothing heals faster than vampire blood, and Leon's is extra potent for us since he's our mate. Thane lets out a shaky breath, nods, and tugs me closer. "Leo?" I whisper. We already lost Talon, and I lost a sister I never knew I had. The thought of losing a former enemy-turned friend seems too much to bear.

"Alive, for now. He isn't doing too well. But we'll get him home to Emily. He'll be able to spend whatever time he has left with her."

I nod, tears pricking my eyes. Will his daughter hate me because he sacrificed his life for mine?

"Harlow… I know he saved you, but—" Thane starts, but I cut him off.

"No. I am not asking you to mark him, Thane. I don't expect that of you. Besides, it would be weird, since I'm the same age as his daughter," I admit.

Thane hums in agreement, and I grip his shoulder, dragging myself up higher.

"You need to rest. Lay back down," Thane scolds me. He's right. Even that slight movement sends my surroundings spinning, but I think that is more to do with the strange new senses I gained from Thane's serum than anything else. Still, I have something far more important to do than rest.

I bury my face in his neck, and my gums tingle as I partially shift. My canines elongate as I press them against his skin. Thane's breathing hitches when he realizes what I am about to do, but it won't work if he refuses my bite. His fingers tangle in my hair as he offers me his neck. I lick the spot before sinking my teeth into him.

Thane clutches me to him, holding me tightly as my teeth pierce through his thick tissue and bands of muscle. His blood fills my mouth, and I swallow it as I choke on the feeling of the bond becoming fully formed. His feelings smash me harder than ever before. Relief, love, home. Everything I once thought he would never feel toward me. To him, I am home. Little does he know, he is also my home. They all are and have been from the moment I laid eyes on them. I just didn't know it then or believe it could be possible.

Rhen, Raidon, and Leon all feel me mark Thane. Their relief is palpable, along with his. I pull my teeth from his neck, only for his lips to crash down on mine, softly at first, before he starts devouring me. I chuckle and blush, knowing there is a paramedic sitting next to us.

"Mine," I mumble around his mauling lips.

"Yours," he agrees, finally letting me breathe.

I rest my head on Thane's shoulder, missing the rest of our mates. They tried to insist I go to the hospital, but instead, I make the paramedic take us to the airport. I just want to go home. Besides, there are plenty of medical professionals in Raidon's family. When the ambulance stops, and I climb out with Thane, another pulls up beside us. Rhen climbs out backward, shaking his head and looking rather angry.

"What is it?" Thane demands.

"He wants to come with us. He's ignoring the paramedics," Rhen says as he helps Leo climb down, still not facing us. The moment he does, I pounce on Rhen, very unsteadily. It is more like a tackle, as I don't expect to be able to move so quickly. Rhen catches me, anyway, and I lock my legs around his waist. Another car pulls up, and Raidon and Leon climb out.

"Are you sure, Leo? You don't look too good," Thane tells him, and I lift my head. Leo is not healing well now his bond is severed. Half his torso is covered in blood-soaked bandages.

"I am not dying before I see my daughter again," he coughs. Thane grabs him, and Leo growls.

"Shut up. How are you going to climb up the steps? If you're coming, you have to let me help!" Thane snaps at him. "And you'll stay with us until your time comes. Your daughter doesn't need to look after you. We will help," Thane tells him.

"No. My daughter isn't going to watch me deteriorate. I won't let that be the last memory she has of me, Thane. I am simply going back to say goodbye, and then you're going to end me," Leo tells him. Thane stops walking. I glance over at Leo as Raidon steals me from Rhen, who growls at him.

"She doesn't need to watch me die like that. You know well enough how traumatic it is for a child to watch their parents wither away from a lost mate bond. Don't subject my daughter to that," Leo pleads.

"I'll do it," Rhen offers.

Thane looks back at him, his eyes flickering to black. I worry about the impact that will have on Rhen. Rhen isn't usually one who harbors hatred. Sure, he did with me, when he thought I killed Thane's mom, but it isn't in his nature to just kill, despite being Alpha. I can feel he doesn't want to kill Leo. He even likes Leo now.

"No, I'll do it. It's fine," Thane answers, and I peek over at Rhen. He seems relieved, but I have no doubt he would do it, if only to save Thane from it.

CHAPTER FORTY-EIGHT

We go home to my mom's, and we're all exhausted by the time we get there. Harlow beelines for Scarlett and refuses to put her down. We watch her sob for hours when she realizes all her milk has dried up because of the torment she faced over the last couple days and the amount of Leon's blood she had to drink. She still needs time to process the trauma, but Mom and Rhen are finally able to calm her down after soothing her for a good two hours.

I watch as Harlow gives Scarlett a bottle, having finally calmed down enough. Harlow believes she's lost a bonding experience with our daughter. Leon feels guilty and keeps apologizing, even though she reminds him it isn't his fault. Scarlett, however, doesn't seem to care if the milk comes from a boob or a bottle. The girl is just hungry. Thane could probably flop his nipple in her mouth, and she would try to draw milk from it.

Harlow refuses to put Scarlett in the crib my father set up, so she and Scarlett take up the middle of the bed. The rest of us spend the entire night sleeping as still as statues, afraid of rolling over and crushing them. We understand it, but it doesn't make for restful sleep.

My eyes feel like sandpaper when I wake up. Thane wandered

out for a drink a few minutes ago, unable to sleep, and still hasn't returned. I carefully slip off the bed. When I leave the room, Leon and Rhen are curled up and clinging to the edge of the mattress, while Harlow's body is curled around Scarlett's.

The sun is beginning to come up, so there is no point in going back to bed now. I spent the vast majority of the night staring at the shadows on the ceiling, anyway. I wander down the hall, hearing arguing, before I stop at the living room door.

Emily is asleep on the couch, holding her father's hand while he lays next to her. He's been there since we got home. He is in too much pain to move. I watch for a few seconds as Emily whimpers in her sleep. Leo's barely awake, brushing his fingers through his daughter's hair.

I spot Thane leaning against the wall on the other side of the room. He is also watching Leo with his daughter. He nods toward the kitchen and my head turns to the giant, half-closed roller doors Mom uses to block the kitchen light from filtering into the living room. That's when I figure out where the arguing is coming from.

I quietly move across the room. Thane pushes off the wall to follow, and we slip inside the kitchen. My mother and father stop arguing the moment we step inside. They rarely argue, and this looks like a big one. My mother has tears streaking down her face, and my father looks furious.

"What's going on?" I demand. I don't like seeing my mother cry.

"Nothing, dear. Go back to bed," she says, dismissing me.

"After everything, Elaine. Everything he has done. Just fucking ask him!" my father snaps at her, motioning to Thane. My brows furrow as Thane leans on the counter. He braces his arms on it while he stares at them expectantly, also trying to figure out what's going on.

"Well?" I ask her, but she shakes her head, and I turn my attention to my father.

"Elaine?" Thane presses. She glances at him before snatching a tea towel off the counter to wipe her eyes.

"She doesn't deserve to lose her father like that," my mother whispers. Her eyes dart past us to look at Emily. Leo coughs, startling her awake. She fusses over him while he tries to reassure her that he's fine. My mother moves to help, but I motion for her to stay. I take the tea towel and the glass of water she grabbed from her. Moving back to the living room, I help Emily sit her father up and help him drink some of the water.

"Have you got any painkillers?" Emily asks, and my mother rushes into the room with a bottle, fumbling with the lid. I take it from her and open it. Mom then fiddles with his IV fluids and tucks him back in with the blankets.

Emily just stares at him. Leo cracks a half smile at her, trying not to scare her, but nothing he does will console her. She knows she is about to lose him. My eyes flick to Thane who watches with a haunted look on his face.

"You would think they'd have a cure for this by now," Emily murmurs. She looks to my mother like she's hoping there's some miracle cure she just hasn't heard about yet.

My mother smiles sadly. "Maybe one day, sweetie," she tells her, and Emily nods, tears brimming in her eyes.

"It's okay, Bub. It's for the best. Karma has come for me, and even if there was a cure, I would spend the rest of my life in prison for what I've done."

Emily's lip quivers at his words. She's unable to meet her father's gaze as she grabs his hand. Leo sighs, turning his head, trying to look out the window.

"Is the sun up yet?" Leo asks, and I glance toward the huge doors. "I'd like to see another sunrise if that is okay."

I glance to my mother, who nods and unhooks his drip.

"Come on, big fella," I tell him, scooping my arms beneath him. "Emily, open the doors. We can put him on the steps outside."

"I won't be able to hold his weight up," she whimpers before rushing to open the sliding glass doors.

"It's fine, I've got him. You have help," I assure her. Both my mother and Harlow have taken quite the liking to her. Omegas are extremely possessive of their homes and mates, yet that doesn't seem to apply for either of them when it comes to Emily. I believe Harlow and Mom just want to help her, since they've both experienced the pain she's suffering right now.

I was shocked when Harlow even allowed Emily to hold Scarlett yesterday. Mom was showing Harlow how to mix the formula, when Scarlett cried out from her bassinet. Emily moved toward her without thinking, her baser Omega instincts calling for her to protect. Thane got between them, as a precaution, and Leo growled a warning at his daughter as she reached into the bassinet. We all stood there, waiting for Harlow to attack the poor girl.

Harlow simply lifted her head and smiled at Emily. "You can grab her, just be careful of her head."

We all stood there in shock. We thought if any Omega, besides my mother, ever tried to touch our daughter, Harlow would attack, but she didn't. Not even a growl.

Shaking the thought away, I move outside with Leo, sitting on the steps. Mom follows us with blankets and helps me wrap them around him. He sits between my legs, leaning against me. Emily moves to sit between his, resting her head on his knee. We figure Leo only has a few days left after Emily, thankfully, convinced him to not let Thane end him before his time.

CHAPTER FORTY-NINE

I watch Raidon take Leo outside. Charles curses under his breath as he peers at them through the kitchen window. Turning to face him, I lean on the counter. "What were you two fighting about?" I ask, just as Elaine walks in and sets the empty glass on the counter.

"It's nothing, Thane," Elaine murmurs, rinsing the glass.

"You aren't betraying her!" Charles snaps, and I growl at him. He shakes his head, folds his arms across his chest, and leans against the fridge.

"Betraying who? Tell me what the fuck is going on. Is this about Leo?" I demand. Charles clenches his teeth before he sighs. Elaine shoots him a worried glance.

"I have known Leo for years. I know he's done some unspeakable things, Thane, but he had his reasons," Charles says, defending him. I nod. I know Corbin ordered him to kill my mother, but he also saved my mate and daughter.

"I can't mark him," I tell them, feeling guilty but knowing it won't work.

"We aren't asking you to," Charles grumbles. My eyes flick to him before I look at Elaine. She turns her gaze to the window, watching Raidon, Leo, and Emily outside. Her lip quivers.

"I loved your mother," Elaine whispers. "She was like my sister," she says, fiddling with her bracelet. The same one Harlow wears that once belonged to my mother.

"I never lost contact with Leo. I didn't know he was responsible for your mother's death at the time, Thane, but he has helped me a lot over the years. We emailed multiple times, and I'd ask his advice whenever I needed help on my surgeries. He is a good surgeon, and despite what he's done, he's still a good man," Charles tells me.

"I know. I see that now. But I—"

Charles lifts his hand, cutting me off.

"We want you to look past what he has done," he says.

"The fact I brought him back here proves I have done that, Charles," I remind him.

"Enough to let me mark him for Emily and Elaine?" Charles asks.

I blink at him. My eyes flick to Elaine, who can't meet my gaze. Now I understand why they were fighting. Elaine thinks she's betraying my mother and me by asking to save Leo.

"And you can accept him?" I ask Charles. His eyes darken.

"To save him? Yes," he answers, staring at Elaine. I know Charles is a possessive man. He's refused Alpha Packs in the past because he won't share Elaine. By marking Leo, he won't have a choice.

"Elaine?" I ask.

"I'll understand if you say no," she says, nodding and swallowing. I can tell her guilt is eating away at her. She is torn between her love for my mother and saving Leo, knowing she holds the power, if she agrees.

I scrub a hand down my face. They are asking me to allow my mother's killer to live. A person I vowed to end. Who Elaine wanted dead just as much as I did. Arms wrap around my waist, and I jump, glancing down to see Harlow's huge doe eyes peering up at me.

I lean down to kiss her head when she notices Charles.

"Morning," she chirps. She moves to him, standing on tippy toes to peck Charles's cheek before moving to Elaine. She also gives Elaine a peck on the cheek before realizing she's been crying, and that she just walked into a tense situation her groggy mind hasn't picked up on yet.

"Hey, are you okay?" she asks Elaine, reaching for the coffee pot. Charles opens the fridge, handing her sterilized water for Scarlett's bottle.

"Fine, dear. Here, I'll make that while you make your coffee," Elaine tells her, reaching for the bottle in her hand. Harlow's brows furrow, and her eyes flick to us. She holds up the coffee pot and we all nod as she tries to read the room.

"Is everything alright?" she asks, her eyes moving to mine.

"Elaine and Charles want to mark Leo in order to save him," I explain. Her shock hits me, but so does a sliver of excitement before she masks it.

I know what Leo had to do to save her. He touched my Omega, my mate. He laid out every detail on the flight home, as if trying to make it easier for me to kill him when the time came. He didn't try to hide how he touched her, and I can tell Harlow didn't feel violated by it, once she realized he was doing it to keep up appearances. She understands why he did it, and so do I. I'm not happy about it, knowing his paws were fondling and touching her, but I accept it.

"Thane?" Harlow murmurs, noticing Raidon outside the window with Leo and Emily. Her eyes darken, turning clouded.

"Maybe it's time we let go of the past and let the dead rest," I murmur. Everyone's heads turn to me. Elaine's mouth opens and closes as she looks at Charles.

"But—"

I wave her off.

"Mom would accept this, Elaine. You aren't betraying her. She would do the same, knowing he saved Harlow and Scarlett. Mark him. He deserves a second chance," I tell them, staring at Harlow. I've certainly gotten my fair share with her, and she's always found a way to forgive me.

"Son?" Charles asks, and my gaze move to his.

"You have my blessing, but you don't need it," I tell him, and Elaine slams against me. Her arms wrap around me as she squeezes tightly.

"Thank you," she whispers, and I nod, rubbing her back.

I help Harlow make coffee for everyone, and we carry the tray outside. Raidon looks up as we set it on the steps.

"Son?" Charles nods for Raidon to come inside. He points to Leo, but his father waves for him to come in, anyway, and Elaine takes his place to prop Leo up. I know this will be a huge thing for Raidon to accept.

They return moments later, and Raidon seems okay. He grabs Harlow, setting her on his lap. He rubs her arms, trying to warm them. Leon comes out with Scarlett, feeding her the bottle Elaine made. He leans against the door, holding her tiny body. She slurps away at her bottle, bundled up in her pink blanket.

Charles taps Elaine on the shoulder. She looks up and nods. Charles takes her place and Leo groans.

"Always gotta ruin things, Charles. She was much comfier to lean on," he tiredly chuckles before coughing.

"Shut it. You'll have to get used to me touching you, anyway," Charles snaps at him.

"Yeah, I can put up with ya for a few more days," Leo laughs. He is deathly pale, his veins dark beneath his skin, and his eyes are sunken deep into his skull.

"Or maybe longer," Charles tells him. Emily lifts her head up to look at Charles and Elaine.

"You found something?" she asks, hope flaring to life in her eyes. Leo goes to wave her off.

"We have," Elaine says, peering down at her. Her eyes move to Raidon. He nods once to her, and she smiles sadly down at Leo. Leo tilts his head back to stare at her.

"You're gonna let me mark you, Leo," Charles tells him, not giving him the option of choice.

"You want to mark me?" Leo scoffs, looking at Charles over his shoulder.

Charles's eyes remain forward. I know how hard this must be for him. Leo looks at Elaine in confusion when Charles doesn't answer him.

"You want this?" Leo asks her.

"Let us save you," Elaine whispers, looking at Charles. Leo looks at his daughter. His brows furrow.

"You'll mark him?" Emily asks Elaine, and she nods. Emily rises to her feet, slamming against Elaine, making her stagger back as she clutches her.

"Thank you," she says, squeezing her. Elaine brushes her fingers through her hair before Emily lets go, dropping back onto the step next to her father.

"But after what I've done, I—" Leo starts, but I cut him off.

"I'll take care of it," I tell him. He peers up at me, and I suck in a breath, knowing I just promised him no repercussions for killing my mother.

"Please, Dad?" Emily begs, glancing at Elaine and Charles. Leo sighs, looking conflicted.

"And you're sure?" he asks Charles.

"Just shut up before I change my mind," Charles tells him.

"You were always a tough prick," Leo softly chuckles.

"And now I'm yours. Now give me your neck," Charles orders. "I'm not going to be your bitch, Leo. You agree, and you submit to me," Charles tells him, and Leo swallows.

"Please," Emily begs her father, clutching his hands.

"Submit!" Charles orders, smashing Leo with his aura. After losing his mate bond, Leo's aura is practically nonexistent. He's too weak to fight Charles's. It will kill him if he tries. So, Leo must choose: submit and live or refuse and die. Leo growls but bares his neck. Charles doesn't hesitate, sinking his teeth in.

I swallow as Charles orders Leo to mark him back. He does before he turns to look at Elaine. Leo's color has already returned. It always amazes me how tying our lives to our mates' is a cure for most things. Emily breaks down crying, knowing she won't lose her father anytime soon. Leo sits up, now having enough strength to do it himself. Charles moves toward Elaine, no doubt knowing Leo will knock her out when he marks her.

Elaine drops to her knees before Leo, sinking her teeth into his neck. Leo marks her back, and as expected, his bite overwhelms her system. She sways, but Charles is there, waiting to catch her. Leo holds her for a few seconds before looking at Charles. Charles nods once. This will be an adjustment for them. It certainly is for me.

"Thank you," Leo says, staring at Elaine with concern. Charles scoops her up, and Leo lets him. I watch as Charles kisses her cheek, before walking back inside to lay her down. Emily crashes against her father, clutching onto him.

"I'm not going anywhere, now," he breathes. His eyes flick to me, and I nod to him before getting up.

"Where are you going?" Harlow asks, her hand gripping mine. I give hers a soft squeeze.

"I need to go take care of a few things," I tell her, leaning down and brushing my lips against hers before walking inside to change.

CHAPTER FIFTY

Thane's in a weird mood when he returns later. He didn't tell us where he was going or why, just left abruptly after Elaine and Charles marked Leo. Thane has wanted vengeance for his mother's death for a long time. He blamed me for years, and he punished me for it, only to learn I was innocent; that Corbin's pack, Leo specifically, were the ones responsible.

I know it is hard for him to accept Leo and forgive him for what Corbin ordered him to do. Thane swore vengeance on those responsible. Instead, he is choosing to set himself free by forgiving his mother's murderer and one of the men responsible for framing me.

I want to go home, desperately so, and Thane looks relieved when I ask him if we can go back. We help clean and pack everything before setting up the car seat for Scarlett. I sit in the back with her, and Leon and Raidon follow behind us in Rhen's car.

Thane remains quiet, watchful, and contemplative. His mood, however, makes me glance at him nervously.

"I have an emergency hearing tomorrow with the council," he says. His eyes flick to mine in the rearview mirror before going back to the road.

It doesn't answer the question of where he went earlier, but I can guess after he said that. "Okay," I tell him.

"I need you to come with me. I need witness statements and will need you to give yours," Thane tells me.

"For Leo?" I ask, watching the way his hands grip the steering wheel tighter, his knuckles pressing beneath the skin. Rhen glances at him nervously when he finally speaks again.

"Yes, for Leo, but that isn't why I'm telling you this," he says, glancing at me again. "I want you to mark the rest of our mates tonight, please. I know what you went through with Corbin's pack, and that you might not feel up for it, but I need you to do this, Harlow. I don't want you leaving the house unmarked. I won't have you vulnerable again," Thane tells me, and I smile, letting my lips tug up at the corners.

"I can do that," I softly chuckle. Rhen looks over at me, giving me a wink. They have been treating me like glass since I got back. It's annoying because I want things to go back to how they were before.

"That means them remarking you, too. We need to solidify the bond, Harlow," Thane adds. I suck in a breath. That does frighten me a little, remembering how it felt when Corbin's pack forced their marks on me, leaving behind so much marred skin. "Low?"

"Yes, I understand," I tell him.

"Tonight. Promise me! I won't have you at risk. We can't lose you again," Thane growls.

"I promise. Tonight. Just let me settle in first," I tell him. He nods as he pulls onto our long street. Thane doesn't add anything else, but I can feel he is still in a weird mood, so I don't press the matter. I trust he will tell us when he wants to talk about it.

I go to the nursery and settle Scarlett in, making use of it for the first time since she was born. My mates seem a little shocked when I head upstairs instead of to the Den, but I want our bed, and I want Scarlett in hers, knowing they need a decent night's sleep. Once she's settled, I sneak down to the kitchen to look for a snack. Finding a mud cake, I cut off a slice and head back upstairs. I hear the shower running and soft murmurs coming from the bathroom. Shaking my head, I finish the last bite of my cake, deciding to use the shower in Thane's room. I don't want them to fuss over every scratch, and I know they will.

My heart races as I step back into the bedroom with just a towel. All four of them are leaning against the headboard, staring at me. I blink at them. They have such serious expressions on their faces, it makes me wonder if something happened while I was showering.

"What? Is Scarlett alright?" I ask, panicked. I left her for ten minutes, wanting to shave my damn legs.

I rarely get the chance because we often shower together, and there's no way of getting it done in the main bathroom while we are jammed in there like sardines in a can. We need a bigger shower, preferably one with a bench, so I don't have to stand while I shave my legs.

Rhen quirks a brow at me, and I look at Raidon, suddenly uncomfortable with the way they are watching me and not speaking. They're looking at me as if I'm some piece of art on a pedestal they are examining to see if I'm symmetrical or abstract.

"Scarlett is fine. She is asleep in the nursery. I just checked on her," Thane finally says. I nod, exhaling with relief as I move toward the walk-in closet. Raidon moves so quickly he makes my eyes hurt as he jumps in front of the door, blocking me.

A devious smile plays on his lips as his eyes flicker black, a deep thrumming purr emanating from his chest. "Are you forgetting something?" he asks, stalking toward me.

"Yeah, my damn pajamas," I say, trying to sidestep him.

"Anything else?" he questions, making me step back. My brows furrow at his words, and he growls. The noise is extra loud with my newfound hearing, causing me to jump.

"You promised me," Thane growls behind me, and I glance at him. I'm at a loss for what I promised.

I rack my brain. "The council thingy is not until tomorrow," I tell him.

"It seems like someone has a case of baby brain," Rhen chuckles to himself.

"No, Thane said he wanted me to go to the hearing thing and—" I gasp, remembering I promised to mark them tonight. How could I have forgotten? I must have been too preoccupied with seeing the nursery for the first time and settling Scarlett. I also may have taken a nap with her in the rocking chair before taking some time to myself to shower alone.

"You'll be keeping that promise, Low. Now remove the towel," Thane orders.

"Your command won't work on me," I smirk. Thane's eyes flicker dangerously, and Leon shakes his head.

"Hmm, and here I thought she knew better than to test her Alpha by now," Leon snickers, nudging Thane. I glare at Leon as his eyes flicker red with bloodlust.

"I have other ways to make you compliant, Low. So, are you going to make me come over there?" he asks.

"No, you can remain where you are, and they can just line up. It'll be like a drive-thru, take a bite, and scoot to the next," I tell him with a laugh. Yep, call me McDonalds.

"We plan on driving through you alright," Thane warns. My stomach squeezes as lust burns in my belly, yet butterflies quickly dim the feeling.

"I can do it now. Quickly," I tell him, hopping from one foot to the other. I want to get this over with. Thane's right. It needs to be done, but I'm not looking forward to them biting me. I want their marks, and I want to remove Corbin's, but the pain of Corbin's pack marking me is still too fresh in my mind. It replays over and over in my head. I kept begging them to stop, only for the next one to take a bite of me.

Hands fall on my hips as Raidon presses his chest against my back. "That's not what we had in mind," he purrs, nipping at my shoulder.

My stomach sinks. I want to go to bed, maybe eat the rest of that mud cake. I certainly don't want to strip naked and be on display for them.

There's new scars and stretch marks lacing my body, and my skin still doesn't feel right beneath my hands. I feel squishy and far from desirable. I may have shaved my legs, but that doesn't mean I shaved anything else. Not that I'm sporting an Amazonian look, but still.

"We want you, not just your mark," Raidon growls.

CHAPTER FIFTY-ONE

Standing in front of them, I hesitate. They are all eyeing me as if they are about to murder me if they don't get what they want. I don't even know why I'm so nervous, but perhaps it's because this is the first time we're doing it since I've had Scarlett.

"All of us," Rhen growls.

"Together," Raidon purrs, flicking my ear with his tongue. He grips the front of my towel, opening it and letting it fall to the floor at my feet.

They groan. I can feel their eyes on my body, drinking me in. I resist the powerful urge to cover my breasts. They aren't quite as perky as they used to be. My nipples tighten rather painfully at the attention I'm receiving when Thane's Calling slips out, forcing me to relax. My head is already whirling from need, not just because of the Calling, but because of them.

I swallow when Raidon's Calling slips out behind me, cocooning me. Thane's command may not work anymore, but it's clear his Calling still does, and so does Raidon's. They sliver through my body, tightening the hold they have on me. It writhes through my blood and calls me to them, a deep-rooted desire stealing my ability to think straight.

Rhen's nostrils flare, but he doesn't move. He can sense my need. Honestly, I'm more than certain they can all smell my arousal perfuming the room.

"Do you know what we're asking for?" Thane asks. I do know. They don't want one at a time, but all of us. Together. That thought frightens and thrills me.

I all but whimper with need as Raidon's hands move up my sides to cup my breasts.

"Yes!" I breathe as Raidon squeezes them. The sensation from his warm hands is crazy strong, and my knees shake. The Calling turns me into putty. I hate and love it all in one. I crave them, as they call out that primal part of me to mate.

Leon whines as he palms his cock through his shorts. "Stop teasing us, Thane," he groans. I watch his fangs pop out from beneath his upper lip. My gaze snaps to his burning eyes. He wants to feed on me, but his wolf side seemingly wants to play with me as well. With slow deliberation, he nods at me.

"Come here."

My stomach twists with burning lust at his commanding tone, but I stay where I am, waiting for Thane to tell me what to do.

Thane stares at me intently, taking in every inch. "Turn around for us, Omega," he demands.

Biting my lip, I comply and present my backside to him. It just means I get to touch Raidon. His Calling presses me to move closer to him, to devour his flesh. His fingers tangle in my hair as my hands spread across his chest, and my lips follow the path my hands take.

Raidon quietly chuckles, making me realize I am acting more animal than human. Yet his Calling only grows stronger. Some part of me accepts I will never have total control with them, not that I want it because I doubt I would have removed that towel myself, and they know that.

I hear Rhen grunt with appreciation. "You have such a nice fucking ass. I want to lick it. Fuck…" he groans.

My cheeks burn with embarrassment as I am briefly startled back to my senses, reminding me I am stark naked in front of them. The brief panic is forgotten when Raidon's purrs thrum louder. My stomach tightens as arousal shoots through every inch of me, my core throbbing in anticipation. Judging by their tented shorts, I know it is only a matter of time.

"Tell me," Raidon whispers, "do you like getting spanked by Thane, baby?" he purrs, tilting my face to his.

I nod eagerly at his question when I know I should shake my damn head, the Calling overriding my logic right now. "If… if that's what you want," I say.

Thane groans, the sound a deep rumble in his chest, sending electricity up my spine. "Good girl. Face me."

My whole body is a shaking mass of nerves as I turn around. Their tone, their demeanor, it is so erotic. Thane's desire seeps into me, fueling the fire burning through me. My body is throbbing with desire, close to release from just this. They are completely dominant right now, and I suddenly crave their domination, yet fear what that means.

"Are you afraid?" Rhen asks softly. I shake my head.

"Are you turned on?" Raidon whispers, earning a smirk from Thane.

"Y-Yes," I moan, though I know their keen sense of smell was probably able to deduce that before I could say it. Rhen rubs a hand over the bulge in his boxers, and I nearly lose it. Watching him touch himself sends my desire soaring. A desperate sound escapes my throat, and Thane growls.

"They want to mark you, Harlow. And you need to mark them and mate with us. All of us. We won't lose you again," Thane warns me as his eyes flicker. I nod, and my eyes grow wide. "We know after what happened, you may not want to, so we'll keep using the Calling."

I know what he is doing. Thane's wolf needs to show me who is in control the only way it can. His command can't force me to do anything. Yet I don't need to be coaxed or relaxed into submission. I trust my mates. I no longer fear their Calling but revel in it.

"Say it," he rumbles. They are so on edge right now for me to mark them that there is a high chance I will be completely covered in scratches and bruises by the end of this.

"I understand," I choke out. "I like the Calling," I admit as my face flames. That seems to surprise them. I used to hate the Calling when it felt like they used it against me, but now, I seek comfort in it. I know when they use it, I am safe to let go and trust them wholeheartedly. "More," I groan as Raidon's hands travel back down to my hips before slipping between my thighs. I suck in a breath as his fingers tease my slit, his lips devouring my neck.

"You sound so fucking turned on," Leon muses, and I see the way he runs his tongue over his fangs. The sight sends shock waves to my core and leaves a burning ache. I have the sudden urge to bare my neck to him, but I don't dare to move.

"Should I order Raidon to make you come?" Thane purrs, sitting up higher and leaning back against the headboard while Raidon's fingers barely touch my heated flesh.

"I think our girl likes that idea," Rhen murmurs, his eyes dropping to my glistening pussy. "Ask us nicely," he says with a smirk.

"Please!" The word tears from my throat as a low moan.

Thane snarls at my submissiveness as Raidon asks, "Please what?"

"Please, make me come," I beg.

Thane's eyes meet my own, burning a fire straight to my soul. Thane nods to Raidon, and his fingers go from barely touching me to delving between my glistening folds as he shoves two fingers inside me.

CHAPTER FIFTY-TWO

I release a strangled cry and collapse, only for his arm to come around my chest to hold me upright. My hips rock against his hand, desperately seeking anything to rub my swollen clit against.

The lack of friction only seems to heighten my pleasure as my eyes fall shut. His fingers curl upward as his thumb presses against my clit. "Come for me," he purrs in my ear as he adds a third finger, making me cry out. My walls flutter around him, answering his command.

Thane makes a deep sound. "Look at me," he says harshly. My gaze shoots upward, the burn increasing. He releases himself from his shorts, his big hand working his thick erection. His swollen head leaks with pre-cum, and his hard shaft jerks under my gaze as he growls, "You like it when he tells you to come?"

"Yes," I breathe out. My orgasm finally relents, my muscles clenching. I can't tear my eyes away from him. I watch him, my mouth watering to taste him. I want their seed more than my next breath of air, and that thought alone sends my mind whirling. "P-please…"

"Does this turn you on?" Thane ponders in a husky tone. "Do you enjoy watching me rub my cock?"

I nod, licking my lips.

"Please…" I am not sure what I'm asking for. My body feels empty, aching for them. My neck yearns for their bites to mark me as theirs forever. I want to make them mine.

A low whine erupts from my mouth. The sound sets Rhen off. He moves, grabbing me in a flash and throwing me to the bed. My head lands between Thane's open legs, and Rhen's hands part mine, his head dipping between them. He takes a strong inhale and growls. "Dying for this," he says, eyeing Thane.

Thane softly chuckles, and he inclines his head as his hands run over my shoulders to my breasts. Thane squeezes them before he leans over and takes my nipple in his mouth tugging it with his teeth.

And there it is. Rhen's tongue runs up my folds in one swift motion. I arch my back, my eyes closing shut, and my mouth gapes open. I am so wet with need that it almost hurts when I feel the first flick. Rhen nuzzles his nose against my clit, his tongue replacing Raidon's fingers. He takes the bud between his teeth, playing with it. I cry out.

"Rhen, slowly! Ouch!"

A hand tightens in my hair, pulling me roughly and forcing me to look into those burning orbs—Thane. He looks as if he is riding on a knife's edge of insanity, his nose flaring. "Do you want our cocks inside you?"

"Yes—oh!" I exclaim with a scream when I feel Rhen poke his tongue inside me.

"And our bite? Do you want us to sink our teeth into your sweet little neck?" His mouth crashes to mine before I can answer. I moan, kissing him back, desperate for him.

I need to belong to him—to belong to them. Emotions fill my chest with sweet pain. Pulling back from the kiss, he gazes at my face. His body is shaking. His eyes burn with desire.

"I want to be all of yours and yours only."

Groaning, he drops his head to the crook of my neck. I loll it to one side in response, wanting them to mark me.

Rhen's arms wrap around my thighs and pull me roughly toward the edge of the bed. My legs are spread wide, my body exposed. Rhen looms over me, his massive form tense with need. His rigid muscles flex as he strains for control, his face and eyes turning feral and wild. Raidon sits on the bed, pulling me onto his lap, so I straddle him. His lips cover mine, and I rock my hips against his hard shaft, coating it in my slick.

"I don't have enough control to prepare you," Raidon growls as my lips travel down his neck. He offers it to me, and I waste no time sinking my teeth into him. His cock twitches against my pussy, and he clutches me to him as the bond snaps in place.

Fingers delve between my cheeks, finding my pussy. I cry out, my canines slipping from Raidon's neck as Rhen plunges his fingers in and out of me, stretching me. Raidon purrs, his lips nipping and sucking the skin on my neck as his blood drips from my lips.

The idea of Rhen slamming inside me has me arching my back with a whimper. He growls, and Raidon turns me in his lap. Gripping the backs of my knees, he spreads me wide for Rhen, whose eyes are on my glistening pussy. He moves forward, sliding his erection over my slick folds. Rhen makes a low sound of pleasure, sliding over me again, coating himself with my slick. Gripping himself with one hand, Raidon eases forward from behind me, and I feel him press against my pussy. My eyes slide shut in pleasure as I feel him slide in once and pull out.

"Look at me," Rhen hisses, and I snap my eyes open. "Do not close your eyes. You will watch all of us take you."

With a growl, Rhen eases forward, clenching his teeth and resisting the urge to slam inside my tight heat. My slick inner walls grip the throbbing head of Rhen's cock just as I feel Raidon's grip on my legs tighten. He lifts me onto his cock the same time Rhen thrusts into me, forcing both of them into my tight confines.

My pussy stretches furiously, and I'm smashed with Thane's Calling, erasing the sudden pain and forcing me to turn languid between them. Rhen's breath is heavy on my neck as he offers his to me. My canines slip free as I sink my teeth into him, and he moans. His hips jerk, along with his cock that is deep inside me. His blood floods my mouth, and I swallow it, feeling my bond to him solidify.

CHAPTER FIFTY-THREE

Rhen groans my name, a warning on his lips. I moan, rolling my hips, attempting to take him deeper. It doesn't take long until I feel his teeth graze the side of my neck. I feel his tongue lap at the spot but only for a moment. "You're fucking mine!" he snarls.

He bites down hard while he and Raidon slam forward, nearly burying themselves completely inside me. Pleasure shoots through every part of me, my core already clenching in an effort to have them knot me.

"Ah!" I cry out, my hot sheath squeezing around them.

Rhen thrusts inside me again, grunting in pleasure as fingers grip my face. Thane grabs my jaw, and I find a throbbing penis waiting for me. He presses it against my lips, forcing them open, and I swallow his entire length. Thane pulls me closer, watching my every move as he thrusts inside my mouth. His features reflect pure ecstasy. "Does this feel good, baby?"

"Mm," I moan. The vibrations spread through Thane's cock, and he moans in pleasure.

"Do you want it harder?" Thane rasps, fighting the need to fuck me as hard as he can.

"Please," I hum, sucking his cock like a first-class whore. I lick his tip, swirling my tongue on the head before going down. My tongue traces the outlines of his veins against the velvety skin of his cock. Their Calling floods me, overriding any pain I should feel. Instead, I only feel intoxicated with desire.

"Jesus, Low," Thane pants out, slamming harder into my mouth. Tears leak down my face from his rough thrusts. I want this more than anything. The attention of my mates, using me for their pleasure.

Just when I think it can't get any better, I feel fangs sink into my breast, making me gasp and pull away from Thane's cock. I look to find Leon on the other side of Raidon, his fangs in my breast. My hand reaches for him and wraps around his cock. Leon whines, letting out a sigh as his fangs pull out of my flesh. I brush my thumb along the tip of his cock, watching how it jerks under my touch.

Rhen throws his head back with a roar. He snaps his hips against me, repeatedly burying himself to the hilt as I feel his knot swell. His hand presses between us, and I whine, wanting his knot. I know he won't be giving it to me, though.

My breasts move to the rhythm of his thrusts. He forces Raidon onto his back as he lowers himself over my body. Rhen's tongue licks around my taut nipples, sucking one into his mouth before his lips travel up my neck, only to pull away just as Raidon sinks his teeth into me. I momentarily see black, but I don't pass out like when they marked me before.

I gasp, feeling Thane move beside me and press against my lips. They open almost instinctively, taking him into my mouth. My hand slips from Leon's cock as he moves to take Rhen's place when he pulls out of me.

Raidon grips my hips as Leon's cock presses against his, before both shoving inside me. He matches Raidon's pace, slamming into me. I give out a cry as Leon leans forward, sinking his fangs back into my breast, fucking and feeding on me at the same time. I go wild, thrashing between them and whining as loudly as I can with my mouth stuffed full of cock.

My lips move up and down on Thane's cock, never even

stopping for air. Lifting me higher, Leon changes the angle of his thrusts, and it almost knocks the breath out of me.

He bucks hard, hitting me so deeply that I swear I can feel him in my cervix. My back bows as I let out another cry of pleasure. Raidon grunts, snarling as Leon's thrusts make me bounce. He does it again and again, and I cry out each time. I strain between them, desperate to come. They watch me. Their need to fully claim me drives them to ram me harder, and I feel Leon sink his teeth into my neck, marking me as well.

"Come, Low!" Thane roars. His cock slips from my mouth as I let out a loud cry. My body shudders with my orgasm. Leon gives one more thrust, coming inside me with a harsh roar. I feel his cock grow larger, and I widen my eyes. My walls stretch to accommodate their thickened cocks as they start to swell deep inside of me.

"Fuck!" Thane screams and covers my face with his seed and scent, grunting with each jet. Raidon follows close behind him. As he groans, his knot expands inside me, forcing my body to accommodate both of them. Leon leans forward to sink his fangs deep into my neck, marking me as he takes my body hard and fast. He stills as his knot locks him inside me.

I moan deeply. Thane fists my hair, pulling it away from my neck. I loll my head to the side in submission, my mind hazy after being claimed by my four mates.

"Do it. Bite me, please," I beg. With a snarl, all four of them sink their teeth into my flesh. Euphoria explodes through my veins as I suddenly feel their teeth everywhere, marking me body and soul. Thane sinks his teeth into me over their marks, sealing them and locking them in place.

"Oh god!" I cry out, and my body clenches around their knotted cocks.

So. Fucking. Good.

I fall back onto Raidon. A moan escapes my mouth as darkness engulfs me. I am finally complete and claimed — for the rest of the world to see that I am their Omega. Forever.

I am theirs, and they are officially mine.

CHAPTER FIFTY-FOUR

RHEN

Thane lays Harlow's clothes on the bed while I try to coax her awake. She snores loudly as I shake her shoulder. She's drooling on Thane's pillow, but that's better than her drooling on me. I woke up to a puddle on my chest, and she had the audacity to say I drooled on myself when I finally managed to escape her embrace.

She's trying to escape having to go to the council hearing as she continues snoring. A hurricane would struggle to wake her, and I'm pretty sure if one tried, she would flip the storm off and tell it to blow wind up someone else's ass for all the luck I'm having.

Thane chuckles to himself, shaking his head as he walks to the side of the bed she's on and yanks the blanket back. Goosebumps instantly lace her skin from the cool morning air. A mere second passes before his hand comes down on her bare ass. The crack is loud, and I flinch.

She jumps and yelps, rubbing her backside.

"Up!" Thane laughs.

Her eyes turn to slits as she glares at him. She grabs a pillow and lobs it at him, hitting him between the shoulder blades.

"Alphahole," she snarls. Thane turns and smirks at her.

"Time to get up, Low. We need to leave soon. Rhen has been trying to get you up for the last ten minutes," he tells her.

She grumbles and reaches for the blanket before tugging it back up. I press my lips into a line to stop my laughter as I see Thane huff and cross his arms.

"Get up, Low!" he warns as Leon wanders in. Raidon follows behind him with Scarlett, burping her over his shoulder.

"Now, Harlow," Thane growls as she reaches for a pillow to cover her head, blocking him out.

"Now, Harlow!" she mimics, trying to impersonate his voice. She comes off sounding more like a child throwing a tantrum at being forced to go to school. Thane growls and Leon snickers behind me.

"Someone's in trouble," Leon says in a sing-song voice.

"Yeah! He is for not letting me sleep!" comes her muffled voice. Leon bristles, and my gaze falls on Thane, feeling his annoyance. I know he is tempted to test his aura on her.

"You have three seconds to get your ass out of bed," Thane threatens. He shakes his head and curses under his breath when she doesn't move. "1... 2... 3."

"Wow, congratulations, you can count like a big boy," she mocks as she curls up beneath the blanket. Thane snarls, ripping the blanket off her, and she shrieks, trying to grab it back. "Nooooo!" she drags the word out, making it sound like a whine.

"You're being a brat. Now up, before I turn your ass red," Thane warns her. At his words, she covers her backside with her hands but doesn't move from her spot. Thane sighs, gripping her ankles and ripping her to the edge of the bed. She claws at the sheets but can't escape his grip when his hand comes down on her ass again. I cringe at the sound of the slap and almost rub my own ass, just at the sight of her reddened cheeks.

"Slap my ass again, and you can suck your own dick!" she warns him. I don't know what's worse, her whine of pain or the sound she makes as he quickly pulls her over his lap. His hand comes down hard on her ass once more. She shrieks, trying to cover her bright-red behind. Yet her arousal perfumes the air, like a beacon of lust and sin.

"You were saying?" Thane asks. She growls, biting his thigh.

"Yep, she's in one hell of a mood," I tell Thane as he pinches her nose to get her to release his leg.

"Let go!" he growls, pushing her hands away to rub her backside. "Right, Leon, grab me the butt plug from the top drawer. The third one," Thane tells him and Leon laughs.

"Now you've done it," Leon tells her. She lets Thane's leg go, lifting her head.

"Wait, wait! I'll get up!" Harlow pleads, as Raidon laughs and takes Scarlett out of the room. Thane grips her hair, tugging her head back.

"What was that?" he asks her.

Leon wanders over and drags the cool, glass plug up her spine, causing her to stiffen.

"I'll suck your cock!" she blurts as she shudders at the feel of it.

"Hm, I'm listening," Thane quietly chuckles, rubbing her ass and squeezing her cheeks. His fingers trace around the tight muscle of her hole. His other hand presses down on the center of her back as she bucks against him.

"I'll behave, I'll behave!" she shrieks, but I can feel her anger bubbling. So can Thane. She wants to bite him, put him in his place. But he is already in his place, and so is she. Over his knee, right where he likes her.

"That doesn't sound very convincing," he tells her, holding out his hand for the butt plug.

"I'll swallow!" she offers.

"You would have to, anyway," he tells her. He snaps his fingers at Leon, who snatches the lube off the bedside table. Harlow bucks when she feels the lube drip between her cheeks.

"Oh, you better sleep with one fucking eye open, Thane! I am going to shove that fucking thing right up your ass," she growls as he traces it between her cheeks, coating it in the lube. She tries to cover her ass with her hands again, but Thane easily grips her wrists with his free hand, holding them in the small of her back.

She bucks before growling at him. When he doesn't let her up, she bites his thigh again. He groans, only for it to turn into growl, and I snicker when he shoves the butt plug inside her. She whimpers and lets him go. "No! You asshat," she snarls, kicking her legs before she bites him again. He slaps her ass, and she cusses him out.

"You have quite the language this morning," he tells her, and she growls. "Want a bigger one?" he warns. She shakes her head, and he lets her wrists go to grab her hair, tugging her head back.

She seems like she's about to cuss him out again but changes her mind. "Leon, grab—" she starts, batting her eyelashes at him and making him smirk, "a smaller one?" she purrs.

"Not a chance," he tells her, and she pouts.

Thane pulls her to sit on his lap. His hand tangles in her hair and he nips at her mark. "If you remove it," he warns, running his tongue along her jaw, "it'll be my dick next time, not a plug." He slaps her ass, and she grits her teeth. I know she's going to make him regret that later.

"Now get dressed. We have the hearing in an hour," he tells her. She huffs, snatching up the dress he set out for her and heading into the bathroom.

"I'm surprised you didn't make her suck your dick," Leon groans, sounding a little disappointed. It must be a nice reprieve for him. It's usually his ass over Thane's lap.

"Oh, she will. She'll just do it on the drive there," Thane assures him before turning to me. "If she isn't out of there in ten minutes let me know, and I will drag her ass out," Thane tells me as he leaves the room.

CHAPTER FIFTY-FIVE

Thane is gonna pay. I can still feel his fingers etched into my skin. And sitting is very uncomfortable. Although, I actually don't mind the plug. I have no idea why Leon made such a big deal about it when Thane told him to get it out.

We have been stuck here for hours. Thane has influence within the city, but he still needs to prove that he isn't letting a cold-blooded killer loose. I've recounted the events with Corbin's pack—and how Leo was instrumental in my safe return—for the council three times. When they finally give the verdict that Leo is free to go without repercussions, I let out a breath of relief, excited to get home. Yet as I move to rise from my seat, Thane grips my knee.

"Now, moving on to the Omega laws," the Council Elder says. I sit my ass back down, looking at Thane. He leans into me.

"You want the laws changed? This is how we do it. I'm giving you a voice here, so use it," he whispers before getting up from his seat and moving to the front of the room.

Rhen drapes his arm across my shoulders, his fingers massaging the back of my neck as I listen intently. There are twelve council members; six of them are women and the other six are men. They are all Alphas, and they don't seem too impressed with Thane wanting to amend the laws.

"Mr. Keller, these laws have been around for… well, for as long as I can remember. Omegas are a rarity, and you want us to just let them be free to do as they please? As if they aren't necessary for our survival? We owe it to werewolf society to keep these laws in place. What you are asking for could make Alphas extinct," the Elder, Cole, says.

"Like we are currently doing to the Omegas," Thane argues.

"They are born for us!" Elder Cole retorts.

"Says who? You? Because you believe an Omega will never choose you if we actually allow them a choice? If we look to our history, Elder, Omegas were once revered. Not seen as objects, or an Alpha's possession. Now, they are simply toys!" Thane snaps at him.

"The laws were put in place to continue Alpha bloodlines. A small sacrifice to preserve our way of life. Your way of life, too, Mr. Keller," Elder Cole says, and Thane shakes his head.

"Is that what you will tell your daughter when she is shipped off to a sanctuary next year, Cole? That she is no longer allowed to have her own life but is now expected to become an Alpha's fuck-toy. Are you going to be the one to force her to her knees, or will you ask the sanctuary to do it?"

I watch his mouth gape open.

"Mr. Keller, you are out of line!" he roars, his face turning an angry shade of red. The women, however, listen intently to what Thane is saying. A few of the younger members even nod at his words.

"Really? Well, how about we ask one? Ask my Omega, Cole. Let her explain what her education was like, and we'll compare it to the traditional education an Alpha receives." Thane tells him. Elder Cole shakes his head as one of the women speaks up.

"I want to hear it," she says, her eyes moving to mine. She nods to me while Elder Cole sits up straighter in his seat.

"You are not seriously entertaining this. We need to preserve our bloodlines."

"What about the Omega bloodlines? Have you heard the recent statistics for how many Omegas die each year from forced bonds?"

Thane questions.

"Which is why we created the serums—to acclimate them," Elder Cole retorts.

"Still not a guarantee. We lose more every year," Thane responds. Elder Cole stands to argue, his thinning gray hair wisping around his skull. It makes me wonder how old his daughter is. He looks ancient, but Thane spoke as if she is still young. I shudder at the thought of being paired with someone old enough to be my grandfather.

"How about we call a small recess? Afterward we can hear from your mate about the Omega facilities," the woman says, standing. She flicks her dark hair over her shoulder and the woman beside her also stands. Thane curses when they leave and storms back over to us.

"The women are interested in listening. So is Tatum," Rhen reassures him.

"Yes, but Cole holds the majority ruling. Even with my vote, he'll be the tiebreaker. I know he intends to go against me, like he did with my mother. If he does, I may just kill the old bastard."

"He has an Omega daughter?" I ask Thane, and he nods.

"Yes, she's twelve."

"So next year she'll be forced into a sanctuary, right?" I ask Thane. I chew my lip before reaching into his pocket. Thane watches me, amused, as I steal his wallet. "How long is the break?"

"Fifteen minutes, why?"

"I have an idea," I tell him, turning on my heel.

"Wait, Harlow!" Thane calls out, but I wave him off. "Fuck! Go with her! I can't leave in case they come back early," I hear Thane tell Rhen, who jogs to catch up with me.

We stop at two different stores before returning just in the nick of time. We walk back in as the council members are retaking their seats. Elder Cole seems disinterested as the woman calls me up. I take my bag, stuffed full of goodies, and move to the front of the room.

"Hurry up. Let's get this over with so we can vote," Elder Cole says, glaring down at me.

"It would be easier if you came down here to help me. I need a volunteer," I tell him. Thane cuts me a look before turning to look at Rhen, who chuckles to himself while shaking his head. One of the women gets up, surprisingly, and grips Elder Cole's shoulder.

"Come on, what's a little demonstration?" she purrs. He rolls his eyes but gets to his feet.

"You are aware this isn't how council meetings are held?" he snaps at me as he stomps down the steps.

"No, but you are aware that Omegas are rarely allowed in the council, so how would I know how they are held, Elder?" I ask him. He clicks his tongue and shakes his head, walking down to the small area in front of the council tables, where I'm standing. I grip the little table and drag it over. A few of the council members sigh and shake their heads.

"Your daughter is twelve?" I ask, and he nods. "So old enough to go to sanctuary next year?"

"Yes, she wants to study politics," he tells me.

"Even though she'll never be permitted to hold a seat on this council?" I ask. He should know that. Is he just giving her a false sense of hope, or did he really think she will be the exception? "And you expect them to teach politics at an Omega Sanctuary?" I ask him.

"Of course. It's a private school, one of the best sanctuaries."

I reach into the bag to pull out a porn magazine. "Well, I never got the chance to study politics, Elder Cole. And neither will she, but I can tell you what she'll be learning. At her age, I'm sure you were studying to be a council member. Or maybe, with your prepubescent brain, you wanted to be an astronaut." I shrug and hand him the magazine. "This is what I was taught at thirteen. Where a dick goes and how many my body can take," I tell him.

CHAPTER FIFTY-SIX

"Well, sex ed is to be expected, of course," Elder Cole nods.

"They hand magazines like this out?" the woman asks. "I'm Milena, by the way," she tells me, quickly introducing herself.

"Yes, Milena, and much worse," I tell her.

"At thirteen?" she asks again to clarify.

"As I said, that is to be expected," Cole says motioning to the magazine. She holds it up to him. It is an Omega with an Alpha Pack of five men.

"This? Really, Cole? At thirteen?" she snaps at him before tossing it up to the other Alphas.

"Want to see fourteen?" I ask her, reaching back into my bag as she turns toward me. I slam a huge rubber dildo, complete with knot, onto the table, and it suctions to it.

"You are out of line, Omega!" Cole yells at me.

"Mrs. Keller," Thane growls in warning. "She is my mate, and you will address her as such." The Council Elder grits his teeth, glaring at me, but I speak before he has a chance.

"So, this is out of line in a room full of adults, but it's okay in a classroom full of children?"

Cole clicks his tongue, refusing to look at the dildo, as if it repulses him. Milena grabs it, shaking it in his face. "This! This is disgusting!" she growls at him. He slaps her hand away and she drops it back to the table.

"This is what your daughter will be taught at fourteen: how to get an Alpha off using her mouth and hands. Wanna give it a go, Elder Cole? You could do a demonstration. I'm sure you'll enjoy it because I loved those classes. Taught me so much. And they should really help your daughter with council politics. I'm sure these skills will be valuable in council chambers, right?" I ask him, which makes him gape at me in horror. He looks at the other council members, who seem just as appalled.

"No, this is outrageous—"

"Have you ever been inside an Omega Sanctuary?" I ask him, and he shakes his head. "So, while you were learning literacy and numeracy, I was learning how to take a knot, how to get on my damn knees for an Alpha. I was also taught to be quiet, compliant, and submissive to prevent my Alpha from killing me. That's the same thing your daughter will be taught. Now picture your little girl on her knees before you. Is that the future you want for her?"

Elder Cole steps toward me, shaking his finger in my face. "You disgusting little—"

One second he's scolding me, and the next he's gone. A loud bang echoes through the room as Thane slams him onto the desk. The sound makes me flinch, and Milena shrieks. Rhen grabs at Thane's shoulders seconds later.

"Remember whose mate you're speaking with, Cole!" Thane snarls, his grip on the man's throat tightening. Cole's eyes water, and his face turns purple. Thane's entire body trembles with his rage. The other council members stand as if they are about to intervene. One look from Rhen, however, makes them retake their seats.

"Thane," I whisper, gripping his arm. He turns his gaze from Cole, who is clawing at his hand. Thane's eyes flicker, his canines retracting as he growls.

"Remember who put you on this council, Cole," Thane snarls

at him. He then grabs the dildo and slams it on Cole's balding head, suctioning it to his skin. I have to press my lips together to stop my smile. Milena snickers as Thane lets him up. "Now answer her," Thane growls.

Elder Cole coughs, fingers prodding at his throat. As he does, the rubber dick wobbles on his head, which only makes the situation all the more hilarious. Elder Cole straightens, peels the dildo off his head, and sets it on the table. I'll give him one thing; he is good at keeping his composure while embarrassed.

"What was the question, Mrs. Keller?" he asks, straightening his tie as if nothing happened. Glancing at Thane, he nods for me to continue.

"I asked if those skills will help your daughter with council politics?" I repeat. He presses his lips in a line and shakes his head. "Those are the only so-called skills she will learn in an Omega Sanctuary. She'll be taught to obey and take whatever her Alpha gives her, even if she doesn't want it. Her body won't be hers. It will belong to her Alpha, even if he hurts her. And she can't run, because that's a crime. Yet in staying, she may risk her life."

Elder Cole stares at the dildo on the table, and he sucks in a breath. I look at the other council members, who are watching intently.

"And what if she is forced into rotation? That is the standard sentencing, set by this council, for countless 'crimes' an Omega might commit," I say, and Elder Cole swallows. We all know what a punishment that is. "She will become an Alpha's plaything, shipped from one Alpha to the next until there is nothing left of her. Is that the life you want for her? Are these the laws you want to uphold?" I ask him.

"They are paid for such services, Mrs. Keller, and some—"

"Some choose it, yes, but the vast majority of Omegas in rotation are sent there by this council! For minor crimes, like failing to pay fees or running from their duties," Thane cuts in. I have no idea about the numbers, but it's clear this is something Thane has researched.

"Overrule me, Cole. Any of you," Thane says, addressing the

entire council, "and when it's your daughters' turn in the sanctuary, we'll see how you feel when I order rotation for her."

"Are you threatening us, Mr. Keller?" Tatum asks.

"If it was good enough for my Omega, it's good enough for your daughters," Thane tells them. "You'll sit by and watch them be sold off to the highest bidder. That's what they're born for, right?" Thane asks as the council members glance at each other. "I have seen firsthand what they teach girls in those places. From the age of eight!" he says, tossing a stack of photos on the table. I recognize the rooms because they're from the sanctuary I grew up in.

"These photos were taken while I hunted Corbin. They are from his brother's sanctuary. These classrooms are for elementary school girls!" Thane states. Milena picks them up, looking through them before handing them to the other council members to look at.

"Eight years old! You call yourselves Alphas, but you allow this? Alphas are supposed to protect their packs, their Omegas, not send them off to be raped and abused by other Alphas. That is basically the point of these places. They are nothing more than glorified pedophile rings, and we allow it! Turn a blind eye to it! There's no oversight. They are hidden away from the public, so wealthy Alphas can have their pick of virgins when they go to auction."

Milena nods in agreement.

"We failed them!" Thane suddenly screams. His fist comes down hard on the table, making everyone jump. "Just like you will fail your daughters if we don't make this city a haven for Omegas. Give them a choice, educate them, but not with this shit," Thane says, picking up the dildo and dropping it.

"Your Omega is from a sanctuary, Mr. Keller, purchased from an auction," Cole retorts.

"And I have to look at her every goddamn day, knowing my fathers failed to stand beside my mother. That the very council my family founded subjected her to that!" Thane snaps, his hands fisting at his sides. "We did this. We can fix it."

"This city is small compared to the rest of the state, Mr. Keller. These laws won't pass in the state, let alone the whole country," another man speaks up.

"You're right, at least not anytime soon, but it's a fucking start. How many Omegas are reported missing every year? How many run? We don't even know the actual numbers anymore because most flee with their children. What if they had somewhere safe to run to? Alpha bloodlines are dying because we force Omegas to run and hide. We show them that we won't protect them, and you expect them to hand themselves over?"

"Our bloodlines wouldn't be so decimated if Omegas didn't fear us! They don't need us, we need them. It's about time we start showing them how important they are, how valued, instead of beating them into submission and expecting them to stick around or not kill themselves. Do any of you know the stats on Omega deaths from last year?" Thane asks. They all shake their heads. Thane growls, turning to walk back to grab a document from his briefcase before dropping it on the table in front of Milena and Cole.

"Last year, twelve percent of Omega deaths were from suicide. Sixty-eight percent were at the hands of an Alpha. Don't you see a problem with that? I wonder what statistic your daughters will fall under. Because their futures don't look too bright, no matter which way you look at it."

Chapter Fifty-Seven

My back aches from sitting in this chair. The council shut hours ago, and they are still in deliberations. I stretch my arms above my head and turn to spot Harlow walking into the room. Rhen took her to stretch her legs and get her something to eat when we realized this was going to take longer than expected.

My eyes trail over her, and I smirk as I take her in. My gaze roams over her body, stopping at her face. She raises an eyebrow at me, catching me eyeing her.

Harlow moves to sit in one of the pews, and I crook my finger at her to come to me. She purses her lips but wanders over, glancing nervously at the door the council members will return through. She probably thought they'd be back from deliberations by now. My arms snake around her hips and I squeeze her ass. Harlow glares at me but the council isn't here, nor would they see anything behind my high desk if they return unexpectedly.

"More comfortable?" I ask her. Her cheeks flame as if she's worried someone might overhear and understand the question I asked. She nods. "Hopefully it won't be too much longer, but if you want, I can have Raidon come and get you?" I ask. We've already offered this multiple times, but she insists on staying, wanting to hear the verdict.

"No, I'll stay," she whispers.

I nod to the chair beside me, but she shakes her head, turning to go back to the pews. As she goes, I notice her skin is laced with goosebumps. The air-conditioning is on high in here, and even a few of the council members complained about it being too cold earlier. I barely feel the cold, but it's obvious Harlow is freezing. Reaching out, I grip her hand, and she stops, turning her attention to me. "I want to stay," she assures me.

Harlow is only wearing a little black dress, making me notice the tinge of blue on her skin. I shake my head, shrugging off my suit jacket to see Rhen about to do the same. He tosses his arms up in the air, realizing I am giving her mine. Yep, she is definitely cold. She wastes no time taking it from me and moving back to the benches behind me, taking her seat.

Rhen places a cappuccino on the desk before taking his seat beside me. I take a sip and wonder about the council deliberations and how they will vote. After seeing Harlow's demonstration, I can assume Milena and the other women will support us. It's a tossup as to whether or not Harlow's testimony had any effect on Cole and the other male members.

I have known Cole since I was a kid. He was friends with my fathers, yet they shared vastly different views on Omegas. My fathers were just not vocal about their views, which led to my mother's downfall with the council. Instead, she had to resort to blackmailing and digging up dirt on the members, and in the end that got her killed.

They've been debating for four hours, likely arguing over which laws to erase and which to keep before they bring it to a vote. They know what my vote is, so they didn't bother asking. I sit up as they finally re-enter the room. Anticipation fills me as I wait to hear their decision.

"Before we vote, we'd like to ask a few questions, Mr. Keller," Elder Cole says.

"Yes?" I ask, more than willing to answer anything they want.

"Exactly where do you plan to house all these Omegas? If we make this city a haven for them, we will have Omegas coming from all over the country seeking to escape their obligations."

"They can stay at the Omega refuge I'm building in my mother's name. I've already doubled the construction crew, so it should be completed by next week," I answer, even though I know it won't house the number of Omegas that will travel here to seek refuge.

"How many can it house?" Milena asks, glancing up from her documents.

"Roughly three hundred, maybe more," I say. She nods and purses her lips.

"That won't be big enough. We'll have to figure something else out," Cole says, as he flicks through a folder. Tatum leans over, tossing a document in front of him.

"We can divert council funds. We should be able to afford to adjust our budgets and push a few community projects back until next year. Having more Omegas here could be a good thing. It will draw attention to the city, bringing in tourists and Alphas looking for Omegas. That revenue can be used for extra security and to reimburse the council. Can we also put aside some of that revenue into a fund for the Omegas?" he asks Cole, who nods. "Is there an existing fund? How do you plan on financing this refuge?" Tatum asks, turning to address me.

It is Rhen who gets up, however. He moves toward the council table and hands them a folder. "The Keller family has been putting aside half their company's net profits since Hana first petitioned the council. That hasn't changed since Thane took over. Each month, money is set aside, invested, and pushed back into the fund. The interest gained on the returns alone is enough to cover any expenses the refuge has."

"What about schooling? These women—as you said before—have had no proper education since at least the age of twelve, and that does not include orphaned Omegas raised in facilities," Clara, another council member, asks.

Clara and Milena are both roughly Harlow's age, which works to our advantage. They are from a newer generation with a fresh set of eyes on how to direct our future. Rather than letting the city remain stagnant, as Cole would have it, they are more open-minded and eager for change. Cole bitched and moaned when they joined the council because they challenged him on everything, which is exactly why I pushed to have them voted in.

"We'll open an Omega school, and we can train the adults for council and city jobs, or for jobs within my company. That gives them added protection, will help us keep tabs on them, and employ those who want to work. There will also be free courses offered through the refuge: self-defense classes, counseling, and a drug and alcohol rehabilitation program. We have resources they can use," I explain. They nod, yet I can tell they are still worried about the impacts to the city, as they should be. This is a big change.

"And what of Alpha offenders? Those who refuse to acknowledge the new laws?" Cole asks.

"Like anything else, it would depend on the crime as to whether they get fined, prison time, or banished from the city. We can also make sure all Omegas have access to free healthcare to get pheromone blockers and other essentials that will keep them safe and also stop sending the city's Alphas into rut."

Tatum and Milena nod.

"And what of the Omegas who want to join packs or go into rotation? Some of these women have been in rotation for years. Some choose that life," Cole says.

"Those who want it can choose rotation. We'll just find ways to make rotations safer, and make sure the Omegas are properly compensated. As for those who want to find a pack or a single Alpha, we can hold meet-and-greets. We'll make sure the choice is ultimately up to the Omega, and any requests for claiming must be reviewed to ensure the Omega isn't being coerced or under command," I tell them. Saying it out loud, it sounds like a lot, but it is manageable.

"There is no perfect way to do this. It will be a learning experience, not only for us but for the city and the Omegas. There will be mistakes. We just need to make sure we learn from them and quickly make any necessary changes to prevent further mishaps," I tell them. They all look at each other, but I see Cole nod.

They deliberate for a few moments, and I glance at Harlow, who has been quiet since they came back. I wonder what she's thinking.

I can't tell through the bond because her emotions are all over the place, as if she's in shock that this is even happening.

Harlow looks at me, and I nod for her to come over. Her relief through the bond is palpable, and she quickly gets up from her seat, moving to my side. She goes to take the empty seat next to me, but I pull her into my lap, uncaring that the council members are right there. I feel her body warm with embarrassment at the action, but they aren't paying us any attention, too busy debating and trying to figure out what is essential and where they can make cuts.

"I feel like throwing up," she murmurs, her nerves suddenly coming through loud and clear as she fiddles with my mother's bracelet on her wrist. "What if they say no?"

I know she is worried about Scarlett. Elaine tested her blood, and like her mother, she is Omega, but our daughter is never setting foot in one of those places. I will forge her documents if needed.

"They won't. We have enough proof, enough supporting documents, and it won't cost the city much. Half the work is already done. It's mostly legalities now," I assure her. She chews her lip, squirming on my lap as she tries to hop off. I growl, nipping her shoulder as Elder Cole clears his throat, and she quickly slips off my lap.

"We do this, and our city will come under hot water fast. So we'll have to take precautions, Thane, and you must attend all council meetings until everything is finalized. But the council has unanimously decided: the laws surrounding Omegas will be abolished, and new ones will be written to protect them. We'll start sending out closure notices for all rotation facilities within the city limits, and start the referral services," he tells me. I can hear Harlow's heart racing, as if it wants to leap from her chest in excitement.

Tatum slides a calendar over to Cole, who quickly flicks through a few pages before looking back up. "Next week at 5:00 PM, we'll hold another meeting to discuss employment agencies and security risks. Until this is fully managed, weekly meetings will begin starting then."

"I'll be here, and so will Harlow," I tell them, glancing at her. She nods, gripping my hand beneath the table. Her relief is so immense it vibrates out of her and nearly steals the air from my lungs. I know it is for Scarlett. Now she will be safe, and so will every other Omega living in this city.

We climb in the car, finally leaving after a long day. For once, I feel a sense of accomplishment after the hearing. This is the first time I've done something that truly matters, that will impact lives and make a difference. It only makes me want to do more.

Harlow remains quiet as I glance at her in the rearview mirror. If only I had done this years ago, or if my mother had succeeded, she never would have ended up in that place. I can't fix that, but I can ensure I change it for the next generation, and that is exactly what I plan to do.

And once I gather enough evidence to prove this is safe and that it works, I will go to the state council, then to the Supernatural Parliament.

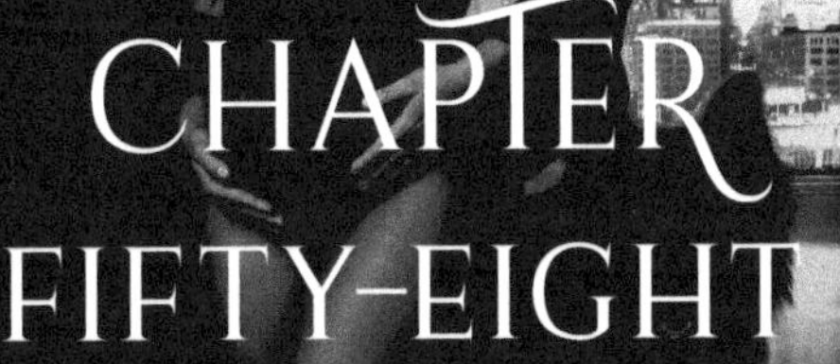

CHAPTER FIFTY-EIGHT

ONE MONTH LATER

I'm sparring with Leo, and I am drenched in sweat. My clothes stick to me like a second skin when he finally stops. Glancing at the clock on the wall, he pulls his whistle from his pocket.

He blows the whistle, signaling the end of class. Murmurs amongst the other Omegas break out through the enormous room. A few even let out sighs of relief as they move toward the bathrooms to change and leave. Leo really made us work tonight.

Exhausted, I flop back down on the mat. Leo walks over, peering down at me with his hands on his hips and an amused expression on his face. "I would get up if I were you. Training may have finished, but you know someone will be here soon to pick you up."

I groan, quite content with dying here on this mat. I had a good run. I will risk their wrath.

"Come on. You don't want your mates to think you're slacking," Leo scolds. I roll my eyes at him and sit up. Leo softly chuckles at my reluctance to move. Every muscle aches, I am saturated in sweat, and I know my ass will hurt when I peel it up off the mat.

We're at the Omega refuge. Leo is one of the self-defense trainers here. Thane makes me attend every single class, never allowing me a night off. Despite most of the Omegas here only having to train three times a week, Thane makes me train all five, with no exceptions. Leo runs three classes a week. Raidon and Rhen alternate between the other two days.

Leo offers me his hand and I grab it, letting him pull me to my feet.

"Elaine told me Charles got your medical license reinstated?" I question, and he shrugs as we make our way across the room to the bleachers.

Pushing the hair that escaped from my ponytail off my face, I snatch my water bottle off the bleachers, and drink deeply.

"Charles got me a job at the hospital, but I turned it down," Leo tells me, drinking his own water before moving to pack up the mats.

I follow, helping him clean up and pack away all the equipment. "So, you don't want to go back?" I ask him.

"I can do more to help here. Besides, I already asked Thane if I can work as the refuge's doctor on staff as well as handle the training, so I'll have plenty of work to do," Leo tells me with a shrug. He grabs one of the blue mats, dragging it to the closet while I remove the velcro tabs on the next as he returns, bending down to grab it.

"Because of Emily?" I guess, and he smiles.

"Yeah, she loves it here. She signed up for some of the night classes they offer, and Elaine got her a job at the clinic as a secretary four days a week," Leo tells me, and I smile.

"Anyway, go on. One of your mates will be outside waiting. I'll finish up here," he tells me, taking the mat I'm unsuccessfully trying to drag to the closet.

Exiting the gym, I move down the long corridors toward the rec room, which is being painted today. I know Thane is coming to pick me up, but I have no intentions of going to meet him. Rhen, Leon, and Raidon all made excuses about being unable to pick me up, knowing they'd already be here.

Strolling into the rec room, I find the artist almost finished. Raidon is sitting on the couch with Scarlett, who is happily munching on her hand as if it is the tastiest thing in the world. Leon and Rhen are helping clean up and setting 'wet paint' signs out.

Leaning over the couch, I kiss Scarlett's cheek, and she blows raspberry spit bubbles at me before going back to gnawing on her hand.

"Where is mine?" Raidon pouts when I stand. He lifts his face up, and I smile, leaning down to kiss him.

'Low! I've been out front for ten minutes now!' comes Thane's voice through the mind-link. I ignore him, and Raidon gives me a knowing look.

I walk over to watch the artist finish before he packs everything up. When he's done, I pay him, only to hear Thane's angry voice again.

'Harlow!' he barks through the mind-link.

"Oh, he is going to be pissed," Rhen laughs as Leon trots over to me.

"Hmm, you smell so divine. All nice and sweaty for me," he says. I push him away as he nips at my skin, knowing if he keeps going, it will alert Thane that they are also here.

'Harlow!' Thane growls in annoyance. I know I am pissing him off because he rarely uses my full name, always calling me by the nickname he gave me.

"I can't wait to show your mother tomorrow. She'll love it," I tell Raidon, and he nods, gazing up at the giant mural on the wall.

"Yeah, he did an amazing job," Raidon admits, his eyes scanning it. "He's gonna love it," he assures me with a smile. I nod, hoping he's right because it took me ages to think of.

'What are you doing? Do I need to come in there?' Thane snaps. I can feel his annoyance. *'Right, you better have a good excuse for bloody ignoring me!'*

I feel how pissed off he is through the bond. I can also feel him getting closer, making me giddy.

'You seriously think you're being funny right now? Where are you? Wait, I can feel you're close. Why are the others here?'

I continue ignoring him as he opens the mind-link to our other mates. *'I swear, if you all run from me, I will turn each of your asses red,'* he growls at us, earning a laugh from Raidon and Rhen.

'*Maybe I like being spanked,*' I retort.

'*Oh, I wanna watch you spank her,*' Leon chimes in.

'*Your ass will be the first one over my damn knee for lying to me!*' Thane growls at him.

'*I'd like to see you bend me over your knee,*' Raidon mocks.

'*Don't tempt me, Raidon,*' Thane growls.

Rhen laughs, and I turn to see him reach down and grab Scarlett. Raidon reaches for her, wanting to keep her as a shield, knowing he's safe from Thane while holding her.

"Nope, you antagonized the beast; you can deal with him," Rhen scolds.

"Because you're a chicken little brown noser," Raidon taunts.

"No, I just know better!" Rhen chuckles.

'*Uh, why are you in the rec room?*' Thane asks, and I peek out the door to see him walking down the corridor.

I turn my attention back to the mural and laugh when I see Leon trying to take Scarlett from Rhen. When he realizes he isn't going to get her, he hides behind Rhen. I lean on the door frame, and I hear Thane growl as he comes up behind me. His arms wrap around my waist, and his lips press against my neck.

"You're in so much trouble," he growls, nipping at my mark. "You all are—" His words cut off when he lifts his head and sees the wall.

CHAPTER FIFTY-NINE

On the wall is a giant mural of his mother. I spent days digging through the storage boxes in the Den, trying to find the perfect photos. The artist also painted our daughter in Hana's arms. Thane stands beside them, his arm draped over his mother's shoulder.

The background of the mural is the Omega refuge, which was built in Hana's honor. In each window, there's a symbol for every pendant from the bracelets our mothers shared. It took me ages to convince Elaine to hand over her bracelet. Zara asked for Sophia's and brought it with her when she visited last week. Each one of their challenges is displayed. It shows how much things have changed and how much still needs to be overcome.

Thane lets me go, making a whimpering noise I've never heard from him before. Rhen moves closer to him, and he instantly grabs Scarlett.

"That's your Nana," he whispers to her, kissing her cheek. "You all did this?" he asks, looking at our mates, but they point to me.

His lip quivers as he turns back to look at the painting. I wrap my arms around his waist, feeling his body tremble as he fights a war with his emotions.

"Your mother would be so proud of what you have done. I certainly am," I tell him. He nods, staring down at me.

"I never would have done it if it weren't for you, though. It would have always been an idea, not an accomplishment," he tells me. I nod, already knowing that. Thane started the plans for this place when I was locked in the basement. He started building the refuge while he still hated me. He had no intention of killing me or putting me into rotation, no matter what he threatened. He couldn't stand me, but he wasn't going to let me go either. Despite knowing that, it doesn't make this place any less meaningful.

"Thank you," he whispers, turning and wrapping his arm around my waist to tug me closer. He kisses my forehead as Rhen, Leon, and Raidon come over.

"So, does this mean I'm not getting spanked now?" Leon asks, and we all laugh.

ANOTHER MONTH LATER

We are being run off our feet. Thane is trying to hire extra staff to run the refuge, but with so many Omegas arriving in the city every day, we now have to look into alternative housing. We have a few exchange homes set up, with trusted female Alphas and Betas, and nearly every hotel is booked out. The council has also added extra security throughout the city.

Once word got out, our Omega population tripled within two months. Thane was supposed to go to the state council next month, but he's been fast-tracked to the Supernatural Parliament instead. Two other cities have also changed their laws, becoming safe havens for Omegas. Even places that haven't changed their laws yet are starting to shut down the facilities.

"Ready?" Zara asks. I put away my tablet and climb out of the car with her.

We've just come from our parents' gravesites. Thane is having their bodies exhumed and moved to the city. Last week he showed Zara and me their headstones. Mom and Dad no longer have to hide anymore, and they will soon be laid to rest under their true identities.

Zara stops, and I turn my attention to the huge building. I hate this place, hate it with a passion, but I need to do this. We scoured through every inch of this place for the last three days, keeping any evidence of the crimes committed within this facility for Thane to take to the Supernatural Parliament. Curtis was sneaky. He even had a black book filled with officials who helped cover his family's crimes.

Thane is talking to the project manager with Jake. My and Zara's other mates stayed back at the hotel, playing daddy daycare with all the kids so Zara and I can do this.

Looking up at the facility, I am relieved it is being demolished. Zara grabs my hand, and I stare down at them clasped together. Hers is shaking slightly, and I rub my thumb across it. Our mother's bracelet glistens in the sun on her wrist next to Hana's on mine.

After shutting down Tal's club and emptying their apartment, we found out Bree took Mom's bracelet from the crash. It was hidden inside the secret compartment of a jewelry box. After going through Bree's stuff, we learned how truly unhinged she was. Bree had intentionally set our car on fire after the accident and got Mrs. Yates to help cover it up. Since Mrs. Yates falsely reported her car stolen, we were able to get her charged with conspiracy and accessory-after-the-fact.

Turns out she is in love with Mr. Black and was willing to do anything to help Bree. She was also the one who covered up my and Zara's identities at the facility, but not out of guilt. She was worried Zara or I would take our mother's place. Her obsession with Mr. Black is shocking, and it all came out when she was arrested.

Thane and Jake come over to us. They hand us hardhats and safety glasses before leading us away from the site. We move back to the cars, which is a safe distance from the machinery about to tear this place apart. We can't erase the past, but we can erase the place that caused so much trauma for so many people. Today, that is what we do.

"Ready?" a voice says over the radio in Jake's hand. Jake looks at Zara and me, and we both nod.

"Knock her down," he calls back as Thane's arms wrap around my shoulders, his lips pressing to my cheek.

"3 … 2 … 1" he whispers as the huge digger brings its bucket down on the roof, caving it in. I lean back against him. It only takes an hour or two before the place is reduced to rubble.

"No one will ever set foot in that place again," Zara whispers.

"Or any place like it by the time I'm done tearing apart the Supernatural Parliament," Thane assures her, and Zara smiles.

I nudge Thane and he peers down at me. "I wanna go home," I tell him, and he nods.

"Come on, then. I don't particularly want to watch the cleanup," he tells me, and I agree. My feet and lower back are aching, yet I needed to do this. So did Zara. It is like we are finally burying the past and letting it go all in one.

CHAPTER SIXTY

A FEW DAYS LATER

I am two seconds from storming out of the living room as Rhen stands there waiting for something—anything—to happen, which never will.

"I give up. This is stupid, Thane." I motion to Rhen. My back is hurting, and I'm exhausted from pulling on some invisible force I apparently should have. I stare down at my bunny slippers and growl when Thane speaks.

"Again, you have an aura. You just need to figure out how to use it," Thane scolds me. We have been at this for days. Sure, I can resist his and anyone else's aura now, but using my non-existent one seems pointless.

"If I had an aura or command, it would work by now. Your serum makes me immune to you. It doesn't make me an Alpha, Thane. I'm still an Omega," I retort. I am tired, and I want to go to bed. We have been at this for hours.

"Try Leon again," Thane says, and I roll my eyes.

"Fine, just hurry up. I want to go to bed," I tell Leon, waving him forward as Rhen sits.

Leon gets up from the lounge. Thane has been trying to get me to magically pull an aura out of my ass every day since we got home; trying to teach me, an Omega, to use a command. Like that'll ever happen.

Sighing, Leon steps up to play guinea pig. Closing my eyes, I focus on forcing my non-existent energy out and onto him. I am beginning to wonder if they are just mocking me at this point because Thane seems to have set an impossible task.

I'm Omega. I can't command a damn butterfly! Peeking one eye open, I groan, and Leon jumps.

"Wait, that was it? You already tried?" Leon asks. I shake my head.

"Wow, congrats, you're stronger than an Omega," I say dryly. Anyone would think he actually expects something to happen. "See, it's pointless."

"It's not pointless. You're not even trying," Thane growls, standing.

"That's because I don't know what I'm doing. How am I supposed to feel my aura, energy, or whatever, when I don't know what I'm feeling for?" I deadpan. Good thing he's good-looking because, sometimes, I swear he lacks vital brain cells—the ones that make him remember I am an Omega.

Thane moves across the room, and I see Raidon yawn, also bored with watching me struggle. Thane grips my shoulders, pulling me in front of him and turning me to face Leon.

"You have been marked by all of us, and you have my serum in your system. You can command him."

I shake my head. "Clearly I can't, or he would be on his knees for me," I snap.

"Is that an option?" Leon purrs, wiggling his eyebrows and licking his lips at me.

A smile sillily at his offer. "By all means." I motion to the floor, but Thane growls. I groan, leaning back against him. "Fine, show me again." This is ridiculous and a waste of everyone's time.

"You just love the Calling," Rhen snickers, and I smirk. Yep, any of them can lull me into blissful relaxation any day and I'll never complain.

"Are you going to focus this time? Last time, all you did was dry hump my leg, and wrap your lips around my cock," Thane questions, and I shrug.

"I can do it. I don't mind using my Calling," Raidon volunteers, raising his hand. He drops his arm when Thane glares at him. I like Raidon's and Leon's idea better than standing here.

Thane presses his chest to my back. His Calling slips out and I melt into him. His hands fall on my hips to steady me, his voice in my ear. "Now look for that psychedelic feeling, the vibration, tug on it," he tells me, but I don't want to. I want to stay here. "Low, focus. The energy you feel, the tingling in your limbs, is me tampering with your essence. Now push against me. Try to resist it," Thane says, speaking nonsense.

Who would want to be pulled from this state? He's barely touching me, and my panties are already ruined. Instinctively, I try to turn, gripping the front of his boxers. Thane groans, grabbing my hand and turning me back around.

"I still stand by what I said. I'm happy and willing to volunteer. If she wants to grope me, I won't complain," Raidon purrs. His voice sounds distant as I become drunk on Thane's aura.

My hand grabs his cock behind me. "Low! You can have it later, now focus!" Thane snaps, yet my hands have a mind of their own. Thane sighs, pinning my arms at my sides. "Low?"

"Yes?" I all but moan, and he groans in frustration.

"Focus!"

"Hmm, focusing, focusing," I mumble, wishing he had a dial so I can turn it up a little more.

Thane jams his fingers in my ribs, making me shriek and jump. "Focus. Push on the Calling. Try to shove it back at me," he tells me.

I sigh but do as he asks. Only, when I do, I nearly collapse because it's like I walked into it, making it ten times stronger. My face tingles, and my body buzzes as euphoria washes over me. I hear Rhen chuckle as Thane's arms wrap around me to hold me upright and steady.

"Now, that low-frequency buzz making your skin tingle when

you push back against me is your aura, your command," Thane whispers, kissing the side of my face. He drops his Calling, and it's like a bucket of water is tossed on me. I pout, wanting it back.

"I don't see the point of this. It's not like I can really do much with a command, besides maybe order another Omega," I admit. I will never be able to make anyone submit, so it makes little sense as to why he has me practicing this, anyway.

"Because it's a deterrent. Besides, if, for some reason, you have to use it, it may buy you enough time for one of us to get to you," Thane explains. "Plus, it makes your resistance to Alphas even stronger."

"But I'm already resistant to command now," I whine.

"Yes, but what if several command you all at once? Or all of us do? Practicing with your aura, even a weak one, will strengthen the side of you that obeys. Make you more resistant."

I roll my eyes. It seems like a waste of time to me. It's not like I go anywhere without them, unless it's the refuge, and there I have Leo with me.

Leon stands back up, stepping in front of me. Closing my eyes, I focus on the tingling sensation I felt when Thane used his Calling on me. Moments pass before I start to feel my skin buzz.

"Good girl. Now, hold on to it," Thane tells me, so I know I latched onto the right thing. "Now try to project it. Think of Leon and try to push on his aura with it."

I do as he says, feeling the spark of touching Leon's aura as it easily fights mine.

A shudder runs through my body, some deep-rooted instinct

telling me to back away, a nagging feeling telling me I am taking on someone stronger, dangerous. Leon's aura instantly flares up, pushing back, and he curses, making me drop mine.

"Sorry, I didn't mean to do that," Leon murmurs.

"It's fine," I tell him.

"Okay, an aura is one thing, but you need to put the command behind it. Without a command, it's just pressure," Thane explains.

I look over my shoulder as Thane steps away from me. "Leon, sit down. I can ignore mine. I'll try with her," Thane says.

"I can only just barely touch Leon, and you want me to touch yours?" I say, shaking my head.

"If you can hold it, it will strengthen you. Then, maybe you'll see that you have a command."

Thane stands in front of me and my shoulders slump. This aura and command thing exert so much energy for doing absolutely nothing.

"Close your eyes," Thane tells me, and I do. I find my aura and project it out. I feel it touch Thane's and instantly retreat when I feel him tug on it, like he's calling it out. It makes me gasp.

"Hold it. I'm not resisting you, Low. Keep pushing," Thane urges and so does his aura.

"Now try to command me."

My brows pinch, and I try to do as he asks. It's like trying to catch air as I push my will forward. As soon as I tell him to submit, it's like someone flicks a switch and my Omega side forces its way through, telling me to submit to the bigger predator.

Thane's hands grip my arms and sparks rush across my skin. I open my eyes and exhale in a huff.

"See, after a while, you'll get used to it. You can resist our commands. You just need to practice resisting and projecting the auras," Thane says.

"But aren't they the same thing?" I ask him, finding all this very confusing.

"No, an aura is energy. It's similar to physical energy in a sense, a battle of willpower. A command is an order. It's not just touching them with your energy, it's commanding theirs," Thane tries to explain.

"Come on, we can go to bed. We'll try again tomorrow," he tells me. Rhen and Raidon both jump up off the couch, followed by Leon. Walking up the stairs, I hear Scarlett cry out.

Leon rushes past us all in a blur to settle her and I stop on the steps.

"I'll go make a bottle," Thane says, heading back toward the kitchen before I can.

I finish climbing the stairs and move to the nursery to check on her. I find Leon sitting in the rocking chair with her. Thane wanders in a few seconds later with her bottle and takes her from him.

"Get to bed. I'll feed her," Thane tells a yawning Leon. He nods, and I step aside as he moves toward me. I watch Thane give her the bottle, his index finger stroking her little nose as he purrs, rocking back and forth.

Slipping the door shut, I wander to our room and crawl into bed, face-planting into the pillow. Raidon climbs in beside me and Rhen beside him. Leon stumbles over, falling on my other side when Raidon slips his arm beneath my head. I roll, pressing my ear to his chest, getting comfortable.

When nothing happens, I smack his chest, and he chuckles.

"You know, you are quite demanding and bossy for someone so small," Raidon purrs at me.

Ignoring his comment, I smack his chest again, wanting to be lulled into blissful sleep. Seconds later, his Calling slips out, and a sigh escapes my lips. I snuggle closer to him with Leon's arm draped over my waist.

Yet before I manage to fall asleep, Raidon does, making me growl as his Calling slips away. I'm about to crawl over to see if Rhen is awake, just as Thane comes in, climbing in next to Leon.

I climb over Leon, making him grunt when my knee squashes his ribs. He rolls into me, causing me to face-plant onto Thane before he's even lying down. He lets out a grunt at the impact, and he nudges Leon to move over. He reluctantly rolls into Raidon, and Thane lays down, tugging me closer.

Thane tugs the blankets up and I tap his chest. "So impatient," he mutters as I starfish on him. "I better not wake up covered in drool again," he mumbles.

"No promises!" I tell him, drumming my fingers on his chest. His Calling slips out, and I melt against him. "Maybe you do have a dial or button?" I mumble.

"Huh?"

I shake my head and yawn before falling into darkness, listening to the thrum of his Calling.

CHAPTER SIXTY-TWO

Thane

My eyes open, and I blink up at the ceiling, not sure what woke me. I close them, trying to go back to sleep. I kick the blanket off, the heat of Harlow's body making me sweat, when I suddenly feel her teeth and tongue drag down my chest.

Leon groans beside me, rolling into me. I slowly come to my senses as Harlow moves down my body. She bites my hip, and I lift my head, trying to figure out what she's doing when her lips wrap around my cock.

"Fuck!" I groan when her scent finally hits my nose.

My pupils dilate, and my vision clears. Her tongue slides up my shaft as she devours my cock. My fingers tangle in her hair, and her nails scrape down my thighs, carving me to pieces as my cock hits the back of her throat.

"Harlow!" I groan. I try to pull her back up my body, but she is possessed by instinct, driven by her senses as she takes what she wants.

My hands tighten in her hair as I pull her head up. She has a certain innocence, especially when she looks at me with her doe-eyes. However, I find as I pull her head back, she is anything but. No, now she is lust and sin, threatening to suck the soul out of me via my cock.

Glowing eyes peer back at me in the darkness and she purrs. Her claws slip from her fingertips and into my thigh, refusing to let go. She is quite content sucking on my cock for now, so I let her.

I awkwardly twist my body without jostling her, reaching for the lamp to flick it on. Raidon and Rhen are stirring, waking to her heat. Leon sits up abruptly, his eyes blood red. His hunger is the first to take over. Bloodlust and a deep need to feed on her zap through the bond.

Leon reaches for her, half out of it, and my hand grips his wrist, startling him to his senses. He shakes his head, palming his face as he recognizes he was about to attack her.

I let him go, and he exhales and swallows.

"How long has she been like this?" he manages to choke out. His blood-red eyes are now staring intently at my neck.

"Not long. She just woke me up," I admit, offering him my neck. Leon wastes no time sinking his fangs into me. The bed dips, and I know either Rhen or Raidon are now awake, finally responding to her heat.

Her lips leave my cock with a pop, and she crawls up my body. She straddles my hips, her fingers gripping my cock before sinking down on me. A growl escapes me as pain flares up my shaft. The tip of my cock hits a wall, breaking through it. I hiss, wondering what she did. All I can think is, too tight, but she pays me no mind and just takes what she craves.

I want to take her. To devour her. I want to slam my cock inside her and tell her she's mine, but she has other plans. Her strangulation hold on my cock makes me hiss, but she is too far gone. Pain flits through the bond from her, but she is crazed with heat. The pain only enhances her pleasure, and I know something is wrong.

"Slow down, Low." I curse as she rocks her hips. Leon moans, pulling his teeth from my neck, and I can finally see her. It doesn't take long to realize why Leon stopped when I see Harlow's lips wrapped around his cock as she leans across me to take him in her mouth.

She gags on him, taking him to the hilt. Through the bond, I can tell her heat is enhanced by my serum, which now runs through her veins. Everything feels different to her now. She struggled a fair bit the first week, her senses stronger. She is stronger, faster, so I know Leon has to stop her before she passes out.

Alpha instinct is vastly different from Omega, and she's acting like an Alpha in rut: incapable of stopping, even if she wanted to. Omegas are the same in heat. Their baser instincts take over, and now she is not only fighting her Omega instinct, but the impulses I fight on the daily. It intensifies her heat, making it ten times worse.

Tears slip down her cheeks, and her heart races from the lack of air. Leon grips her face, trying to push her away. She growls at him, and Rhen is quick to grip her hair, tugging her head back. She gasps for air, her chest rising and falling heavily as he forces her to breathe.

However, breathing doesn't seem to be a priority for her right now, as she fights him. Rhen responds by kissing her on the lips. It's tender at first, meant to lure her in, but then he quickly ups the tempo, devouring her. His tongue darts out, slithering between her lips. She makes a noise, and I groan as she rolls her hips against me. Pain slivers up my shaft again. I'm somewhat stuck after she impaled herself on my cock without care.

Rhen lets her go, and her hands fall to my chest. Her lips part, and before I know it, my tongue is inside her mouth, swirling with hers. She flinches, tensing up completely before shuddering. My desire is just as strong as her need. She can't keep up with my hunger, and I feel like I am fighting with her tongue. Tasting her, I smirk. Her flavor is like dopamine to me.

I am buried inside her. She envelops my entire cock. I can feel her slick juices around me, and it causes me to grunt as she lifts her hips, slamming back down on me.

"More," she gasps into my mouth, her skin heating beneath my fingers. I feel the bed dip between my legs as Raidon moves behind her.

His entire body trembles as her pheromones fill the air, the sweetest drug. He holds himself back, trying not to hurt her. She is causing herself enough damage with the way she's savagely fucking me. I try to stop her from pulling up again, and his hands slide over mine on her hips. I move my hands to keep her flush against me.

Leon is entertaining Rhen, his lips wrapped around his cock as

Rhen fucks his mouth. Harlow's claws slice through the sheets as she tries to push back against Raidon when I feel his cock nudge against her entrance. She whines, wanting more, but I keep my arms locked around her so she doesn't impale herself back on him.

Harlow groans when I feel his cock slide in against mine, and so does Raidon, her inner walls squeezing us in a vice. Harlow pushes back against him, and Raidon grips her hips, holding her still.

His eyes move to mine, feeling my knot swell already. We've barely started, which is why I've been trying to slow her down. She is going to tear herself apart. I know my serum enhances everything, but I didn't realize how much worse it would make her heat.

"Careful, Raidon. If she pulls off me, I'm gonna hurt her," I tell him. I'm unable to move, partially locked inside her tight confines. I try to ignore her slick inner walls trying to milk me.

"What's wrong?" Rhen asks, his voice husky with lust. Leon sits up, looking where I have her pinned to me. They look at Raidon, who hesitantly moves, trying to give her what she craves without me breaking her.

He builds up a rhythm. Faster, harder. Harder, yet barely pulling out of her, so she rocks between us both. Harlow shudders, and I curse, feeling Raidon struggle with her heat as pain strangles me.

She is sending us into a rut, her pheromones growing potent. "More, don't stop," she whines, but I can smell her blood along with her arousal. Raidon stills. His eyes go to mine, worry flitting across his face as she fights against me, wanting to ride me.

Having no choice, I flood her with my Calling and knock her out. The moment she goes limp, Raidon pulls out of her. His fingers delve back in as he tries to dislodge me from her.

"Please tell me she didn't knot me," I say as Rhen's Calling slips out, keeping her sedated. Worry bleeds through the bond when they finally realize something is wrong.

"Yep, she locked you behind her pubic bone," Raidon tells me.

"Just do it," I say. I grit my teeth, feeling him force his fingers deeper. She wakes when my Calling slips away, but Raidon and Leon flood her, along with Rhen. My knot isn't full, but she slammed down too hard on me the wrong way, forcing my knot. I feel immense relief when Raidon unlocks me, and I slip from her.

"She tore a little, but she's okay," Raidon tells me. I exhale, tracing my fingers up and down her spine. Rhen moves her hair from her face, and her scent grows stronger. "Grab the ties. I won't have her hurting herself," I tell them, knowing she is already fighting the sedation.

CHAPTER SIXTY-THREE

All four of them grab hold of one of my limbs. They pin me to the bed as my eyes flutter open. Heat like wildfire crawls through my blood, and my whole body aches.

I am high on their scents as I breathe them in. Their presence alone is my addiction. There is no one I feel so at ease with as with them—like the world no longer matters, and we are living in our own plane of existence together.

Every inch of me feels overstimulated because they are everywhere. It's like my body belongs to them, and there is nothing I crave more than that.

"Hey, we're right here," Thane whispers, his lips crashing down on mine. I try to move my hands but find them tied to the headboard.

Rhen's hands slide up my thighs, and he spreads my pussy lips open. I hear a loud buzzing noise infiltrate my ears and I try to figure out what it could be. My curiosity is quickly sated as I feel it buzz straight through me. The device is vibrating against my clit, immediately pulling a moan from my lips. My eyes shoot wide open, and my hips lift to chase the vibration. I moan loudly as the heat ravages me.

When I peer down, I see Raidon and Leon each straddling

one of my legs and leaning over me. I feel their hard cocks against my thighs, making me squirm as their mouths move to my hips. They start to lick upward, perfectly in sync, before they arrive at my breasts. I'm lost to the sensations. They needily and readily stimulate me even more, drawing loud moans from my lips. The sensation is unbelievable, unlike anything I've ever felt before.

The vibrator is still buzzing away at my clit, covering my skin in millions of goosebumps. I am unable to stop myself from moaning, and my noises travel in all directions. I tilt my head to look up at Thane, and he leans down, capturing my lips. I desperately want to touch him, but my hands catch on the soft restraints holding me to the bed.

My eyes flutter shut again. I'm overstimulated. It's difficult to focus past what is happening between my legs. Raidon and Leon's hot mouths are all over my body, licking and nipping, soothing the heat that won't ease off. I'm gasping and quivering, the vibrator sending shocks through me that make my whole body spasm, but I want nothing more than just their touch.

I whimper for it, and they seem to understand. Leon and Raidon sit up and grip the backs of my knees, pulling them up and spreading me wide for Rhen's hungry gaze. Rhen pulls the vibrator away, tossing it to the side. Then, their hands find me. Raidon's fingers move to my entrance, playing with the soft, wet flesh, teasing my slit before sliding his fingers inside me. Leon's press where the vibrator was just moments before, toying with my clit in circular motions. It drives me wild, making me tingle all over as Thane's lips latch onto my nipple.

Raidon curls his fingers inside me and begins to pick up a steady rhythm. Leon does the same to my clit, his rhythm matching Raidon's until I am practically screaming. My vision is hazy. The world around us has disappeared.

My body is now sputtering, shaking, and vibrating. Pleasure courses through my bloodstream and travels throughout my body, setting every inch of me on fire.

Rhen leans down, placing his hands by my shoulders and capturing my lips. His mouth leaves mine and starts kissing down my body. I shiver, focusing on every inch of me that he tastes. He is tender, yet quick and eager, kissing a trail down my body until he is suddenly between my legs.

He kisses my mound, soft and fluttery, and then he presses his tongue to the tender flesh between my legs. He uses his fingers to spread my lips and locate my clit. He licks it, drawing loud moans from my lips.

I look to my left and see Thane. My eyes focus on his cock, and I moan as I watch droplets of pre-cum start to form and spread. I stick my tongue out, wanting nothing more than to taste him. I don't need him to thrust into my mouth, but he does it, anyway. Gently holding the back of my head, Thane helps me move up and down his shaft, tasting every inch of him.

I slowly become aware of what's going on between my legs. Pleasure spreads like wildfire, setting my body ablaze. Rhen is very skilled at what he's doing, circling his tongue against my clit. Raidon's fingers enter me and spread me open, causing my pussy to pulsate against Rhen's mouth. His breath hits my flesh, feeling like heaven. I cry out as my orgasm ripples through me, only to end too quickly.

"Thane," I all but scream around his cock, needing more, needing their knots. I want to claw them apart and feast on them as each passing second gets even hotter. Hunger for them swallows me whole. I hear fabric tearing as my claws slash through the restraints. My hand comes down on Rhen's head, and my fingers tangle in his hair.

Raidon's fingers slip from me, and my legs are shoved open wider as Rhen's lips crash against mine before I can pounce on one of them. The bed dips as they move. Rhen rolls, tugging me on top of him. Never have I felt so out of control, my senses on fire.

I feel a hand on my ass. A firm grip squeezes me. Thane's palm is somewhat raw, squeezing and caressing my skin. As Leon and Raidon palm my breasts, Leon's fangs graze my shoulder. Thane squeezes me, both hands now on my butt cheeks. He begins to massage them in his grip, slapping his hand flat against me.

CHAPTER SIXTY-FOUR

I flinch, but at the same time, I roll my hips against Rhen beneath me. His cock slides through my slick when I feel Thane lift my hips. Rhen's hand slips between our heated bodies as he positions himself at my entrance. I try to sink down on him, but Thane's hands tighten, preventing it and forcing me to go down on him slowly.

"Slow, Harlow. Let us," Thane says, pressing his lips to my shoulder. His Calling seeps out behind me, but the frequency is low, just lending me enough to slow the heat trying to destroy me.

Raidon grabs hold of my jaw. He tilts my head up a little and brings his thumb to my mouth, forcing my lips to part. He pushes his thumb in deeper. He doesn't have to say anything for me to know that he wants me to suck on it. So, I do.

I moan when I feel the tip of Thane's cock against my entrance. It feels so intrusive and so demanding. My body flutters, and my muscles stretch and start to ache. I feel weak in my knees and weak in my arms, which makes it hard to focus on what's going on around me.

Raidon kneels beside me, and my tongue darts out as his scent hits my nostrils. His hands slide into my hair, holding it back as he lowers my face toward his cock. My lips latch around the tip of him, and my tongue traces the veins hungrily.

Time stops for a moment. Then, all at once, they thrust their hips forward. Raidon's cock in my mouth and Thane and Rhen in my pussy, in one violent thrust. All my senses are overwhelmed. My heart beats faster, and my stomach churns. It feels like electricity. There is absolutely nothing I want more than to just give in and lose myself to this. And I do.

What they're doing seems rehearsed. They pull out, still in sync, and then begin to thrust back in again. Raidon's cock slides over my tongue, and I taste it while my pussy squeezes them. My hands skim the mattress, searching for Leon.

Thane grabs ahold of my hips from behind me, while Raidon, in front of me, grabs ahold of my hair. He tugs it to keep me at the right angle. I make a noise, choked up, but so fucking horny at the same time. My sounds are muffled, though, by the cock in my mouth. The cocks inside my pussy are bringing me so much pleasure that my mind is starting to reel.

They pick up speed. It's a similar rhythm, but their arousal has now taken the upper hand, and they go slightly out of sync. They are using my body for their own pleasure now, but I can tell they still worry about hurting me by the controlled way they thrust into me.

Their thrusts are firm and strong, but not too fast. I feel them filling me, every inch of them, which is exactly how I like it. I press my tongue against the cock in my mouth as Raidon's grip tightens in my hair, and his cock twitches in my mouth.

"Fuck!" he curses as long jets of his seed coat my tongue. Some part of me hoped it would help ease my heat, but it has the opposite effect. Instead, it acts like an aphrodisiac as I swallow it down.

Raidon's cock leaves my lips with a pop. I reach for him, but he grips my chin, his lips brushing mine softly. He pulls away when I feel new hands in my hair. Sparks rush along my scalp, and Raidon lets me go before I feel Leon's cock press to my lips, making me groan. My lips part, taking him in.

Thane's pelvis slaps against my ass, and I feel him throbbing inside me, sliding in and out. The tip of his cock repeatedly punches my most pleasurable spot over and over again, driving me crazy.

I am gasping, my skin is tingling, and my heart is beating so fast I can feel myself getting dizzy. I moan again, creating a vibrating sensation around Leon's cock inside my mouth. He seems to like it because a moan escapes his lips. My ears pick up on it, and I gasp. His moan is followed by a grunt as he thrusts into my mouth.

Thane's cock, buried deep inside me, pulls out and slams back in. Rhen and Thane are taking me in the most delicious way imaginable. I moan louder now, whimpering out with pleasure, and I nudge back against Thane. His grip on my hips tightens, forcing me to slow.

"Good girl," Thane purrs. His voice sounds hoarse and sexy. His hands pull my cheeks apart, so he can watch himself slide in and out of me. Rhen hums, and they pick up their pace again.

The room smells of sex. I no longer know where I am. It's like I've been lifted out of my body and brought to heaven, just to experience the most intense bliss I have ever felt.

Thane angles himself just right, and he starts to repeatedly slam into my g-spot. I am wailing with a cock halfway down my throat. I'm so close I can barely think, when I feel Rhen's knot expand. Thane groans as his knot also expands. Rhen's hand slips between us, not allowing his knot to enter, making me whine.

I feel like I'm floating on a cloud, transported to a plane of utter bliss. I feel them everywhere, and it's the best thing in existence. They apparently feel the same, because Rhen is suddenly pulsing inside me. Their thrusts slow a little, and their moans grow louder, filling the entire room.

I clench the sheets while they continue to pump in and out of me. I feel myself slipping over the edge as Rhen's cock coats my insides with his cum, warmth filling me. My whole body sputters, and I moan so loudly that I cause vibrations against both Leon's cock in my mouth and Thane's cock in my pussy.

They moan simultaneously at that, whimpering and groaning as they shiver. I imagine the looks on their faces, filled with arousal and pleasure. They grunt, and Rhen quickly slips out of me—with perhaps only a few seconds to spare before Thane's knot forces its way inside me. He starts to come. There's an explosion in my mouth and in my pussy. The sensation is unbelievable as I feel his knot lock in place. I swallow and quiver as the saltiness of Leon's cum coats my tongue.

After their orgasms are ridden out and swallowed down, Thane yanks my body back against his and lies beside me. The pleasure seems to last an eternity. Even when they move off of me, it's like the pleasure is now ingrained in my body.

Thane moves us to our sides and spoons me, his arms wrapping around my front. He kisses my neck while Rhen, now in front of me, starts to kiss my lips, tasting Leon's remnants inside my mouth.

My skin cools rapidly, making me shiver as the heat dies down. My body aches as my fingers run down Rhen's chest. He chuckles, letting his Calling slip out. I feel the bed move as Raidon leans down and kisses my temple. "Sleep, love."

"Thane?" I murmur and hear his Calling answer me before I ask him. I slip into the darkness.

My entire body aches as I wake up. Every part of me hurts as arms slip beneath my body, lifting me. I don't want to get up yet. I'm quite content to remain in bed all day, but that isn't an option. I hear water running before I'm submerged, making me hiss at the sudden sting.

"There's a council meeting today. Attending is part of the agreement, babe. We can't miss it, or I would have let you sleep," Rhen tells me as he sits with me in the bath.

"Where's Thane?" I mumble, wetting my face and trying to wake up.

"Making you something to eat. Raidon is feeding Scarlett, and Leon went out to get more formula and diapers," Rhen tells me. I nod my head, leaning back against him.

"My heat felt different this time," I mumble.

"Yes, we know. Thane thinks his serum enhances it."

I figured as much because, usually, the pain is excruciating. However, this felt different, more like a craving. There was more desire than pain, though that was there still. It's just that instinct was overriding the crippling agony that usually writhes through Omegas.

"Tip your head back," Rhen demands as I reach for the loofah. I scoot forward between his legs and tip my head back so he can wet my hair. His fingers massage my scalp as he lathers my head, and I begin to wash my body, knowing that if he woke me it means we need to leave for the meeting soon, which in turn, means I slept all day.

CHAPTER SIXTY-FIVE

THREE DAYS LATER

The city is holding a fundraiser and its first meet-and-greet. Omegas may not need Alphas the same way they need us, but they are essential when we go into heat. Omegas could live happily enough on suppressants, but it isn't a perfect solution. Even I know that.

We've gone over the details to ensure no Omegas are coerced or commanded at these functions. Thane wants to ensure that, ultimately, Omegas have a choice. The city is adjusting so well to the changes that many other cities are now doing the same thing.

Even so, we have a long way to go, but I have no doubt Thane will see it through. I know Thane feels like he is taking over where his mother left off, finishing her purpose, which has now become his. Ours. Thane has taken on the challenge, and I know he won't stop fighting until he succeeds. Especially now that he has even more reason to fight: Scarlett.

There was a huge outcry after Thane publicly revealed what truly goes on in the sanctuaries. The number of people outraged by the treatment of Omegas is surprising. Even more surprising—it is the female Alphas.

Alphas, the very people we were sold off to.

None were willing to step forward to fight for Omegas before Thane. They had no reason to do so. But now that they've heard our stories, they are quick to step up and say no, enough. They are stepping forward and fighting alongside him. This is not a battle he will fight alone.

The hardest part will be fighting the corruption within the government. In hindsight, there isn't much difference between the black market and what was legal. It is still trafficking, and most Omegas in the sanctuaries aren't willing participants.

One thing has also become apparent: Omegas aren't as rare as we thought. Many, like my mother, decided to take their chances on the run, refusing to bow down to the corrupt system and Alpha ownership. We also learned many Alphas have been keeping their children a secret, fearing they'd end up in the sanctuaries. So they kept their Omega daughters and sons out of public view.

"Come on," Thane says, offering me his hand. I groan, not wanting to move from my spot on the floor. I'm helping design flyers for the meet-and-greets in the coming weeks.

"No, come on. You promised we could try again," he tells me. I grab his hand, letting him pull me to my feet. He grabs the front of my robe, which falls open when I stand. It is starting to get cooler at night, so I've been wearing more layers.

I love the colder nights. Nothing beats the crackling sound of wood on a fire. Although we will have to get baby gates once Scarlett starts crawling. She loves watching the flames flicker from her rocker. It makes me worry she will want to crawl into the giant fireplace. Raidon says he will put them up when we need them.

Rhen sets his newspaper aside and Leon turns the TV off.

"Just like yesterday. You almost had it," Thane assures me, and he is right. I managed to hold him under my aura, even though it didn't really have much effect on him. He said it felt unnatural, but he definitely felt it. So now we just have to perfect it. Thane wants to ensure I can't be commanded by anyone.

One-on-one, I can't be commanded by an Alpha. I thought I was completely immune until Thane got Rhen to command me alongside him, proving me wrong. It's a loophole to the serum. Another one being that when I use my aura, they have the ability to pull on and manipulate it.

So, Thane says I need to learn how to control it. He doesn't want me to be vulnerable to anyone, not even them, which I think is silly. I trust them with my life. I think this is more about him trying to soothe his guilt over the past, despite my forgiving him. He also believes figuring out how to use it will be a deterrent if I can hold it.

Using my aura will throw people off and hopefully give me enough time to escape. Since Omegas normally can't use an aura or command, it will make an attacker waiver and second guess what I am, as long as my pheromones don't get in the way.

It reinforces the need to practice. Raidon drags the coffee table out of the way, and Thane pulls me to the center of the room. "Okay, just like yesterday," he tells me, rubbing my arms.

Closing my eyes, I try to pull on my aura, searching for it. My heat the other day seemed to do the trick, though, because since then I have been more aware of the light buzzing on my skin, the essence behind it.

"Good, Low. Now push on mine," Thane tells me. I focus on projecting it, trying to force it over him. His aura makes mine buzz as it draws mine out further.

"Now, try to get me to submit," he says, and I almost roll my eyes at him. That will not work. Maybe, by some miracle, I can make him sit, but submit? Not a chance. His Alpha aura won't allow for that. It would be like challenging him.

"I won't be able to hold it," I murmur, trying not to lose focus as I feel the edge flicker, wanting to retreat.

"Just try it. No harm in trying," Thane says and I sigh. My body shakes as I try to hold it over him. A bead of sweat runs down my back as my aura pushes against his. I might as well be pushing against a brick wall; his aura is impenetrable. Thane isn't a normal Alpha, but an Alpha-of-Alphas.

Gritting my teeth, I try to push on it, feeling it flex as it pushes against his free will. "I can't," I force out.

"Hold it, Low. You can do this," Thane says softly. His fingers grip mine firmly, tugging me closer. "Focus. Hold it. I can feel it," he assures me.

"Yeah, but as soon as I try to command you, it will drop," I tell him. I squeeze my eyes shut tighter, as if that will actually add more strength to it and not give me a headache.

"Try. Just try it once, and we'll call it a night," he tells me.

I sigh, my entire body heating as I try to focus. I can hear Scarlett babbling happily in her rocker, hear the soft music it plays as it rocks from side to side. Using my aura, my senses enhance every little thing.

Even his touch feels stronger, the sparks rushing across my hands and up my arms. I can hear the beating of his heart, mine, and our mates. Yet Thane's thumps faster than normal, beating rapidly and loudly.

"Try, Low. I need you to at least try," Thane murmurs.

His aura won't allow it, yet I know he won't let me stop until I at least try, so I sigh and speak the word. "Submit!" I tell him.

I wait for the pain to start, as it often does when playing with his aura or trying to command them. It is unnatural for both them and me, yet as I say it, I feel his aura drop slightly. I try to jerk my hands from his, but he just tightens his grip.

"Hold it," he tells me, but I shake my head. "Hold it, baby," Thane whispers, and I open my eyes to find him kneeling before me.

"Stop it," I grit out, knowing the only way this is even possible is if he's allowing it. My aura is no match for him.

"I need you to hold it," he says.

I shake my head, tears brimming in my eyes. I can feel him struggling with his own instincts to not fight me. He is surrendering to mine or at least trying to.

"Say it," Rhen says, and my eyes flick to him. My hands are clammy, and I'm sweating. My silk nightgown sticks to my skin. I glance down, and it's like Thane is fighting a war.

"I don't need you to do this," I whisper to Thane.

"No, but I need you to," he tells me. "I don't want you to be my mate. I want you to be my Luna," he says, and I suck in a breath.

"Now, make me submit." He squeezes my fingers, and I swallow, knowing what he's giving me. If I make him submit, he'll no longer be my Alpha. We will be truly equal. His command will never work on me, and I will be able to control his Calling. Even if all of them command me or use their Calling on me, it will have no effect unless I allow it.

My voice trembles as I fight not to drop my nearly nonexistent aura. "Submit," I stammer, pushing against him, and I feel all resistance drop from him.

I can tell it is causing him pain. I feel his agony through the bond as he fights his own aura, refusing to let it resist mine before he bares his neck to me. This is what Charles meant when he said this is something almost impossible for an Alpha to do.

It goes against everything that is ingrained in their very being. It's why Alphas usually fight to the death. They'd rather die fighting than submit and survive. And yet, Thane does it, and I feel my own aura strengthen as he submits, giving me control over him and our mates.

Tears drip down my chin at what he's giving me, what he makes me do. My aura drops the moment he submits, and my legs give out from under me. Thane's arms catch me before I hit the ground and pull me close.

"I love you," he whispers. His entire body is covered in sweat. His skin sticks to mine, which is just as sweaty.

"I love you, too," I murmur.

Hands tug at my hair, pulling my head back. Raidon leans down, brushing his lips against mine, while Thane buries his face in my chest.

"Now you're our Alpha," Raidon mumbles against my lips. Pulling back, I see Rhen gripping Thane's shoulders, whispering something to him and trying to calm him. His entire body shakes as he clutches me. Thane lifts his head, and I see tears etched into his skin. He peers up at Rhen, who smiles softly at him, leans down, and kisses him.

"Thank you," Rhen murmurs, making me wonder if this is for them, too. Thane isn't just making me his equal but giving me power over them. I know he wouldn't have done that without telling them first.

Leaning forward, Thane looks up at me. His lips tug at the corners as he kisses me, his tongue tangling with mine as he stands from his kneeling position. I wrap my legs around his waist as he straightens, and his hands fall to my ass, squeezing it.

"Yours," he whispers.

"Mine," I say, smiling against his lips. "Hmm, that means I dominate you now," I tell him with a laugh.

"Except in the bedroom," he says, chuckling.

"I can live with that," I tell him.

"And the kitchen. Don't let her have that either," Leon chimes in. I shoot him a glare over Thane's shoulder.

"Yes, I definitely call rank in my kitchen," Thane quickly says.

"My cooking is not that bad," I whine.

"It could be better," Raidon mumbles, and my eyes narrow at him. I look at Rhen.

"I'd still eat it," he says, and they all stop to glare at him. He shrugs.

"See, and you reckon you're not the brown noser!" Raidon exclaims. "Even she knows her cooking is sh—" I raise an eyebrow at Raidon when he motions toward me. "Edible," he finishes. "If you like charcoal," he adds with a laugh.

"For Scarlett's safety, I think it's better if I cook," Thane says, defending their remarks on my lack of cooking skills. "But I'll teach you," he tells me, pressing his lips to my cheek as he climbs the stairs.

Leon retrieves Scarlett, who wants out of her chair, her legs kicking furiously.

CHAPTER SIXTY-SIX

FOUR WEEKS LATER

"You're pregnant," Raidon tells me as I heave my guts up, his hands tangling in my hair.

"Scarlett is barely four months old," I retort.

"You went into heat, we fucked you, so now, you're knocked up," Raidon chuckles.

"That's not a guarantee!"

"Isn't it?" he laughs.

"We can't have another baby right now. They'll be the same age! Scar—" I heave, upturning my stomach again, my hands clutching the toilet bowl.

"Only for a few months," he tells me, unfazed by my vomit, unlike Rhen. I threw up in front of him the other day, and he, in turn, threw up in the bathtub. His retching made mine worse, and we turned into a synchronized dance, both of us unable to stop until we had nothing left. Leon came in afterward to find us laying on the cold tiles, feeling like death. Then Thane got stuck cleaning up the mess we made.

I shake my head, hoping he's wrong. "Please don't be pregnant.

Please be a stomach bug," I whine. I don't want to be sick every day. Scarlett didn't make me this sick. Plus, we have short pregnancies, lasting just sixteen weeks, and Scarlett is only just starting to crawl.

Hearing footsteps, Raidon tugs slightly on my hair and I look over my shoulder. "Rhen, don't you come in here. I'm not carrying your ass out," Raidon calls.

"Again?" Rhen asks through the closed door.

"Yep, for the past twenty minutes."

"She's pregnant!"

"I am not!" I retort, and Raidon laughs.

"You are, and to prove it, Thane should be here any minute with a pregnancy test."

I roll my eyes at him before finally making it to my feet. I rinse my mouth and brush my teeth. But before I can leave, Thane walks in with a box of pregnancy tests and a cup. I glare at Raidon as Thane hands me the cup. Moving to the toilet, I sit, only to find them staring at me.

"Get out!"

They don't, and I scrunch my face up. "Can't even pee on my own," I mutter as they turn their backs to me. I pee in the cup and set it down, only for it to disappear before I can even pull my underwear up.

I growl at Thane, who took the cup. Raidon bites the wrapper, tearing it off and pulling the testing stick out. He gives it to Thane while I wash my hands. He then opens another two.

"I'm sure one is enough," I tell him.

"Nope. You'll just say the test is faulty," Raidon retorts. I huff, moving to sit on the edge of the bathtub.

Thane looks at his watch and I exhale as we wait. "Why are you upset? This is a good thing," Thane says, glancing at his watch again, as if it will make the three minutes go faster.

"Says the man not puking his guts up every morning!" I tell him.

"I'll talk with Mom and Dad. We'll get you something," Raidon tells me.

"Is it safe to enter?" Rhen calls out. Raidon pops his head out the door and nods at him. Rhen wanders in with Scarlett. I hold my arms out for her, and he passes her to me. I bounce her on my knee when Thane's watch finally beeps. He glances down at it while Raidon plucks the tests out.

"What's it say?" Leon asks as he walks in. They all huddle around my pee cup, and I shake my head at them. Leon does a happy dance before spinning on his heel and moving toward me. He plucks Scarlett out of my arms, juggling her like a tea bag. She cackles, jamming her fist in her mouth.

"Mommy's having a baby," Leon coos.

"Told ya," Raidon smirks.

"Could still be wrong," I mumble under my breath.

"What was that?" Thane asks with a laugh.

ONE WEEK LATER

The ultrasound technician moves her doppler over my stomach. We estimate I should be about five weeks along, assuming I fell pregnant during my heat. That means we should also be able to tell the gender today. I've been terribly ill for the last two weeks now, and I'm not gaining weight despite the medications I'm on.

"Yep, she's five weeks along," the woman says, pressing some buttons.

"Then we can find out the gender?" Thane asks. The woman nods, pushing her glasses up her nose. I glance at Rhen, whose eyes are on the screen, arms braced on his knees. He turns to me and smiles when he feels my eyes on him.

"So, the gender of baby A is–"

"Baby A?" Raidon asks, and my head turns to look at the screen. She points to the image, and I notice the extra baby.

"Yep, twins," the woman confirms as she moves the device over my stomach again.

"Now, Baby A is…" she says, adjusting the device a little. "A boy."

I smile, looking at Thane, who winks at me.

"Hear that! You're gonna have a little brother!" Leon tells

Scarlett, who has no idea what he's telling her.

"And baby B is… also a boy," the technician tells us.

"Another boy!" Leon tells Scarlett, who gives him a huge, gummy grin. She started teething recently, and her gums are all swollen. She chews on everything she can get her hands on, including the furniture.

"Now I'll just turn this up to check their heartbeats," she says, turning a dial. Both heartbeats are nice and strong as we listen to the thumping. A giddy feeling makes me tingle all over, excitement slivering through me.

EPILOGUE

HARLOW

ALMOST TWO YEARS LATER

Our entire family stands in the backyard, gathered around a table covered in food and presents. It is Scarlett's second birthday.

"Happy birthday, Scarlett. Hip, hip hooray," everyone sings. Scarlett leans forward, lips pursed as she tries to blow out her candles. Thane's standing behind her and helps. She claps her hands, and he fixes the party hat on her head.

"Who wants cake?" Thane calls out. He spent two days making a unicorn-dinosaur cake that Scarlett insisted she wanted. It has a T-Rex body with a unicorn head and horn. The twins waddle over to Thane as he helps Scarlett cut the biggest chunk. Her dark, curly hair blows in the breeze as he sets it in her bowl.

The twins are just learning how to stand and have to use Thane's pant legs to pull themselves up. Scarlett notices them and grabs a piece of her freshly cut cake. She leans over and holds it out to Xavian, who was given Rhen's middle name. Thane named him while Leon demanded to name Emeric, which is Raidon's middle name. This caused many arguments because Raidon wanted to give him Leon's.

They eventually agreed on Emeric so long as I agreed to have another baby later, which turns out to be now. I'm nearly full-term with our second daughter, who will be named Falon.

"Xavian, let Scarlett eat her cake. Daddy has some for you here," Thane tells him as he gnaws on Scarlett's hand, slobbering all over her fingers. Thane scoops him and Emeric up in one arm, perching them on his hip while he grabs their bowls. Raidon moves to help him as Scarlett holds the mushed-up cake to Raidon, wanting to feed him some.

"All yours, baby girl. Eat it up," he says, yet she continues to thrust the cake at him. He pulls a face, reluctantly eating the mushed-up and slobbered on cake. "Mmm, yum," he tells her. Thane chuckles at him.

"Happy birthday, Scar!" Zara leans down, kissing her cheek and dropping a tiara on her head. Zara has six kids in total now. She insists she is done, but Jake keeps pestering her for one more. I watch as Zara helps Scarlett open her present, who holds it up to show us while I move to take a seat. My lower back is killing me from standing half the day.

So much has changed in the last two years. Thane got the Omega laws officially overturned in the Supernatural Parliament. Omegas can no longer be considered an Alpha's possession. We now have free will and laws that protect us. He accomplished what his mother always wished. What she fought and died for.

Hands grip my shoulders, and I peer up at Leon. He leans down to kiss me, and I growl at him when he tries to deepen it. He chuckles, pulling back and moving to clean up Scarlett, who is covered in cake and frosting. Thane is feeding Emeric while Raidon feeds Xavian. I look around for Rhen and see him walking toward me. He places a piece of cake in front of me.

Everyone is sitting at the table eating. Before cake, Leo and Charles spent half the afternoon chasing the kids around on the climbing frame and playing with them in the bouncy castle with Emily. Elaine is sitting next to me, and her hand smooths over my huge belly.

"See, think of all the tummy rubs you could get," Sam tells Zara, nodding to Elaine's hand.

"Not a chance. I am not a breeding machine. I am done," she tells him, shooting him a look. I chuckle as they continue to bicker. Her other mates join in, but she remains firm.

"How much longer now?" she asks, changing the subject and looking at my belly.

"A week," I say.

"Still want me to come down? Jake can drive me," she offers. I was at her last birth, and she arrived a few minutes after my twins were born. I smile, nodding.

"Of course," I tell her, and she nods back.

Zara and I try to get our families together for a weekend every month. We alternate between her house and ours. Family gatherings are huge now and something I don't take for granted.

I always make sure to find the time, and I know Zara feels the same. We both wanted cousins and relatives growing up, but living on the run, we didn't get that. Now, we make sure our kids have it, because to us, family is everything.

The End

About the Author

Fueled by caffeine, barely-contained sanity, and the chaos of raising five kids, along with a penchant for the wicked. Jessica Hall is an international best-selling author from Australia. Her writing spans a few genres, from dark and seductive paranormal romance to gritty contemporary mafia and the dark and taboo that push boundaries.

Known for writing stories that ignite desire and stir the soul, Jessica Hall invites readers to explore a world of forbidden fantasies, emotionally charged twists, and characters who don't just break the rules—they shatter them. Whether it's commanding Alphas, morally gray antiheroes, or heroines with more bite than their enemies, every page promises a thrilling escape into the deliciously dark and dangerous.

If you crave stories that toe the line between love and obsession, innocence and sin, you're in the right place. Just don't expect happily-ever-afters to come easy—or without a fight.

After all, a mind like hers can only create magic—*or madness.*

Connect with Jessica Hall

Website: https://www.jessicahallauthor.com

Facebook: https://www.facebook.com/jessicahall91

Instagram: https://www.instagram.com/jessica.hall.author/

Tiktok: https://www.tiktok.com/@jessicahallauthor?is_
from_webapp=1&sender_device=pc

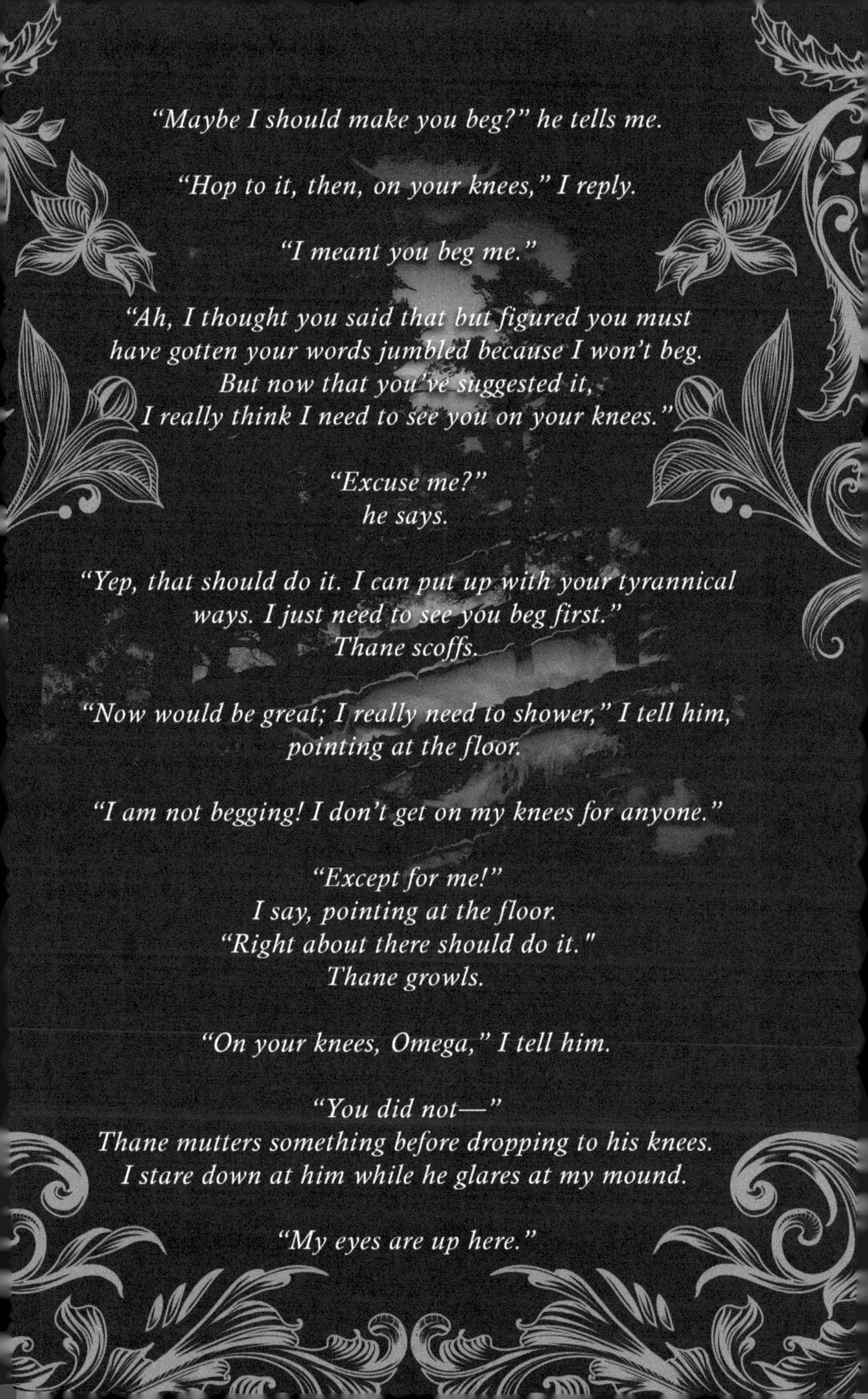

"Maybe I should make you beg?" he tells me.

"Hop to it, then, on your knees," I reply.

"I meant you beg me."

*"Ah, I thought you said that but figured you must
have gotten your words jumbled because I won't beg.
But now that you've suggested it,
I really think I need to see you on your knees."*

*"Excuse me?"
he says.*

*"Yep, that should do it. I can put up with your tyrannical
ways. I just need to see you beg first."
Thane scoffs.*

*"Now would be great; I really need to shower," I tell him,
pointing at the floor.*

"I am not begging! I don't get on my knees for anyone."

*"Except for me!"
I say, pointing at the floor.
"Right about there should do it."
Thane growls.*

"On your knees, Omega," I tell him.

*"You did not—"
Thane mutters something before dropping to his knees.
I stare down at him while he glares at my mound.*

"My eyes are up here."